Accidental Encounter

ROSEANN COTTON

Acknowledgements

The ladies in the critique group, Chrysalis, deserve my utmost thank you for their blunt critiques/suggestions. Although initially deflating, their feedback proved most beneficial. I extend my gratitude to beta readers Mary Jean Rivera and Brenda McConnel. Author and editor, Christina Weaver, came through once again to be an invaluable and encouraging help. I could not have written this book without her generous assistance.

Lastly, I want to acknowledge my mother, Rosemary, and my Aunt Rose, the inspirations for this story.

Chapter 1

T he alcoholic monster Rachel called her father struck his wife once again. Rachel wanted to stop him. It was hard staying in her bedroom, but what could she do? Her mother wouldn't fight back for fear her husband would turn his wrath onto Rachel and her brother, Cliff. There was no escape. It was the 1930s. Mother, daughter, and son depended on the monster.

These horrific recollections of her nightmare childhood remained rent-free in Rachel's mind all these years later. Now, as a thirty-one-year-old adult, Rachel developed an unreasonable intolerance of anyone drinking beer in her presence, especially her husband, Lee. In her mind, consuming only one bottle of his favorite beer once a week was one too many. Anxiety that Lee would follow the same path as the monster remained a constant companion.

"Ta-da!" Lee said, removing his hands from his wife's eyes. He pecked her cheek, proud of the bookcase he'd made as a surprise.

Rachel smelled the odor of alcohol on his breath. She focused on the amber liquid in the bottle sitting on the end of the workbench. As usual, the sight of the beer triggered her hatred for the beverage. "You broke your promise . . . again."

Lee's face etched with disappointment at Rachel's reaction. "I put in much effort the past few weeks making the bookcase. I deserve a celebratory drink. Honey, I've only had half a bottle. No biggie." He reached out to hug her. She turned away.

"It is to me." She grabbed the container and dumped the remaining contents into the laundry sink. She dropped the bottle into the garbage can. That's when she saw another empty bottle. She held it up, waving it back and forth. "Only half a beer?"

Lee ran his hands through his military buzz-cut hair in frustration and turned his back to her. He took a deep breath and touched the bookcase. Turning his face toward her, he spoke in a controlled voice. "Rachel, I know I promised when Gina was born that I wouldn't drink, at least not in front of you and the kids. I'm okay with that, but I'm tired of feeling like a criminal. A few beers a week doesn't mean I'm an alcoholic. I'm aware of how much your father's alcoholism affected you, and I've tried to accommodate your wishes."

"No, you haven't." She pointed to the bottles.

Lee's teeth clenched and his eyebrows narrowed. "Nothing I do pleases you." He tapped the workbench.

Rachel walked to the bookcase. She ran her hands over it. "You did a superb job. I like the light brown stain. I now have a place to keep my books."

"So, you're pleased with my surprise?"

A slight grin surfaced as Rachel nodded. "Thank you."

"You're welcome." He leaned over and kissed her cheek.

"Go gargle. Your breath stinks."

The following Friday, Lee read a story to the three kids and tucked them into bed. He left afterward to join his navy buddies at best friend Howie's house for their weekly poker evening. Rachel leaned against the doorjamb, watching. She kept her expression neutral, not showing the hurt and anger festering in her stomach. Cards every Friday night! No matter what!

"See ya about the usual time," Lee said, kissing Rachel's forehead. "Don't wait up." His smile didn't reach her eyes. She put on her corduroy robe, then settled in the lounge chair with a page-turner mystery novel.

Several hours elapsed before she jerked awake when the book fell to the floor. Her eyes burned and she rubbed them. Tucking in a bookmark, she closed the book and frowned. Almost one o'clock. *Lee should be home by now.* He'd never been this late before. Rachel paced the living room carpet, her fists straining the pockets of her robe. She called Howie. Voice shaking, Rachel said, "I'm sorry to bother you, Howie. Has Lee left?"

"Rachel?"

"Yes. Lee's not home." Her voice rose, and she choked on her words.

After a pause, Howie said, "Lee left over an hour ago."

Her voice stuck in her throat.

"Rachel, are you still there?"

"Yes. Howie, was Lee drinking tonight?"

There was silence on the other end.

"He was drinking, wasn't he?"

"He drank a couple of beers all evening."

"But that's enough to impair his driving. He might have run into a tree or a telephone pole." Before Howie could answer, she added, "Or driven the car down the steep embankment near the playground."

"Rachel, stop it. Calm down." He cleared his throat. "I'm sure there's an explanation."

Howie's attitude irritated Rachel, even though she knew he made sense. She hung up and went straight to the bathroom, where she lost her entire dinner. Rachel stepped outside, hoping to see Lee turning into the driveway. She visualized the smile of relief and then the scolding tone when she told him how worried she'd been. She secured her robe tighter as the chilly March air nipped at her. After a bit, she trudged back inside. She paced until her legs gave out. She collapsed on the couch into a fetal position, clutching a throw pillow, and eventually fell asleep.

The sound of the front door opening woke Rachel when Lee arrived home at sunrise.

Relief engulfed Rachel for a moment, then rage took over. She stood. "Where were you? What took you so long to get home? Were you sleeping off the beer?" She spewed the questions at him as she stomped to stand inches in front of him.

Lee stepped back, holding his hand up to stop the flow of anger. In a soft voice he said, "On the way home, I became dizzy and had shortness of breath. I pulled to the curb and closed my eyes for a moment. But I guess I conked out. I'm sorry I worried you."

Rachel noted Lee's pale face and trembling hand. Her diatribe stopped. He didn't seem drunk, but he appeared sick. Sweat beaded his forehead.

The ire drained from her. "It's Saturday. Go lie down." She forced her tone to remain even. She watched him walk toward the bedroom, relegating a major decision she'd made to the back burner of her mind . . . for now.

Chapter 2

O n Sunday evening, after Lee tucked the kids into bed, he joined Rachel in the living room, carrying a bottle of beer.

Rachel's lips curved into a frown as she focused on the bottle. "Turn off the TV," Rachel said.

"You rarely miss watching *The Ed Sullivan Show*. What's up?"

Her expression was serious. Rachel cleared her throat. "I'm taking the kids to Oregon." Rachel's decision to return to her native Oregon was a bold move for a wife to make in the 1950s.

"To visit your mother and Aunt Regina?"

"No. I'm moving there."

Lee grinned and patted her thigh. "Stop joking."

"I'm not."

This bombshell stunned Lee since she'd silently tolerated his love affair with beer for the nearly ten years of their marriage. She loved Lee and had no desire to divorce or tear the children from their father. But no way would she take a chance of subjecting the three children to the horrendous childhood she'd endured.

Lee turned his body toward Rachel. "What are you saying?"

"I can't stand your drinking anymore. Friday night I was worried sick when you didn't come home."

"I told you what happened. I fell asleep." Lee stood, paced, then paused while his brain processed this shocker. He stared at the beer. He dumped the contents into a hanging spider plant. "See? I can live without alcohol. You're more important to me."

"Humph. You're aware of my feelings about alcohol, but you continue to imbibe. There are always a few beers in the garage. You won't quit."

"So, you want to leave because I enjoy a couple of beers a week?" Then, the D word. "You want a divorce?"

"No. If we move away, you won't spend time drinking with your brothers, Howie, and your navy buddies."

Lee stomped into the garage and removed three beer bottles from the shelf. He slammed them against the brick fireplace. Amber liquid splattered onto the bricks and carpet. Shards of glass sailed throughout the room, a few landing on Rachel's lap. "There! All gone!" He saw the shock register on Rachel's face before she could hide it. "There's no way I'll let you take away my children." He wiped beads of sweat from his forehead. A spell of dizziness overtook him. He eased himself onto the sofa, his breathing shallow.

Rachel noticed his discomfort. She knelt in front of him, touching his hands. "Are you all right?"

"I'll be okay in a few minutes, at least physically."

Rachel ended the discussion for now. "A week from today is Easter. We'll talk more after the holiday. On Saturday I'm taking the kids to get new Easter outfits."

During the next week, Lee abstained from alcoholic beverages. Rachel was aware of his effort and felt encouraged. But she remained skeptical his abstinence would last. This year, 1956, Easter was on April Fool's Day. When she resumed the discussion about leaving for Oregon, she would make clear moving was no April Fool's joke. She was serious as a heart attack and would follow through on her threat.

On Saturday, Rachel gathered the kids for a shopping trip to pick out Easter outfits. Eight-year-old Gina wanted a pair of patten leather shoes and a matching purse. Younger brothers, Eddie and Barry, balked at wearing a suit and tie.

"Do we have to?" Barry asked.

"Of course," Rachel answered, running her fingers through his dark, curly hair. "Easter is a special day, and it's proper for males to wear a suit."

"Okay," Barry said, "but I'm taking off the tie before we go to Uncle Dominick's for the ham dinner."

"Me, too," Eddie said.

On the way home, the children begged their mother to stop at the playground. "We haven't played on the swings and merry-go-ground since last Halloween," Gina said.

"Pleeease." Eddie gave her his sweetest smile.

"Yeah. Can we?" Barry asked.

Rachel glanced at her watch. Almost noon. Lee would expect them home soon. She surveyed the three smiling faces. She caved. "Okay, but only for a little while. Daddy is expecting us home for lunch. He's fixing your favorite... hot dogs."

"I wish he was here. He pushes the merry-go-ground real fast," Eddie said.

Rachel parked herself on a bench. Happy visions of Lee playing with his kiddos popped into her mind as she watched them swinging, sliding, and whipping round and round on the merry-go-round. These pleasant musings warmed her heart. How could she tear father and children apart? What was she thinking? He was an amazing father and treated her with love and respect. *Lee doesn't deserve my hatred of alcohol held against him.* She stood. "Hurry kids. Daddy's waiting." She raced home to tell Lee she changed her mind about leaving and how much she loved him. That moment never happened.

Chapter 3

—◦✦◦—

Rachel walked to the casket, flinging her upper body over it. "No!" she screamed as if the sheer force of her torment would bring Lee back. "He can't be dead. Lee!" Her knees buckled, sinking to the well-manicured earth. Brother-in-law Vince lifted Rachel, holding her tightly as he guided her to a nearby bench. Emptiness, numbness, and absolute grief overtook her entire being. All these emotions threatened to plunge her into anguish from which she could not escape.

Lee's siblings lobbied to bury him in the family plot. Rachel preferred the Philadelphia National Cemetery to honor his over twenty years of service in the Navy. Considering what Lee would have wanted guided Rachel's decision. His family came first.

On a sunny April day, the two hundred-plus mourners gathered for the funeral mass at St. Michael's Catholic Church in Vineland, New Jersey. They filed outside to the freshly dug grave. Lee's three youngsters stood on tiptoes to place red, white, and blue carnations on the casket. At the conclusion, the attendees reflected and commented on the collage of pictures. *Leonardo "Lee" Eduardo Favretto, February 25, 1912–March 31,*

1956, was written in fancy script. Friends and relatives offered condolences as they passed by Rachel.

"So sorry."

"Lee was a wonderful man."

"Cherish all your memories."

"If there's anything we can do . . ."

The heartfelt expressions, hugs, and kisses didn't register with Rachel. She remained oblivious, her eyes focused on the mahogany casket. She ignored Sophia, Lee's older sister, as she gathered Rachel's three children. "I'm taking them to the hall for the reception."

Rachel stayed behind after the mourners had departed. Vince stayed with her. "I never got to tell him I changed my mind," Rachel wailed.

Vince sat next to his sister-in-law. She laid her head against his chest, her tears dampening his brand-new suit jacket. "What'd you say?"

Rachel sat erect. "I never got to tell him one last time I loved him and would not leave him." Her hands covered her face. "It's my fault he passed."

"What are you saying? The autopsy report will no doubt show Lee died of a heart attack." Vince turned his head back and forth. "Hard to believe he had one. I thought he was in good physical shape."

"It's not fair! Even though he was thirteen years older than me, I figured we'd grow old together. Why did God take him from me and the kids?"

Vince bit his lips, turning his head from side to side.

"If I hadn't taken the kids to shop for Easter outfits and stopped at the playground, I would have been home to call for help. Instead, I found him unresponsive and not breathing!"

"That doesn't make it your fault." Vince tried to convince her.

"Yes, it does!" Rachel yelled. The icy fingers of guilt over what she'd done gripped her in their clutches. Turning to face Vince, she unburdened her soul. "I threatened to leave Lee and return to Oregon with the kids."

"Are you serious?" Rachel's revelation cut him like a knife. "Why? I thought you were the perfect couple."

"I hated his drinking. It brought back thoughts of my father and the horrific childhood Cliff and I suffered. I would not go through that again. My father worshiped the almighty bottle. I remember all the beatings with a leather belt and the welts on Cliff's back. And the times he yelled at me for something as simple as leaving a few crumbs on the table. And the way he slapped Mom around. My brother and I hated him! He died when I was sixteen and Cliff was thirteen. All I felt was relief and didn't cry. Not one tear. Cliff laughed."

Vince paced a few steps from Rachel and stopped. He said nothing for a moment, then turned to face her from the distance. "Sure, Lee liked a beer, but that doesn't mean he drank in excess." She watched as the compassion left his eyes and they hardened. "Lee told us you had a thing about drinking. I thought he exaggerated. I didn't know you were holding it over his head." He rubbed his palms over his face and back into his hair, making it stand on end in places.

"You thought about divorcing my brother because you figured he drank too much? Unbelievable. He was not an alcoholic."

Rachel faced Vince. "My hatred for alcohol clouded my thinking. You can't imagine how guilty I feel. I've cried a bucketful of tears, knowing he went to his grave with my threat weighing on his mind."

"You put him through hell." She noted Vince's accusatory voice.

She bowed her head, salty tears flowing unchecked from her eyes. Vince handed her his cloth handkerchief, and she dabbed her eyes. "I'm sure I caused him stress. I don't think I can forgive myself or overcome the guilt." She stood and brushed her skirt to smooth any wrinkles. Standing at the casket, she rubbed her right hand over the glossy surface. The sweet fragrance of the carnations drifted to her nostrils as she rested her head on the top.

Eventually, Vince gave Rachel the folded American flag that had adorned the casket. He escorted her to the reception hall, wrapping his arms around her for support. She turned her head for one last glimpse. "You will always be in my heart. I will love you forever and a day," she said in a somber tone.

That evening, Rachel tucked the children into bed after a discussion in the boys' bedroom. It had been a Herculean effort to put aside her intense grief and comfort them.

"What'll happen to us without Daddy?" Gina asked.

Uncertainty about the family's future reigned high in Rachel's mind, but she didn't want them to worry. "Things will work out." She must convince herself as well.

"I'll take care of you," seven-year-old Eddie offered, hugging his mother.

"Me, too," Barry said.

"Daddy is an angel in heaven. Let's say a prayer to him," Rachel said. She knelt, and the children followed suit.

"Wait!" Barry yelled. "I'm going to get Leo!" He raced into Gina's room and gathered the spoiled orange and white tabby cat. "Leo loved Daddy too."

"Don't forget, it's my turn to sleep with him tonight," Gina reminded him.

A short while later, Rachel sat on the couch and stared at the plastic bag containing Lee's personal effects. She couldn't bring herself to deal with the items for now. She turned her attention to the bowl of sympathy cards sitting on the coffee table and reached for one. It was from the Schuberts. They'd written how much they appreciated Lee helping to search for their missing dog when fireworks spooked Thor. Card after card related similar stories. Each one felt like a spear in her heart.

Rachel's mother, Kathryn, walked into the living room. "I spotted this card behind the canisters." Sitting next to her daughter, she wrapped her arms around Rachel and guided her head onto her bosom.

Eventually, Kathryn got up. "I'm going to bring you a glass of warm milk." She handed the sealed envelope to her daughter. Rachel recognized Lee's handwriting. She clutched the oversized envelope in her hand, teardrops spattering on it. With shaky hands, she held it out to her mother. "Please open it."

Kathryn exhaled and unsealed the envelope. She pulled out an anniversary card embossed with a bouquet of pink roses, Rachel's favorite flower, and handed it to Rachel. Out fell two tickets to see *Marty,* the 1956 Oscar winner for best picture. *My God! Two days ago was our tenth anniversary.* She had forgotten. She read the verse under which Lee had written *I will love you forever and a day.* As Rachel held it close to her heart, she rocked back and forth, wrinkling the card.

"Mom, will the pain ever end?"

There was only one word to describe Kathryn's marriage . . . nightmare. She had felt no sorrow when her husband died, only regret she hadn't somehow moved heaven and earth to leave the marriage. "There is no time frame. Everyone responds to grief in different ways. In time, your aching will ease. You'll never forget Lee. He'll always remain in your heart. Cherish the years you shared with him and your memories." She smiled. "You have three reminders of your love for each other . . . Gina, Eddie, Barry."

Words spilled out of Rachel's mouth. "Mom, you don't understand. I thought about leaving him and going back to Oregon if he didn't stop drinking and told him so. I wasn't about to put up with another alcoholic. And he took off every Friday evening to play cards with his navy buddies. I resented that." She blew her nose. "I took the kids on Saturday to shop for Easter clothes. When we returned, I found him lying on the kitchen floor. Quite traumatic for the children." She buried her face in her hands, struggling to continue.

"I realized I was unreasonable and overacting. I hurried home to tell him how much I loved him and had changed my mind." She sighed. "Looking back, he complained a few times of slight chest pain, dizziness, and shortness of breath. I should have insisted he see a doctor. The stress I caused him no doubt contributed to his death. If I'd been here, I could have called an ambulance, and he would have survived whatever it was." She closed her eyes, thinking about his last moments. *Did he suffer? Was he frightened? What was his final thought?* "I will know until the day I die I didn't get the chance to tell him what he meant to me. Don't you see? He went to his grave with my threat hanging over his head."

"My dear, don't you ever blame yourself. I'm positive Lee had a severe medical problem. Probably his heart. I'm sure Lee knew you loved him and wouldn't follow through. Believe that."

Her mother wiped the tears from Rachel's cheeks. "I know it's too soon to broach this subject, but I'm hoping you might return home to live. I miss you and my grandchildren. I'd love to help you raise them."

"You're right, Mom. Too soon. I'll need time to make decisions."

"Will you be okay financially?"

"It'll be rough. I'm getting a death benefit, and Lee had a small life insurance policy. I'm eligible for a percentage of Lee's Navy pension. His commander is going to help me navigate all the paperwork."

Kathryn patted her daughter's thigh. "Well, I'm headed to bed. Or would you like me to stay with you?"

"Go on. I can't sleep. And thanks for being here, Mom."

Her mother kissed Rachel's forehead. "Love you."

As Kathryn walked toward the bedroom, Rachel asked, "Why didn't you ever remarry?"

Surprised, Kathryn stopped and faced Rachel. "Why do you ask?"

"You've been a widow for fifteen years. Are you lonely?"

"Now and then. But I don't dwell on it. I keep busy managing Aunt Regina's café, and I enjoy volunteering at the old folks' home. One lady is teaching me to knit."

"You deserve to be happy."

"I had such a rotten marriage, I'm afraid to try again. And besides," she chuckled, "who'd be interested in me at my age?"

"Don't be ridiculous. You're attractive, with only a smidgeon of gray hair, and at fifty-three your life is far from over. Look at Aunt Regina. She's quite active at seventy, isn't she?"

"I suppose so. She has Gerald, even though they're not married. Don't worry, I'm content with my life. But a piece of advice, Rachel," her mother offered. "If you ever have another chance at marital happiness, take it. You're only thirty-one. Too young to remain a widow." She patted her lips as a yawn surfaced. "Good night."

"Although I stupidly thought about leaving Lee, I loved him to the depths of my soul. I need time to figure out my life without him. My primary goal now is to be strong for the children's sake, not wondering about another man."

"I understand."

"Please don't tell anyone about my foolish notion. Only you and Vince know."

Kathryn winked.

Rachel reached for the anniversary card. She rubbed her palm over the paper, trying to smooth the wrinkles. As she re-opened it, the two *Marty* tickets fell onto her lap. She ripped them into a million pieces and tossed them into the air. She pulled her knees up to her chest and wrapped her arms around her shins. Her bloodshot eyes squeezed to shove out more tears. How could her mother suggest she remarry? Her heart belonged to Lee.

Chapter 4

❦

"**I** miss Daddy," Gina said one evening three weeks after Kathryn had returned to Oregon.

"Me, too," Eddie agreed, snatching the last piece of garlic bread from the plate as Barry reached for it.

Barry punched his older brother's shoulder. "That was mine!"

"Too bad. I got it first."

Rachel watched the interaction. She noticed Eddie picked fights with his siblings. It had been a running theme for a while. She worried that Lee's death affected his behavior. The children rarely argued or fought before his passing. Lee was one of those fun parents . . . wrestling with the boys, shooting baskets with Eddie, spinning the kids around in his arms until they were dizzy, and reading stories to them with great enthusiasm. Lee loved his kiddos with the force of a thousand hurricanes.

"Stop it!" Rachel exploded. She snatched the bread from Eddie and sliced it in half, handing a piece to each boy. She willed herself a million times a day to control her emotions in the kids' presence. This time she was powerless. Covering her face with her hands, she tried to suppress the tears.

Gina jumped up and hugged her mother. "Mommy, please don't cry. You still have me, Eddie, and Barry."

Rachel looked at her three dark-haired children. She wasn't the only one who was suffering. The kids had lost "the best daddy in the whole wide world" as Gina maintained. Their loss was also acute, if not greater than hers. It was cruel and didn't seem right. She reflected only a handful of adults had offered any condolences to them. They deserved to receive more than a sympathetic smile. Rachel decided she had to get out of her haze and pay more attention to them. *God, give me the strength to raise the children without their father.*

Rachel said, "We all miss Daddy. But it's going to be okay because we have each other." She spoke these words, hoping to convince herself.

Insomnia gripped Rachel. Lying in the bed she shared with Lee and where she'd conceived their children proved problematic night after lonely night. She turned on the bedside lamp and reached for the framed photograph of Lee. She focused on his smiling face. It reminded her of what she lost and what she'd done to him. Sadness was a constant companion. Not a day went by without her heart crying for what was. Where there was love and laughter, there is now a painful hollowness. She crawled out of bed and stepped outside onto the porch, staring at the stars sparkling like diamonds. Lifting her head upward, she implored Lee. *Please forgive me.*

Rachel returned to her bedroom. As she passed the dresser, the plastic bag containing Lee's personal effects caught her eye. Carrying the bag to her bed, she made herself comfortable. She dumped the contents on the bedspread. His wallet, a few coins, and his watch tumbled out. The coins totaled fifty-five cents. Enough for a trip to *Dairy Queen* for ice cream cones. Lifting the wallet, Rachel stroked the genuine leather exterior. The first thing she saw inside was his driver's license, then a picture of his three kiddos. She pulled out a five-dollar bill and two ones. Yay! She would use this "windfall" to treat herself to several flats of pansies and petunias.

As she closed the wallet, she noticed a white piece of paper peeking out from one slot. She pulled the wrinkled paper out and unfolded it. A smile appeared as she read the salutation. She read what she assumed was a love note to her. But wait! The handwriting didn't match Lee's. Too feminine.

My Dearest,

I live for the few hours I can spend with you on Friday evenings. Every day I dream I'm wrapped in your warm embrace. I'm not sure how you'll react, but I may be pregnant. What if I am? Will you acknowledge the child? What about your wife and children? We'll discuss this situation Friday. Till then . . . Love, DK

A coldness hit Rachel's core. She reached up a hand to clasp her throat. Her mind stuttered for a moment.

It couldn't be true! Had her stance about his drinking driven Lee to this betrayal? She reread the words. How long before his death did the woman write the note? When was the child due? DK? No name to identify the woman. She challenged her brain. The initials did not relate to anyone she might know. And only moments ago she'd begged Lee for *his* forgiveness.

She swore her heart would explode inside her chest as she rushed to the bathroom, where the contents of her stomach spewed into the toilet. She splashed cool water on her face, then reached for the hand towel. Her wedding ring caught on a loose strand of thread. While untangling her ring, another bombshell surfaced. Lee's wedding ring was not among his personal effects! Was he wearing it when she found him? She couldn't recall, but if he was, *she* hadn't removed it. Where was it? He *never* took it off unless he was working on a motor vehicle.

What moments ago were precious reminders of her husband, now tormented her. Despite the painful discovery, her heart still belonged to Lee. She couldn't switch off her love for him like a light bulb. Rachel wanted Lee back more than she'd ever wanted anything. *I need an explanation.* Rachel stuffed the jarring note inside the wallet and dropped Lee's effects inside the plastic bag. She buried it beneath several pairs of socks, then slammed the drawer shut. She stared at her wedding ring, contemplating its removal. It remained on her finger.

Rachel plopped onto the bed and stared at the ceiling. No matter what, one thing was certain. She would never reveal this secret to anyone. She would not ruin Lee's reputation. Relatives, friends, and colleagues all respected Lee. His three children worshiped him. She would carry this devastating secret to her grave.

It was at this moment Rachel longed to free herself from the memories encased within the walls of this house. *I'm moving back to Oregon.*

Chapter 5

For the next few months, while secretly making plans for the move to Oregon, Rachel put on a cheerful demeanor for the sake of the children. On the last Saturday of July, the family attended Gina's ninth birthday party at Dominick's, Lee's older brother. Mother Nature had threatened a thunderstorm, but the day dawned cloudless and sunny. A mixture of flowers and native plants dominated the backyard. Rose bushes circled the immense oak tree, the central point of the yard. A volleyball net stood waiting for the teenagers' competitive games.

Uncle Vince arrived, handing Gina a present as long as she was tall. "But wait to open it with the other gifts." Gina bounced up and down, squealing with delight. She wrapped her arms around his waist. "Thank you."

Vince sat on the picnic bench next to Rachel. She patted his thigh. "You spoil the kids, Vince. But I'm grateful for you being here for them and showing them love. Thanks to you, they don't mind changing Leo's litter box." They both laughed.

"I'll be there for you." He enclosed Rachel's hands within his, leaning to kiss her cheek.

"Hot dogs and hamburgers are ready. Come and eat!" shouted Uncle Dominick.

The kids made a beeline to the table where "grill sergeant" Dom piled the patties and dogs onto a platter.

Rachel watched Barry grab a hot dog. "This is too black. You burned it."

Uncle Dom grinned and rubbed his hand through Barry's hair. "Trade it."

Barry dropped it back on the platter and grabbed one to his liking. Vince placed the wiener in a bun and squirted ketchup on it. Barry sat on the ground and gobbled it down, then ran to the picnic table, heaping his plate with potato chips.

"Yum, yum," Dom said. "As usual, Carmela, your potato salad is out of this world."

"I second that," Sophia complimented her younger sister. "What's your secret?" The entire family appreciated Carmela's culinary excellence.

"I'll never be a Slim Jim, thanks to my wife," said her husband.

Carmela tapped her head, grinning. "Recipe's up here and will stay there."

When everyone had devoured the assortment of food, the teenagers engaged in an invigorating game of volleyball. The menfolk headed to the basement to play poker.

Rachel retired to a comfortable lounge chair. She smiled, watching the younger children pummel each other with water-filled balloons. She leaned back, reminiscing how much Lee's playful antics thrilled his kiddos. *If only . . .* Eddie threw a balloon at his sister.

"Eddie Favretto! You got my dress wet!" She picked up a balloon and ran after her brother, aiming at him. The balloon landed at Eddie's feet.

"Ha, ha," Eddie teased her. "You missed." He grabbed another balloon and headed to torment one of his cousins.

Tears filled Gina's eyes as she ran to her mother.

Rachel fanned the wet area in the air. "Honey, it will dry. Stay here so you're out of target range. Eddie!" She called out and he turned to face her. "Keep those bombs over there!"

Aunt Sophia summoned everyone to gather around the picnic table to sing *Happy Birthday*. Gina giggled with glee. "Goodie! Cinderella's on the cake! Is it chocolate?"

"Of course," Aunt Carmela answered.

"When I turn eight pretty soon, I want a Superman on my cake," Eddie declared.

"And I," Barry chimed in, "want a big dinosaur when I turn seven."

Carmela laughed. "We'll see when the time comes. I love making cakes for all my nieces and nephews."

Vince lit the nine candles. "Make a wish before we sing."

"I wish Daddy was here."

Until this moment, the Favretto family had focused on having fun, pushing Lee's absence into the far interior of their minds. A brief cloud of gloom gripped the celebration before Sophia stepped behind Gina. She prompted the family with arm gestures and began singing "*Happy Birthday to you . . .*" The group joined in and clapped when the song ended.

"Now you can blow out the candles," stated Vince.

Gina inhaled and blew out all nine.

"Here you are, dear." Carmela handed her a knife. "You get to cut the first piece." Gina sliced a huge portion, then licked frosting from her finger.

Eddie asked, "Can I have one that big, too?"

"We need to make sure there's enough for everyone," Carmela answered. "Gina's the birthday girl, so she gets a larger piece. But you can have as much of my homemade vanilla ice cream as you can eat."

"Goodie, but I like chocolate better."

When Gina finished opening her mountain of presents, the guests headed home. Rachel and her sisters-in-law stayed to help Adeline clean up.

Vince threw a basketball toward Eddie and Barry. "Come on, guys, I'll show you the finer points of dribbling. Gina, care to join us?"

"Nah, I'm going to play with the new doll you got me."

Rachel began clearing the picnic table. She carried a bowl of leftover baked beans and a plate of raw veggies to the kitchen.

"How are you and the kids coping?" Adeline asked as she scraped the small bit of soggy jello into the garbage.

"Honestly, Adeline, I'm hurting. It's been four months and I still can't believe it can hurt so bad. Too often, I wake up crying in the middle of the night. It's hard to accept I've lost a part of me I'll never regain.

Like a puff of smoke, Lee's gone forever." She sighed. "One night I got up and leaned against the bookcase he made for me. I sobbed so hard I thought I'd burst." She continued to paint a glowing picture of Lee. She grabbed a napkin and wiped away the tears.

Adeline put the leftover potato salad in the fridge, then hugged Rachel. "I wish the family could make it better for you."

"How about grief counseling?" Carmela asked.

"Yea, that might help," Adeline agreed.

Rachel gave them a weak smile and said she'd think about it.

"If you don't want to discuss this, I understand," Sophia said, "but we're wondering what the autopsy revealed."

Rachel bowed her head.

"Never mind," Sophia said, wrapping the uneaten hot dogs. "Looks like we're about finished." She pushed back a stray strand of her gray hair.

"There was a complete blockage in his left coronary artery. It caused a massive heart attack. Lee mentioned now and then he had heartburn, dizziness, and shortness of breath. We didn't have a clue he had a serious problem." Rachel sniffed, and Adeline handed her a tissue.

"Come on, ladies," Sophia said, "group hug."

"Thanks," Rachel said when they separated. "I needed that. And I want you to know how much I appreciate all the attention you've given to the kids."

"We love you all and will always be here for you," Carmela assured her.

Rachel pulled out a chair and sat down. "That's why it's difficult to tell you about a decision I made."

The three women exchanged worried glances.

"I'm moving back to Oregon."

Adeline gasped, dropping a half-filled plastic pitcher of lemonade. She lifted her apron to her eyes before fetching a towel and cleaning up the spill.

Sophia sat opposite Rachel. "Why?"

Rachel stretched her arms toward Sophia. She took her hands within hers. "Without Lee, I can't stay in that house with all the memories, even the happy ones. It's not a simple decision. I'll miss all of you, but I always hoped to return to Oregon when Lee retired. My roots are in Oregon. I want to be near Mom and my great-Aunt Regina."

"Any chance we can persuade you to stay?" Adeline asked as she threw the soiled towel in the sink. "We're an enormous, loving family. The men will step in and be there for your boys."

"No. I won't change my mind." Rachel held back one factor affecting her decision. *When the boys grow up, they will attend men's activities with alcohol and I won't have them exposed to drinking.*

"We've lost our Lee and now you and the children," Sophia lamented. "Did you tell the kids?"

"Not yet."

"How do you think they'll react? You'll be uprooting them from the only home they've ever known."

"Families move all the time. They'll adjust."

The kitchen door slammed open. Eddie ran in, beaming. "I made some baskets! Uncle Vince thinks I'll be an outstanding basketball player like Daddy!"

Vince and Barry followed Eddie inside. Vince grabbed the towel damp with the spattered lemonade and wiped the sweat off his face. He filled a glass with cool water. Noticing Adeline's moist eyes, he asked, "Why so gloomy?"

Adeline pointed to Rachel.

Vince looked toward his sister-in-law. "What's up?"

"I'm moving back to Oregon."

The glass slipped from Vince's hand, splashing water on the floor.

The news of Rachel's decision spread like wildfire throughout the Favretto family. They launched an all-out campaign to persuade her to remain in Philadelphia. Or to move to Vineland. Vince was the lead instigator, enlisting Gina, Eddie, and Barry to his side.

Vince visited often, helping Rachel and playing with the kids. On this occasion, he finished mowing the lawn. He turned on the hose and held it over his head. Shaking his head to remove the excess water, he headed to the front porch, stopping to splash the kids playing in their plastic pool.

Rachel brought him a glass of ice water. She joined him on the step.

"Any chance I can change your mind?" Vince asked.

"No. We've had this discussion." She rose, but Vince pulled her back down.

"Rachel, what are you running away from? This is your home. We all love you and the kids and we'll help in any way we can." He wrapped his hands around hers, his tone almost begging.

"I love all the Favrettos and appreciate everything you've all done, but I can't stay in that house." She withdrew her hands from Vince's. "Maybe I *am* running away." *From the thoughts haunting me about Lee's affair.* She turned to face Vince. Maybe Lee had disclosed the affair to him. They were close. "Do you know of anyone we may have forgotten to contact about Lee's passing? Someone with the initials DK?"

"I doubt it. Why do you ask?"

"Never mind. It's not important."

Vince resumed trying to convince Rachel to stay. "Have you considered everything? Where are you going to live? With your mother?"

"Aunt Regina has a vacant three-bedroom cottage next door to her café. It's kind of run-down, but she's letting us stay rent-free as long as I want."

"Convenient."

"Vince, my great-aunt never married or had children. She's always had Pekingese dogs, which she considers her babies. Spoiled rotten. Nothing but the best for them, believe me. Anyway, Mom's parents died in a boating accident when she was twelve. Aunt Regina became her guardian and raised her. And she was there for us while we dealt with my father's drinking. I named Gina after her, Regina Estelle."

"Sounds like you're fond of her."

"Extremely. I remember how upset she was when I moved to San Francisco to become a telephone operator." She smiled. "Since Lee was Italian, my marriage to him thrilled her. She didn't like it when I ended up in Philly after the Navy transferred him. She's almost seventy-one, and I want to be there for her as she ages."

"You have family here."

"But *my* family is in Oregon."

Leaning against the step, Vince said, "I'm going to miss you more than you can imagine. And I don't like the thought of you driving cross-country with three youngsters." Snapping his fingers, he leaned toward Rachel. "Hey! I'll go with you. I can fly back."

"I appreciate your suggestion, but no thanks. I can manage."

"When are you leaving?"

"Hope to be on the road the last week of August. Need to enroll the kids in school."

"That's only a few weeks from now."

"Yeah. I've still got a lot of packing to do."

"What about the house?"

"I'm putting it up for sale. Dominick is handling everything for me."

"It's time you enjoy an evening away from those three rascals. How 'bout I take you to a movie this weekend? You'd enjoy watching *Marty,* this year's best picture winner. I know Adeline offered to babysit whenever needed."

The color drained from Rachel's face. *Marty?* No way.

Vince wrapped his sweaty arm around Rachel and pulled her close to him. He planted more than a friendly kiss on her cheek.

Rachel frowned and shoved him away.

"Rach! What's wrong?" Vince righted himself from her push.

Rachel stood on the step above him. "I don't want to see that movie!"

"Why? Lee told me you loved the write-up about it. He wanted to take you."

She raised her voice. "Our anniversary was a few days after he died. He had bought tickets to see *Marty*."

Vince was silent for a moment. "I'm so sorry, Rachel." He moved to hug her. She held out her hand to stop him.

"I want you to stop trying to change my mind. I'm moving back to Oregon. I'm aware you all love me and the kids, but you have your own lives and families to take care of. Mom and Aunt Regina want me home. I doubt Cliff cares one way or another. Anyway, my great-aunt is getting older and though she has my mother and a long-time boyfriend, she can use my help too." She let her voice plead her case. "I want to be busy and feel needed, not just by my kids. Sorry, Vince. I'm going."

Vince reluctantly accepted Rachel's decision. "Ok, but I'll keep trying to convince you to let me go with you. I'll miss you and the kids. I'm coming for a visit. That's a promise." He planted a quick kiss on her cheek, then sprinted to his car.

Chapter 6

The Favrettos gathered at Dominick's for a combination farewell and birthday party for Eddie and Barry. Hugs, kisses, and moist eyes were plentiful as the Favretto relatives gave their emotional goodbyes. Rachel thanked the family for all their love and support. Sophia volunteered to keep the kids overnight so Rachel could concentrate on packing the last few boxes.

"Mind your aunt," she said to the children.

She projected a brave persona during the party but broke down as she headed toward the cemetery. She knelt beside Lee's marble headstone and traced her fingers over the engraved lettering. She thought of all those times Lee was silly, twirled her in his arms, horsed around with his kiddos, and his daily expressions of affection. She couldn't believe he was having an affair, but the note showed otherwise. Despite the evidence, her love for him hadn't died, and she buried the infidelity in the deepest corner of her mind. *I will love you forever and a day.*

The next morning, Rachel filled a tote bag with necessary toiletries and a first aid kit. She stacked the suitcases near the front entrance along with a few toys, a bag of cat food, and Leo's carrier. She filled a grocery sack with a supply of snacks. Last, she ran her fingers across the folded flag that had draped Lee's casket before placing it into a red cloth bag.

The movers arrived at eight, and an hour later Vince appeared with the children.

By noon, the men had completed loading the furniture and boxes. They secured the truck doors. "We'll be on our way, Mrs. Favretto." They confirmed the destination in Oregon, while Rachel signed the inventory receipt.

"Take care of our stuff," she warned them.

The man saluted her. "That's our business."

As Rachel walked toward the house, the Nelsons, their elderly neighbors, approached her. "We've enjoyed knowing you and are going to miss your family. We hope whoever buys the house is as friendly as you folks." The wife hugged Rachel. "May we take the children to our house? We made treats for them."

"Of course."

Picking up Leo, Barry fell in step behind his siblings as they followed the couple to their house.

Vince loaded the suitcases into the trunk. Rachel leaned against the living room wall and slid onto the carpet, surveying the empty interior. She didn't know if parting from this home was a wise decision, but hoped distance would help ease the emotional pain of Lee's death and affair. Memories flooded her as she saw images of the laughter, playfulness, and love that abounded within these walls. The happiest memories hurt the most. The tears she tried to stifle appeared with the force of a breached dam.

"Everything's loaded and ready to go," announced Vince. When he saw Rachel, he rushed to her. Pulling his sister-in-law up from the floor, he embraced her.

She clung to Vince for support. She was sure her shaking legs would collapse.

Vince put a few inches of space between them. He made a fervent appeal to Rachel. "I can make things better for you. I'm willing to move to Oregon. Whaddya say?"

Rachel shook her head. Giving him a weak smile, she said. "That's thoughtful, but your work is here, and the family would miss you. There is no need to uproot yourself." She hoped that whatever he felt for her was friendship. She suspected he had deeper feelings for her than he should. This move would put an end to any thoughts he might harbor along those lines. She still wondered if he had any inkling of Lee's infidelity. "How often did you join Lee on Friday nights to play cards?"

"What?"

"Never mind."

Vince held out his hand for her to take. She complied, but instead of shaking hands, Vince pulled her close to his body. The kiss was brief at first. But when it became firm and impassioned, Rachel pulled away. Her fears had been well-founded.

"I should apologize. I've taken a liberty I shouldn't, but damn it, I can't stand the thought of you leaving. I want to remain in your life. And who knows? Maybe someday you'll want to be more than a sister-in-law."

Rachel turned away. Vince stepped in front of her and opened his mouth to speak, but she waved her hand back and forth, shushing him. "Lee was my soul mate, and I loved him. I can't imagine loving *any* man ever again. You're like a brother to me and nothing romantic will ever happen between us. You must accept that."

In a hunched posture, he said, "I plan to visit you and the kids. Don't want them to forget their favorite uncle." Pulling out his wallet, he handed five crisp twenty-dollar bills to Rachel. "Extra dough to help with your expenses."

Rachel folded the bills in half and shoved them into his shirt pocket.

"I insist." He crammed the cash into her purse.

"I'll reimburse you when the house sells." She stepped outside.

"I checked out the Frazer and changed the oil the other day. The spare tire is fine. You should arrive in Oregon with no problems. I'm going to worry about you traveling so far." He tried for the umpteenth time to convince Rachel to allow him to accompany her.

Rachel pooh-poohed Vince's concern. "Don't worry. I'll be careful. I promise."

"Look what we got!" Eddie yelled as he led the way across the yard from the neighbor's house. "A bunch of chocolate chip cookies and brownies!"

The Nelsons waved to Rachel from their porch. "God bless you all!" they shouted.

"Thank you!" Rachel called to them.

"And I got a stuffed cat," Barry said. "I'm going to name him Snuggles like I wanted to name Leo."

The Nelsons had given each child a homemade stuffed animal, along with the goodies.

"You thanked them, right?"

"Yep," Gina answered.

"Time to head out. But first, go potty," Rachel ordered.

"I don't have to pee," Barry said.

His mother pointed to the door. The three trudged into the house. Then the sound of arguing who would get to sit in the front seat drifted outdoors.

Gina emerged first. "Do you think whoever lives here will have a pet?" she asked. "I hope so. Leo sure loved it here." She took a nostalgic stare at the only home she'd known. Her brothers almost knocked her over as they raced toward the car. Eddie and Barry jockeyed for the front seat.

Eddie pushed Barry aside and seated himself in the front. Vince opened the Frazer's back door and gestured for Barry to climb inside.

"I don't wanna sit in the back," Barry said.

"You'll take turns," Rachel said. "Eddie, since you're already here, you can be first. Barry, you and Gina will have your turns. Put Leo in the carrier and set it in the back."

Vince leaned inside the car and hugged his niece and nephews. "Practice your dribbling, Eddie. I expect all of you to behave and help your mother."

"I'll miss you, Uncle Vince. Will you visit us?" Gina asked, wrapping her arms around his neck.

"Count on it." Vince exited the car. He pulled sunglasses from his breast pocket and put them on.

Approaching Rachel, he hugged her for an eternity, then stood back, holding her hands. He tried once more. "Let me go with you. I'll worry about you and the kids every moment. Promise you'll phone me when you've arrived in Alder Creek."

"Will do." Rachel stepped into the car and closed the door to any further pleading. She rolled down the window and handed Vince the house keys. "Please give these to Dominick."

"Miss Stubborn." He had to accept her decision. "Call me for any reason. Godspeed."

"Thank you for everything, especially your involvement with the kids. And I want you to visit." As she drove off, she glanced in the rear-view mirror. She saw Vince remove his sunglasses and rub his eyes.

Hardening her heart, she looked forward. *No looking back. We are bound for Oregon or Bust. Well, we'd better not be busting anything.*

Chapter 7

A week from today was Labor Day. Rachel planned to arrive in Alder Creek by then.

They traveled only as far as Youngstown, Ohio before dark. Rachel refused to drive at night, so they stayed in a cheap motel west of town.

For the next two days, they journeyed through Ohio and Indiana, then entered Illinois, where a traffic jam in Chicago delayed them. *I should've taken a different route,* Rachel scolded herself. By Wednesday evening, they reached Omaha, Nebraska. They spent the night in a quaint motel, then headed north to I-90 the next morning. Rachel knew a miracle would occur if the children didn't become restless and misbehave during the long trip. Sure enough, the squabbling and complaining emerged.

"Move over," Barry told Eddie, shoving him. Eddie reciprocated.

"Boys, there's plenty of room. Both of you sit by the doors," Rachel said. "Barry, you count all the red cars. Eddie, white. And Gina, count the black."

Hours later, they were approaching Rapid City, South Dakota.

"Mom," shouted Barry. "I have to pee!"

"Can you wait till we reach a gas station?"

Wiggling back and forth, Barry yelled, "No!"

Sigh. "Okay." Rachel drove a few hundred feet before pulling off the highway and parking.

"Stay close to the car," Rachel said. Barry bolted out the door and pulled down his shorts.

"Eddie, take Leo out of his carrier and bring him over to that pile of dirt. Don't let him takeoff," Rachel ordered. "And stay away from the road."

Rachel stepped from the car and leaned against the hood. She spotted a road sign. *Mt. Rushmore, next exit.* Hmmm . . . She'd wanted to visit the site someday, and they were so-o-o close. *Nah, forget it. No sidetracking. Besides, it's already five fifteen. No doubt closed.* A loud shout from Gina interrupted her thoughts. "Leo's taking off!"

Rachel turned and saw all three kids running, trying to capture Leo. The cat scampered toward the highway. To her horror, Barry was chasing him, his head bent down, focused on the speedy feline. Rachel screamed and rushed toward him. "Barry! Stop!" His mother's screaming distracted him. He tripped on a large rock and fell forward, landing on the loose gravel. He jumped up and darted into oncoming traffic. His mother grabbed him and backpedaled to the safety of the graveled shoulder.

"You're squeezing me too tight, Mom!" Barry said.

Rachel couldn't speak. Her breath hadn't filled her lungs and her mouth felt as dry as dust. She had considered leaving Leo with Vince. She knew cats do not travel well. This episode made her wish she had done so. But it was only a fleeting thought. Lee had pranced into the house last Christmas holding a kitten. The excited kids had argued over naming it. Rachel got the honors, and she had chosen the name Leo after her hubby. It was his last gift to his kiddos.

Gina stopped beside them, scolding Barry. "It's all your fault Leo got away. You had to pee!"

Barry kicked his sister. She returned the favor.

"Enough!" Rachel shouted. The screech of skidding tires caught their attention. They looked toward the highway in time to spot Leo scamper from a near miss and head toward the grassy median strip dividing the highway.

The car pulled to the shoulder and after a moment, the driver exited his car. "I almost hit that cat! Does it belong to you?" His face reddened, and he curled his fingers.

Rachel pushed her children behind her and stood straight to face the approaching man.

"I'm glad you didn't," Gina spoke, peeking from behind her mother and looking up at the towering, bearded man. "Would you help us?"

Rachel watched the man's gaze take on their frightened group. His shoulders relaxed and a slow smile spread across his face. Rachel's tension eased when his fingers uncurled and he wiped his palms on his jeans.

"I'm sorry I yelled. It startled me when your pet ran in front of my car." He wiped his forehead with the back of his hand.

"Can you help us with Leo?" Gina asked.

"You don't have to. It was our fault he got out. We've caused you enough trouble," Rachel said.

"Yeah, I can help you out, little lady." The man snapped his fingers. "It so happens, I lucked out today and caught a couple of salmon. Be right back." He walked to his car and returned with the enticement and set it on the ground.

It didn't take long for Leo to come to the edge of the highway. Much to Rachel's relief, no cars traveled toward them as Leo bounded across the road to the fish. Before he even got more than a sniff, Gina grabbed him. She ran to the car and put him inside the carrier. "You shouldn't have run off!" She admonished the meowing cat.

"Thank you so much for offering your catch."

The man picked up the fish. "Don't worry about it. All is well. Make sure you keep your cat," he stared at Barry, "under control." He touched the brim of his cap. "Ma'am." He turned and sauntered back to his car.

Rachel examined Barry. A slightly skinned knee was the only sign of injury. "Come on kiddos, back inside the car. Barry, do you need a bandage or will you be okay?"

She watched as he contemplated the value of being a victim or a big boy. He straightened. "I don't need a bandage." He headed for his spot in the car, with the rest of them following.

Rachel sat staring out the windshield. She inhaled ten deep breaths. Her heart had slowed to its normal beat, but her nerves remained on edge. She was in no mood to drive much further but had no choice.

"Mount . . . Mount Rush . . . more," Gina sounded out the words on the sign ahead on the side of the road. "What's that?"

"It's a place where men carved an enormous sculpture on the side of a granite mountain."

"What's a sculp . . . sculptor?" Barry asked.

"A statue carved out of stone, clay, or wood. Like the one of Jesus in church. Only Mt. Rushmore is much, much bigger and not like other statues. It shows the faces of four of our past presidents."

Gina said, "Let's go see it."

"No. We've got to keep going. Besides, the evening is almost here. I'm not sure it's still open."

"We wanna go! We wanna go!" the children chanted in unison, bouncing up and down.

Hells bells. Why not? Rachel caved. "All right. Mt. Rushmore, here we come!"

Forty-five minutes later, Rachel found a vacant spot in the parking lot. The family exited the car, Gina carrying Leo with a tight grip.

"Where are the statues?" Eddie asked. "There's only a bunch of cars."

Rachel walked a few paces, gesturing for the children to follow her. She pointed upward.

"Oh, there are the faces!" Gina shouted. "Straight ahead. Look up."

Barry ran toward the cement walkway.

"Wait for us!" Rachel yelled.

When the foursome reached the viewing area, Barry exclaimed, "Wow! How'd the guys get so high?"

"They used a tall ladder, Dummy," Eddie replied, extending his arms toward the sky.

Rachel laughed. She took a pamphlet from a display and perused it. "A man named Gutzon Borglum and four hundred workers created this monument. It took them fourteen years." She showed them pictures in the brochure.

After twenty minutes, Rachel herded the children back to the Frazer. "I want to take a picture of you with the faces in the background." She lifted them each onto the car hood and focused the box camera on the trio. "Gina, hold Leo on your lap. I want to see your face. Barry quit acting silly. Now, smile everyone." She snapped the camera. "One more."

While driving back toward Rapid City, Rachel entertained the idea of visiting Yellowstone. Lee had promised to take her there someday.

She pulled into the first motel with a vacancy. While the children slept, she spread the map, calculating the distance to Yellowstone. It was about five hundred forty miles away, a nine to ten-hour drive. Tomorrow begins Labor Day weekend. Would the traffic along the route be horrendous? This was an unplanned excursion she couldn't pass up. She didn't tell the kids about the detour. The next morning, she proceeded west on I-90 toward Wyoming.

She drove through the day, fielding the restless kids and their bickering.

"Stop the fighting. Each of you try to spot a prairie dog."

"I don't like dogs." Gina ignored her and continued coloring in her book.

"I like dogs." Eddie peered out the window, his head moving back and forth.

"Me, too," Barry said, kneeling next to the window.

"They aren't like a German shepherd or a poodle. These are like small gophers. Try to spot a small group of mounds like a gopher hill and watch if a little head pops out. Sometimes they sit on the edge of their home, looking at what's going on around them."

For about a half-hour, the sighting of a prairie dog kept the kids' attention. Rachel kept her eye on the edge of the road in case she noticed something before the boys did.

At about seven that evening, Rachel steered the car into the parking lot of a dilapidated motel. A sign advertised *Rooms, $7.95*. Rachel believed the rate was excessive after surveying the exterior. Weeds poked through the cracked cement. The two small garbage cans overflowed with excess trash scattered near the cans. A stray dog sniffed through the mess. She turned, ready to beat feet, but the sight of the children half asleep in the seats changed her mind. *I'll settle for anything.*

She rang the bell on the counter. A man sporting a long gray beard and a balding head appeared. Munching on a piece of chicken, he got right to the point. "I have one room left, and it only has one double bed."

A spasm of irritation crossed Rachel's face. "Nothing with two beds?"

"Nope."

"Is there another motel close by?"

"No other motels between here and Yellowstone, lady. Take it or leave it." He tapped his fingers on the counter.

Rachel sighed. "All right. Any chance you have a folding cot or extra blankets?"

"No cot, but there are a couple of blankets in the room's closet." He shoved a registration form in front of her. She completed it and handed him eight dollars. "Keep the change."

"Geez, a whole nickel!" He plopped the key attached to a piece of a two-by-two-inch chunk of scratched wood on the counter. "Room 15. Be out by 10, and no pets!"

"What about . . .?" Gina began. Rachel interrupted her. "Come on, kids." She guided them out the door.

"Does that mean we can't take Leo inside?" Gina whispered, worried.

"We'll sneak him in." She directed them to the car and drove to the only empty parking slot.

"I'm hungry," Eddie whined.

"After we put our suitcases inside, we can walk to a small grocery store I saw a couple of blocks away. I'll buy a loaf of bread, peanut butter, jam, and bananas if they have any."

"Cookies too?" Eddie displayed his sweetest smile. "The ones the Nelsons gave us are all gone."

Rachel unlocked the door. She cast her eyes around the room. She ought to give the proprietor a piece of her mind. But she shouldn't have expected much after seeing the exterior. Shaking her head, she scowled at the frayed carpeting, peeling paint, tattered curtains, and stains in the sink and toilet bowl. She hoped this wasn't one of the seedy motels where rooms rent by the hour. Pulling the frayed bedspread back, she examined the sheets. Nothing crawled away.

They walked to the grocery store. She bought bread, peanut butter, jam, and a few apples. They could have a treat tomorrow at Yellowstone.

After their dinner, such as it was, and a small tiff about sharing the one bed, the children conked out. She didn't worry about extra blankets. The muggy heat licked every part of Rachel's body. She tossed and turned in the oversized chair, her feet propped on top of a suitcase. After a restless night, Rachel arose at seven and massaged her neck. She peered through the curtains. Sunny. She showered, then roused the youngsters. She rummaged through the suitcases for clean clothes, then helped the kids prepare for their showers. Eddie insisted he could manage "all by myself".

"Eddie, help Barry so Gina can take her shower."

Eddie wrinkled his nose but hurried Barry through the shower.

Eager to leave this ramshackle motel, Rachel gave the room a quick go-through for belongings. She secured the luggage and put them inside the trunk. Returning to the room, she dropped the key on the table and led the kids out the door.

"Uh, oh," muttered Eddie, pointing to a wet spot on the carpet. "Leo peed."

Rachel grinned. Poetic justice. *Ha, ha.*

The beauty of Yellowstone is everything Rachel imagined … lush forests, colorful alpine rivers, dramatic canyons, gurgling, bubbling hot springs, gushing geysers, and wildlife roaming in its natural habitat. She was happy she had taken the extra time to visit and have the children experience this natural spectacle. *If only Lee was here.* She bit back a sigh. She'd bought him a book with spectacular photographs of the park. Sharing the book with the kids had been a treat for all of them. Now she was without Lee in this experience.

Along the way to Old Faithful, a herd of bison grazed nearby. One wandered within a few feet of the car, frightening Barry. "It's a bazillion pounds! Will it attack us?"

"No. Aren't they magnificent?" Rachel was in awe and wanted a snapshot. She stopped the car and waited for the bison to saunter away. Grabbing the camera and stepping out, she aimed and snapped several pictures. One majestic buffalo turned to stare at her. She snapped more pictures before it took a few steps toward her.

"Mom, get in the car. It's going to eat you!" Barry yelled from the window, his eyes wide, with white showing around the whole iris.

"I'm coming." She ducked into the car and shut the door. The bison stared at them, shook its head, and turned back to join the others.

"Whew! You got away, Mom." Eddie patted his approval on her shoulder.

"Thanks, Buddy." She shifted the car into gear and they headed down the road.

When they reached the Old Faithful parking lot, Rachel guided the children into the lodge. "When is the next eruption?" she asked the snack bar clerk.

"The last one was about forty minutes ago," he answered. "It can erupt anywhere from thirty-five to a hundred twenty minutes apart. It could be over an hour or a few minutes until the next one."

"How long does the eruption last?" a tourist asked.

"Anywhere from one-and-a-half to five minutes. Have your camera ready."

Rachel would not leave without seeing the famous geyser erupt. "Kids, how about an ice cream cone while we wait?"

"Yeah!" they answered, dashing to another counter.

The children ordered chocolate and Rachel chose strawberry, her favorite. Noticing Leo, the teenage clerk politely told them he could not allow pets inside the lodge. Rachel laid forty cents on the counter, snatched a few napkins, and ushered everyone outside.

Twenty-five minutes elapsed, and the geyser refused to perform. The kids whined.

"What are we waiting for?"

"Can we go now? I'm hot."

"I'm bored."

"When it's going to rup?"

"Rup?" Rachel asked.

"Yeah, the man said it would rup every hour."

"The word is erupt. It means water, after building up pressure underground, explodes into the air."

She handed him the brochure, pointing to the cut-away picture of Old Faithful.

"Why do they call it Old Faithful?"

"Because it faithfully erupts every day, rain or shine, all seasons."

Rachel understood their frustration. Even Leo was squirming. She should abandon her desire to witness the eruption. But she was here *now* and may never have another opportunity. She wanted to capture the children on film standing in front of Old Faithful when it erupted.

"Let's go stand under the shade of that tall tree and wait. It's a little cooler."

As they neared the tree, a deep male voice shouted. "There she blows!"

"Hurry!" Rachel said as they rushed toward the geyser, getting as close as allowed. Rachel positioned the kids so the tall column of boiling water and steam was behind them. "Okay kids, put your arms in the air like you're cheering. Now!" She snapped a picture. She wound the film to the next frame and pressed the button again.

"Neato," Eddie said.

When Old Faithful completed its performance, the crowd dispersed. Rachel and the children returned to the car after a visit to the restroom.

Rachel hoped to reach Missoula, Montana by dark. She glanced at her watch: two forty-five. They should arrive around eight. She'd find a motel room and they would leave early the next morning for the last leg to

Alder Creek. It would be about a twelve-hour drive, but she was eager to reach *home*.

Rachel drove while the children napped. She was thankful for the peace, but she reflected on the cruel card dealt her. It never entered her mind she'd be a widow at thirty-one with three children to raise. She wondered what direction her life would take when she reached Alder Creek. The only thing she knew for certain was her mother and great-Aunt Regina awaited their arrival.

Rachel continued driving at a steady speed, admiring the scenery and occasional wildlife. Her heartbeat increased when a moose ambled through the plentiful fir trees.

A thought she'd put out of her mind reared its ugly head. *What am I going to do to survive financially?* For a moment, a possibility popped out. *A veterinarian.* She let the thought linger longer than she wanted. She'd always wanted to be a vet and had attended classes toward certification before the kids came along. That memory intruded, and she slammed the door on that entire train of thought.

When a mileage sign showed fifty miles to Missoula, the kids awoke. Everyone was hungry and ready for a break. Pulling into a gas station and filling the gas tank, she asked the attendant, "Any cafes around here?"

He pointed west. "Only one, a few miles farther. Just beyond the bakery, on the right. Clyde's Café is next door."

"Expensive?"

"Burger and fries for a quarter."

She found Clyde's Café. A few old men yapping between sips of coffee looked like regular customers. Most were friendly and smiled at them and joked with the kids, encouraging them to eat their burgers.

When she got up to pay, the waitress handed her a brown bag. "What's this? I ordered nothing to go."

"I know, Sweetie. The guys thought you folks would enjoy the treat a little later on. Don't protest or they'll have hurt feelings." The kindly woman winked at her.

Rachel observed the men. She approached their table. "Thank you for the bag of goodies."

The waitress walked them to the door and patted Eddie's head. Gina hugged her while Barry peeked inside the bag of cookies.

They piled into the car, Barry in front. Gina opened the carrier door without her mother's permission. Leo stepped out. Gina picked him up and whispered to Eddie not to tattle.

Twilight faded into blackness. Rachel could see the outskirts of Missoula as they topped a ridge. Rachel turned on the headlights. She debated whether to stop at the first motel she encountered or drive through town. Suddenly, Leo jumped onto her shoulder, then her lap. She swiped at the cat, trying to push it away.

"Barry! Grab Leo!"

Gina lurched over the seat and reached for Leo.

Rachel took her right hand off the wheel and reached for Leo's collar. He jumped onto the floorboard.

Rachel looked down to grab the cat, who made his way between her seat and the door. Worried he'd get stuck, she took her eyes off the road. Leo inched his way into the back and jumped onto the seat.

Rachel focused her eyes on the road again. Two bright spots appeared beyond the headlights. A deer! Rachel slammed on the brakes and swerved to the right.

"Hold on everyone!" she shrieked.

The kids screamed as Rachel lost control and they bounced like ping-pong balls. The car bumped over the shoulder and coasted to a field of overgrown grass, coming to an abrupt stop. Rachel heard Barry's head slam into the dashboard as her face banged into the steering wheel. She heard crying as pain shot through her head and her vision went black.

The car's horn pierced the quiet evening. The deer darted innocently into the woods.

Chapter 8

—◦◦◦◦—

Rachel's eyes fluttered. Disorientation engulfed her. *What was happening?* Everything was hazy. Gentle hands lifted her head off the steering wheel and her body pressed against the seat. *Why was her head pounding?* Her eyes opened, and she sat straight up.

A deep male voice spoke. "There's a nasty bump on your forehead. How do you feel?"

The throbbing in her head overcame the confusion for a moment, and she groaned.

"Are you going to throw up, Mommy?" Eddie asked.

"I hope not." The recollection of Leo jumping onto her shoulder, then onto her lap, and the deer standing on the highway flooded back.

She studied the man squatting next to her. "Who are you?"

"I saw red tail lights shining in the field. I figured whoever was inside wasn't trying to make an alternative route to Missoula. I thought I'd better check things out." His voice held slight humor as he turned off the engine.

"He got Barry a blanket," Eddie said.

Rachel turned to see her son holding a blanket against his forehead. Splotches of blood dotted the material.

Ignoring her throbbing head, Rachel jerked up, reaching for her injured child.

"He needs medical attention," the man said.

Rachel stared at him. "What is his injury?" She cradled the sobbing boy, trying to remain calm so as not to alarm Barry.

"I want my daddy," Barry howled.

The man walked to the passenger side and squeezed in beside Barry. "What's your name, Buddy?"

"Barry."

Eddie leaned over the front seat. "I'm Eddie. I'm his big brother."

"Well, Eddie, you can be my helper. But first, I'm going to get a first aid kit from my truck."

Eddie's eyes followed the man as he disappeared into the darkness. "He's coming back, isn't he, Mommy?"

"Yes." She closed her eyes. For a few moments, she would let someone else take care of her kids while she tried to clear her head of the pounding pain.

Barry scooted away when the man returned, but his calm demeanor relaxed the child as he applied gauze to Barry's forehead. "There! All done. Covers your booboo. I'm proud of you for being so brave."

Barry allowed a meek smile to lift his lips.

"How do you feel, ma'am?" The man squatted beside her.

"My head throbs. Everything is still hazy," she answered. "I'm more concerned about the children."

"That guy put on something soft but it still hurts," Barry moaned.

"We need to get Barry to the hospital. He may have a concussion. Your son should be examined too. Also, you passed out. You need checking as well."

Rachel raised her hand to her forehead. "Ouch!" Her skin was tender to the touch, and her left big toe ached. She ignored her pain and turned. "How are you, Eddie?"

"Okay, I guess. Is Barry going to die?"

"Of course not," the man assured him. "He's a brave guy."

"Gina? How about you? You've been pretty quiet back there." There was silence. Rachel struggled to raise herself to peer into the backseat. No Gina. "Where's your sister?"

"I don't know," Eddie answered.

Rachel looked at Barry. He shook his head.

The man spoke. "Ma'am, I'm taking you and your sons to the hospital in my pickup. Don't think anyone is going to stop and help." He reached for Barry. "No time to waste."

"My daughter!" Rachel's face turned ashen, and her lips and chin trembled. She struggled to exit the car. "Gina! Gina!" she cried out a hundred times as she labored to push past the man. Putting weight on her left foot caused pain to shoot up her leg. She fell back onto the seat.

She pleaded with the man. "You must find my daughter. She's not here!"

The man bent to her eye level. "There's another child?"

"Yes! Gina! Gina! Where are you?" She cried out in a shrill voice.

The man stood, rubbing his hand through his dark, crewcut hair. He dropped to his knees beside her. He shined the flashlight under the car and around the immediate vicinity. "Not there."

Eddie looked at the man. Then his eyes slid to his mother's. He whispered. "Gina let Leo out of the carrier."

"I figured that. The cat caused this total mess. Where is Gina?" She demanded of her son. He shrunk into the seat, staring at the floor mats. "I don't know. The last—"

The man interrupted, bringing Eddie's eyes back to his. "Do you remember what happened?"

"The door opened, and Leo ran out. Gina jumped out when the car stopped to run after him."

Rachel swung her legs to the ground. She watched the man swing the flashlight back and forth, calling Gina's name. Her heartbeat raced, nearly exploding. Had she fallen out of the car and been . . . no, the man had checked under the car and Eddie said she ran after Leo. *Where the hell is she?*

Leaning against the door, she couldn't put any weight on her foot. The pain caused her stomach to churn. She had to place Gina's fate in the hands of this stranger. "She's wearing a two-piece navy-blue sunsuit and brown sandals. Braided hair." Looking upward, she prayed, "God, please protect her."

Rachel sat back onto the seat before she collapsed.

"I found a sandal!" he hollered back at Rachel.

Barry crawled into Rachel's arms. She hugged and kissed him like she hadn't seen him for weeks.

From the darkness, the spot of light bounced, and she heard whining.

"Did you find Leo?" Eddie called as he ran toward the beam.

"Eddie, come back here!" Rachel shouted. He didn't obey but continued out toward the light bouncing ahead.

The three came back, and Barry climbed out of the car, dropping the blanket. The muscular man carried her daughter with ease and familiarity. *He's been around kids. He probably has a bunch of them,* Rachel guessed.

He set Gina on Rachel's lap.

Gina lifted her head and muttered, "Leo . . . my foot . . ."

"Your foot?"

"It hurts."

The man shined the beam on Gina's feet. The right foot was bare and swollen. She winced when he touched it. After checking for other injuries, he smiled at her. He reached out to pat her head, and she jerked it away. "I'm not supposed to talk to strangers." She spoke as if she'd rehearsed it.

He gave Gina a friendly handshake and introduced himself. "Gina, pleased to meet you."

She shot him a suspicious glimpse. "How do you know my name?"

"Your mother yelled your name, and I've also met your brothers, Barry and Eddie. We need to head to the hospital."

"I won't go without Leo!" she wailed.

"Who's Leo?"

"Gina . . ." Rachel told her daughter it wasn't likely Leo would be back.

"An enormous animal might eat him!" Between the missing cat and painful foot, Gina was inconsolable. "Leo . . . Leo . . ." Tears flowed as she buried her face against her mother's chest.

"I'll take another look." The man sighed.

"Can I go?" Eddie jumped out of the car right at the man's heels.

The good Samaritan stopped. "I don't want to leave the women without a man to watch over them." He winked. "They'll feel safer if you stay. If you see lights from another car, holler at me. They might stop to help."

Eddie thought for a moment. He stood erect, tapping his chest. "Okay."

Rachel stifled a grimace. "The cat is orange and white and has a prominent heart-shaped pattern on his fur," she said.

When he returned empty-handed, his defeated stride brought tears to Rachel's eyes.

"We need to hightail it to the hospital," the man said. "It'll be a tight squeeze, but you'll all fit in my pickup. Let's go. We can't waste any more time."

"Leo!" Gina shouted. "We can't leave him all alone." She attempted to go hunt for Leo, but the swollen foot thwarted her attempt.

"Yeah, we can't go without Leo," Eddie said.

Rachel agreed, but common sense prevailed. "Kids, there's no choice. Let's pray he'll be safe during the night. Maybe he'll come back to the car and wait for us." Mollified, the three children calmed down a tad. "I hope so," Gina said.

The rescuer carried Gina to the truck, followed by Eddie and Barry. With the rescuer's help, Rachel hopped on her right foot, and he gently hoisted her inside. He lifted Barry onto his mother's lap. He retrieved the car keys, Rachel's purse, and the kids' stuffed animals, and put the suitcases into the bed of the truck. As he raised his right foot to step inside, Rachel shouted, "The flag!"

"Huh?"

"Lee's flag. I can't leave it. It's in a red cloth bag on the front floorboard."

"I'll fetch it."

Rachel heard the sigh in his voice as he trudged back to her car. *This was important. I can replace the things in the car, but not the flag.*

He handed it to Rachel, and she held it firmly against her chest. She didn't look at him as he got into the driver's seat and started the truck. He glanced for oncoming cars, then gunned the accelerator.

"The flag has special meaning?"

"It draped my husband's casket."

A long silence followed the response. "I'm sorry for your loss."

She tried to nod her head, but the movement intensified the pain. "Thank you."

The man pulled into a nearby gas station to ask for directions.

Rachel watched him sprint to the building and fling open the door.

The attendant, yapping on the phone, acknowledged his presence, but continued his conversation. The rescuer folded his arms and tapped his foot on the floor. Staring through the store's window, Rachel could tell his patience wore thin. He grabbed the handset from the teenager's hand and slammed it onto the cradle, uttering words that had the clerk backing up. The teenager pointed a shaky finger west. The man dashed to the pickup and jumped inside.

"You're welcome!" the fella yelled, as he stepped outside, shaking a clenched fist toward the departing man.

Arriving at St. Patrick's Hospital, the pickup screeched to a halt at the emergency entrance. "Don't move!" he ordered as he dashed inside.

Within moments, several medical personnel appeared with wheelchairs and a gurney. A nurse lifted Barry from his mother's lap and tried to seat him in a wheelchair. Barry kicked his legs and flapped his arms up and down.

Lifting Barry, the man asked, "Remember how brave you were in the car when I put the gauze on you?"

Barry nodded.

"Let's show everyone you haven't lost your bravery." He eased Barry into the wheelchair and pushed it inside.

Rachel's body relaxed slightly as an orderly pushed her toward the emergency area. The lobby was the color of ripe lemons and paintings of religious icons adorned the walls. Cut glass vases overflowing with vivid artificial floral arrangements added luster to the entrance. Three folks focused their attention on a cowboy western glaring from the waiting area television.

Staff put the family inside a sterile cubicle. A nurse pulled together two heavy cloth curtains. A woman with a clipboard fired off questions.

The doctor examined Barry first. He determined the gash on the child's forehead required stitches. Barry squirmed to jump off the examination table when he saw the barrel of a lo-o-o-o-ng needle. He screamed, "I don't want a shot!"

Dr. Faillace, his bedside manner as warm as his fiery red hair, said, "I heard how brave you were in the car after the accident. I'm proud of you." Barry smiled and stopped wriggling. The doctor numbed the boy, then sewed the wound.

An intern pronounced Eddie fit as a bodybuilder except for a prominent bruise on his right knee. Gina wasn't as lucky. She sustained a sprained right foot. "You'll have to stay off that foot, young lady," the intern said. "A tech will fit you with some crutches tomorrow morning."

"Do I have to use them?" She held out her foot wrapped in a stretch bandage.

"Yep, if you want to move around. It is crutches or" –he pushed a wheelchair in front of her– "this two-wheeled chariot." He squatted to her eye level. "You strike me as the active type. You can't put any weight on your foot. The crutches will allow you to move all by yourself, and you'll heal quicker if you stay off it."

"What if I have to go potty?"

"The nurse will show you how to use the call button on your bed. Someone will come and help you."

"Right away?"

"Of course."

X-rays revealed Rachel had a broken left big toe. Dr. Faillace taped it along with the "buddy" toe. "It'll be like a splint, immobilizing it." The skin between her left ear and eye was a bright purple from a contusion, but the doctor ruled out a concussion. "I'm glad you're wearing sandals. Your foot won't fit into your shoes." He patted her shoulder. "I'll tell your husband I'm keeping you all overnight for observation."

Rachel's face heated. She stuttered for a moment, then got the words out. "He's not my husband. He rescued us and brought us here."

The doctor frowned and turned to peek through the opening in the curtain. A plump older nurse stepped in and smiled at Rachel.

"That nice man that brought you here had to leave for his friend's wedding that's tomorrow. He told us where your car is and brought your luggage in from his truck. He hoped you'd be fine. I assured him we'd take care of you."

A pang of disappointment emerged. She shrugged, wincing as pain shot through her toe. "I wanted to thank him."

Chapter 9

———◆◆◆———

By eleven, the medical staff finished settling everyone for the night. Gina and Eddie, sharing a room, fell asleep in a flash. Barry slept near his mother in a child's bed equipped with sidebars. Rachel plopped onto the bed. Although late, she reached for the bedside telephone. After getting the hospital operator, she placed a collect call. After three rings, her mother's voice accepted the charges. She willed herself to stay calm as she described what happened.

Kathryn's scream boomed through the phone lines. "Mother of God! It was a bad idea for you to travel such a distance alone with my grandchildren. Wish I'd talked you out of it."

"Mom, we're all okay." Rachel tried to placate her mother.

"You better not be sugar-coating anything," came the rapid response.

"I'm not." Kathryn's heavy sigh drifted into Rachel's ears. "I won't know until tomorrow about the car's condition. If it's undrivable, I've got to figure out how to get home."

"I'll have Cliff come for you," Kathryn said but abandoned that idea. "Take a Greyhound bus. If need be, I'll borrow money from Aunt Regina and Western Union it to you."

"Okay, Mom. Call you tomorrow with the info. Love you."

The conversation with her mother soothed Rachel. She replaced the phone on the table and hobbled to Barry's bed. Kissing his head, she hoped the inevitable scar wouldn't be too noticeable. She returned to her bed and rested her head on the pillow. Her threat to leave Lee, his death, the discovery of his affair, uprooting the family, and now this accident tested her faith. She wondered if she could function, but she had no choice. The children needed a stable mother.

A nurse woke Rachel. "I need to check your vitals. I'll watch your son while you shower before the others wake. Put the shower cap on so you don't get the bandage wet. Press the help button if you become lightheaded." She gave Rachel a no-nonsense stare.

Rachel nodded. The medicine they'd given her helped. The pain in her head had lessened. She found her toiletry bag in her suitcase and headed to the bathroom.

Clean towels and washcloths hung on a towel rack. Shampoo, conditioner, and soap sat on a shelf in the stall.

As the warm water flowed down her body, her mind filled with the accident last night. *Why did this mess happen?* She dabbed at her eyes and pressed her lips together. *I will not let this wear me down. No more tears.*

A little while later, Eddie entered the room, followed by a nun pushing Gina in a wheelchair. She greeted Rachel. "I'm Sister Celeste, nurse, and head cheerer upper. How are you feeling?"

Rachel turned, her legs dangling over the bed's edge. "There's a slight throbbing in my toe. What time is it?"

"8:20."

Stepping onto the floor too hard, Rachel's broken toe smarted. "Ouch."

Sister Celeste left and returned with aspirin for Rachel. Clad in a black habit with only her hands and face exposed, she had a grandmotherly persona. Rachel liked her at once. The nun opened the Venetian blinds, exclaiming, "Glory to God! A sunny Sunday." Turning, she said, "Dr. Faillace will be here before noon to check on everyone. My hunch is he'll discharge you today."

"I hope so," Rachel said, "but I need to find out about my car."

Barry woke. He sat up and patted his fingers over the bandage on his forehead. "Hey, missus nun, is there hair under that black thing?"

Mortified, Rachel glared at him. "Barry!"

The amused nun approached the youngster, grinning ear to ear. "Of course, my child." Bending down, she let him touch a stray strand peeking from underneath the headdress.

Barry touched it, satisfied.

"Can you help us find Leo?" Gina asked.

"Leo?"

"Our cat. He ran away."

There was a slight tap on the door. A police officer stuck his head inside the room. "Mrs. Favretto?"

"Yes." Rachel turned her head to face the uniformed man.

"I am Officer Clarkson." He held out his badge. "Sorry to disturb you, but I need to ask a few questions and tell you about your car."

Sister Celeste reached her arms toward Eddie and Barry. "Come, children, I want you to tell me all about Leo while you eat breakfast." She slid sock slippers onto Barry and then pushed Gina's wheelchair toward the door. Barry lifted his head and stared at the man towering over him. "Is my mommy in trouble?"

Squatting to Barry's eye level, the mustachioed officer said, "No, son. I'm going to talk with your mother about the accident."

He waited until all were gone, then approached the bed. "May I sit?" He indicated the chair next to her.

Rachel nodded.

"Tell me what happened," he said as his hand held a pen poised over his notebook.

"A deer stood on the highway right in my path. I jerked the wheel to avoid hitting it and the car went off the road." She omitted Leo's part in the scenario.

"Yea, that can be a problem in these parts. I doubt if people pay attention to the signs posted along the highway cautioning about deer." He shifted in the chair. "We conducted an on-site investigation. Do you want the police report?"

"Yes. I might need it for the insurance company."

"A local garage towed the car." Officer Clarkson scribbled the owner's name and phone number and handed the paper to Rachel. "He's not open on Sundays. But he's at the garage today waiting for you to contact him." He stuffed the pen and small notebook into his pocket and left. She reached for the phone. "Hello? My name is Rachel Favretto. You have my car, a green 1953 Frazer that was in an accident last night."

"Yes, it's here. I've inspected it. I suspect some damage underneath, but I need the key to conduct a thorough exam. I'll send my son to pick it up."

"Fine."

Shortly after noon, Steve, the garage owner, arrived in person. Steve's pudgy, good-natured face and friendly smile made Rachel feel at ease, but she pulled the blankets over the thin hospital gown.

"Mrs. Favretto," he said. "Your car has a bent tie rod."

"Tie rod? What's that?"

"It helps push and pull the front tires as the steering wheel is turned. They're an important function to a vehicle's steering."

"Can you fix it?"

"Yeah, but not today. It's Sunday and I don't have tie rods in stock. EZ Auto Parts is open tomorrow even though it's the Labor Day holiday. The store opens at nine. I'll get them first thing. I should finish by noon."

She winced at the thought of the extra expense. She exhaled, resigned to the situation. "Do whatever it takes. Thanks."

Steve shook her hand. "Till tomorrow . . ."

Rachel didn't know which gave her more angst . . . her aching toe or thinning wallet.

As Steve gripped the door handle, he stopped. "By the way, the cops found a trembling orange and white cat with a cute heart shape on its fur. Unique."

"What? Where did they find the cat? Where is he?" She pulled the blanket aside, ignoring her modesty.

"Found him under the car at the crash site. He's in my office, back at the shop. I noticed a carrier in your car. He appears fine except for his nonstop meowing."

"Leo!" Rachel shot her arms toward the sky and jumped up. She yelped as she landed on her injured toe. "Ow!" The gown flapped at her side and she backed toward the bed.

Steve smiled. "How 'bout I bring the cat here, even if the hospital doesn't allow pets?" He winked.

"Oh, would you? The children will be ecstatic! We thought we'd lost Leo forever. Thank you! Thank you!" Rachel gripped his hands between hers until he pried them out of her grasp.

Steve backed away from Rachel. "Back in thirty!" The door slammed as he left the room and raced down the hallway.

Sister Celeste brought the children back to Rachel's room. Rachel still smarted from the painful toe. But her elation about Leo overshadowed her discomfort. *Should I tell the kids about Leo? Better not just in case . . .*

Rachel tempered her smile. Leo's return was going to be a wonderful surprise.

Sister Celeste placed a meal on the portable tray and wheeled it to Rachel's bed. Rachel thanked her and peeled off the aluminum foil. Rachel forced a smile as she looked at the disgusting food. A sheet of lumpy gravy resembling paste covered a piece of meat . . .turkey? Green beans, soggy mashed potatoes, and a stale roll stared at her. An overripe banana completed the lunch.

"Eat. You need your nourishment," Sister Celeste ordered.

The growl in the pit of Rachel's stomach induced her to consume the tasteless meal. At least the orange juice was palatable. All she thought about was reuniting with Leo. The children sat around a small table that barely fit their chairs. Gina scooted into a regular chair to eat lunch.

"I hope a ferocious tiger didn't eat Leo," Barry said.

"Tigers don't live here," Gina informed him in a superior voice.

"Yes, they do," Barry insisted.

"Not true!"

"You're lying," Barry yelled.

"Stop arguing," Rachel ordered. She sat erect, eyeing the opening door. Expecting Steve, her smile faded when Dr. Faillace appeared.

Surveying the family, he remarked, "So many gloomy faces. Is our hospitality not to your liking?"

"Leo's still gone," Gina said.

Steve paused outside the door to catch his breath. He pushed on the door and advanced a few steps into the room, hoisting the carrier like an athlete who won an MVP award. "Look who's here!"

Barry and Eddie jumped up and down, squealing, "Leo!" Gina stood but fell back in the chair with a whimper and a frustrated expression. Steve set the carrier on the floor near the excited girl. She unlatched the door and grabbed Leo, squeezing him against her chest.

"How come she got to hold Leo first?" Eddie pouted.

"It is always polite to let girls be first. Don't you agree?" asked Sister Celeste in a diplomatic, matter-of-fact voice.

"I guess so." He grumbled, glaring at his sister.

After petting Leo, Rachel approached Steve. "Thank you for bringing our pet to the hospital. How thoughtful of you."

"This made my day, my entire week, month, or year!" Steve beamed at her praise. "It warms my heart to see the kids' joy. We'll never find out from Leo what happened," he chuckled, "but the important thing is, you got him back. And," he assured her, "I'll repair your car tomorrow as soon as possible." He stuffed his hand in his pocket and left the room, whistling a lively tune.

Dr. Faillace interrupted the reunion to examine everyone. The doctor lowered his voice. "You're all recovering well. Mrs. Favretto, I'd like to make sure you aren't suffering from headaches. I also want Gina to become more proficient on her crutches. One more night ought to do it."

Rachel frowned.

Sister Celeste gave him a knowing look. Rachel didn't interpret it. "What about Leo?'

The doctor pointed to Sister Celeste and said, "That's your duty." He slipped out of the room before the nun could object.

"Please let us keep Leo in here," Barry begged.

"Let me think about it. For now, make sure he doesn't escape from this room! Keep him in the carrier." She shut the door firmly behind her.

The rest of the afternoon and evening passed with no problems. Leo lounged beside Rachel in her bed while the kids watched TV in the visitor's room down the hall. Sister Celeste stopped by with two bowls to hold food and water for Leo and a plastic box containing litter.

Around eleven the next day, Steve arrived. "Car's good as new, well, except for a few minor dents. Ready to check out of this joint?"

"I was ready yesterday."

Handing Rachel the keys, Steve said, "Gotta go, Mrs. Favretto. My son's waiting outside. We're having the family over for a Labor Day picnic and I'm the chef. My barbecued spare ribs are legendary." He patted his bulging belly. "Should cut down on my food intake, but I'm addicted to fattening cuisine. So glad you got Leo back." He pulled a crumpled piece of paper from his pocket and handed it to Rachel. After perusing the bill, she sighed. The total was less than the deductible, so insurance wouldn't kick in. Another blow to her finances. "I don't have enough money on me to pay the whole bill."

"Pay now what you can spare. Send the rest when you can. The address is on the invoice."

Rachel counted the cash in her wallet. She estimated how much she'd need for gas and food. "Here." She handed him the last twenty Vince had given her.

Heading toward the door, Steve glanced at an appreciative Rachel for one last moment. "Your car's parked in a space opposite the hospital entrance. Enjoyed meeting you, your charming children, and Leo. Best wishes."

Dr. Faillace signed the discharge papers. Within thirty minutes, Rachel was thanking him for allowing Leo to stay in the room and for treating her and the children. "My pleasure." He handed her a paper with medical instructions, along with the bill.

Rachel perused it. The charges were for only one day. Even though insurance would cover it, she pointed out the error. He waved his finger. "The bill is correct."

"I could hug you."

"My wife is the jealous type," he laughed. "Make an appointment within a week for Barry's stitches. You and Gina should visit the doctor as well. If your toe bothers you while driving, don't ignore it. Pull over if necessary or at least take an aspirin. Doctor's orders."

Rachel saluted the doctor as personnel arrived to wheel the family out to their car.

Sister Celeste held Rachel's hands. "God be with you." Handing each child a St. Christopher medal, she said, "Gina, Eddie, and Barry, I am so blessed I met you." She petted the cat. "You too, Leo." Her eyes glistened as she opened the left rear door and gestured for the children to enter. Barry scrambled into the back seat. A candy striper assisted Gina and then placed the carrier on the floorboard. Eddie settled in the front for now.

Placing the flag on the front seat, Rachel positioned herself behind the steering wheel. She twisted the key in the ignition, then turned her head toward the back seat. "Make sure Leo's in the carrier. Don't you dare let him out until I stop the car and tell you it's okay." Her tone accepted no argument.

Sister Celeste pushed the door shut and stepped back, waving until the family was out of sight.

Rachel planned to drive straight through to Alder Creek. She'd pull off the road at a rest area and nap if necessary. As the tires ate up the highway to Oregon, she thought about the nice man who'd rescued them. She hoped he'd reached his destination in time for his friend's wedding.

Chapter 10

R achel gripped the steering wheel as she arrived at Sandy close to nine. Her old digs! And straight ahead, was *Dea's In and Out.* It had the best strawberry milkshakes in town. She'd love to stop and order one to relieve the lump in her throat, as she was only eight miles from Alder Creek. Instead, she settled for a swig of water from the thermos. Besides, she didn't want to wake the children.

Minutes later, Rachel steered the car into the cottage's driveway. She turned off the ignition. *Home at last.* The coast-to-coast journey had been grueling. Maybe she should have allowed Vince to come with them.

Alder Creek, a small hamlet along the major route from Portland to Mt. Hood, was where she'd spent her childhood. Laid-back folks inhabited the two dozen homes dotted along a gravel road. It dead-ended at the Sandy River, a favorite fishing spot for the close-knit community. Aunt Regina's weathered roadside café was the only business. Locals joked if you blinked, you'd miss Alder Creek.

Rachel sized up the familiar surroundings. A smile appeared when she saw the rhododendron bush she had helped plant years ago now measured six feet high.

The children were conked out. Before waking them, Rachel closed her eyes for a few moments of reflection. A pleased grin emerged. She was going to live close to her mother and great-Aunt Regina. But her return was bittersweet. Fate dealt her a bad hand. So, here she was, without Lee, compelled to raise her three youngsters without their father. Her eyes shot open when Barry yelled, "Move over! You're hogging the seat."

Rachel turned to view the action in the backseat.

Eddie kicked Barry. "No, I'm not."

"Barry, Eddie, it doesn't matter," Rachel said. "We're here."

"We are?" Gina asked, yawning and rubbing her eyes.

"Yep." Rachel stepped from the car. "Let's go visit grandma!"

The boys perked up and scrambled out. They fell in step behind their mother but passed by her as she waited to help Gina maneuver the stairs leading to the apartment.

Barry and Eddie spilled onto the floor when Barry turned the knob. Rachel and Gina appeared moments later. They entered while the boys bounced around the room.

"Rachel!" her mother exclaimed, tossing aside her knitting. Mother and daughter embraced. They didn't part until Eddie put the cat in front of his grandmother's face. "Here's Leo." Grandma took the cat and snuggled him against her chest. "Pleased to meet you again, Leo."

Bending, she set the feline down and wrapped the boys in her arms. "I'm so happy you're here." Stepping back, she studied them. "Oh my! You've grown several inches since April."

"I'm almost seven! And I got a cut on my forehead," Barry said, pointing to his stitches. "But I was brave."

"I'm proud of you." Kathryn hugged Gina, then stepped back. "What do we have here?" she asked, pointing to the crutches.

Lifting one crutch, she said, "I hurt my foot and can't walk on it. The doctor said I had to use these. I don't like 'em."

"You'll be running around in no time. I'm glad you're all here at last." She adjusted the two whirling fans that provided scant relief in the stuffy one-bedroom apartment. It had a small kitchen, a living room with a couch, and a couple of easy chairs. A square hooked rug covered the hardwood floor. The décor reflected Kathryn's simple tastes . . . a few throw pillows, matching light yellow curtains, and walls decorated with her grandchildren's pictures. The aroma of homemade spaghetti sauce drifted from the kitchen.

"I've got an enormous pot of spaghetti and meatballs on the stove. And ice cream. I'll bet you're all hungry."

"Oh, boy!" Eddie said. "Hope it's chocolate."

"What else?" Kathryn teased. She waved the kids into the kitchen area. The boys helped to insert the extra leaf.

Throughout dinner, a lively conversation ensued. The children shared accounts of the trip and accident. They talked over one another to share their version.

"We saw some guys' faces on a mountain. And a bunch of water shoot into the air!"

"And a humongous buffalo." Barry stretched his arms wide.

Everyone emptied their plates, and the conversation ran its course.

Rachel stood. "Okay, kiddos, help clean up then we're headed next door to bed. It's way past your bedtime."

Kathryn waved them away. "I'll deal with this later. Gerald assembled the beds, and I made them." She handed Rachel the key.

Rachel and the kids descended the stairs and walked to the three-bedroom cottage. Everyone except Gina carried a suitcase from the car to the house. They waited on the porch as Rachel pulled the key from her pocket.

"Welcome to our new home," Rachel said as she unlocked the door and pushed it open. The kids filed in behind her.

"I want the top bunk!" Barry yelled. Eddie dashed ahead of him, searching for the bedroom.

"No arguing," Rachel said. "You can switch every month."

Gina thumped her way to her room.

Rachel dragged the suitcases to the bedrooms. "Tomorrow is a big day for unpacking. Put on your pjs and brush your teeth. There won't be a lot of time to play until the afternoon. It's always a little cooler in the morning, so we'll finish our work and rest when it gets hotter. Maybe you can run through grandma's sprinkler."

"Me, too?" Gina called from her room.

"Afraid not," Rachel said.

"We'll spray her with water," Barry offered, and the two boys laughed at the idea as they climbed into the bunk bed.

Rachel flung herself onto her bed. A deep sleep took instant charge of her exhausted body.

The sound of voices and the stomping of feet on hardwood floorboards woke Rachel.

"Eat a bowl of cereal while I freshen up. It's in a box in the kitchen. The plastic bowls are in the same box." She shook her head as an argument ensued over who got the last of the marshmallow cereal.

After breakfast, Rachel stood with hands on her hips, surveying the boxes, each marked with the contents. The movers arrived a few days earlier and had stacked the cartons three high in one corner. Furniture sat in the middle of the room with no symmetry. Wiping away sweat, Rachel unsuccessfully searched for the carton containing the fan. She exhaled a deep breath. Time to dive in and unpack. She assigned the kids duties.

Improvements already raced through Rachel's imagination. She'd waste no time fixing this little place into a home they would love. The hardwood floors were dull, and the dark brown paint was depressing and peeling in spots. She'd sweet-talk her mother into sewing two sets of cream-colored curtains.

Kathryn tapped once on the door, then entered. "I'm glad you labeled the boxes. We found the box with the bedding. Hope we put them in the right rooms."

"They are. Thanks, Mom."

The rest of the day flew by as everyone unpacked. The boys became distracted making a fort with the boxes before tearing them down. Rachel made them take a nap to get them out of her hair and give her more time to concentrate on unpacking.

Later in the evening, Kathryn arrived with pizza and cold soda. They spread a blanket on the living room floor as the table was still unassembled.

"It's an indoor picnic," Gina announced.

The boys nodded as their mouths were full of pizza. Kathryn leaned over to wipe the red sauce from Eddie's mouth.

Grandma read a nighttime story to the children and settled the argument about who would sleep with Leo. She then joined Rachel on the couch. She grabbed a *Reader's Digest* magazine to fan herself.

"You look exhausted, dear," Kathryn observed. "Why don't you call it a day?"

Rachel put her feet on the coffee table and leaned back. "I am tired. It was a long trip, and the accident didn't help. Never again."

"Is your broken toe better?"

"I'll be hobbling for a while." Surveying the room, Rachel sighed. "A lot of work still ahead. I can't wait to improve this place, starting with a fresh coat of paint.

And different curtains. They're hideous." She fluttered her eyelids and projected her sweetest smile. "How about making two pairs of curtains? Your sewing skills are impeccable."

"I suppose I can find the time. But don't rush me. By the way, Gerald offered to help with the heavy furniture."

"I welcome his help, but I want to paint first." Rachel stood, searching for something to fan herself. "I'm eager to see him. He's always been there for us, hasn't he?"

"Absolutely. A heads up. Gerald wears hearing aids now. He hates them."

Rachel couldn't fathom seventy-one-year-old, robust Gerald having any physical disability. "Can I count on Cliffy to help? Where is he?"

Kathryn frowned. "Your brother knew you'd be here by now, but he's with his buddies playing pool. Said to tell you he'd be by tomorrow after work."

"Has Cliff's attitude improved, or is he still self-absorbed and selfish?"

Her mother shook her head. "As bad as ever."

"I was hoping he would be a father figure for the kids." Her thoughts wandered to Vince and how he had filled that role.

"I'm concerned your brother is displaying some of your father's traits. They share more than a name. Could be in the genes. He drinks, but I don't consider him an alcoholic . . . yet. But enough about Cliff." Kathryn filled two glasses with water. "Guess this is the only beverage available until you can go shopping for groceries. Cheers!"

"I can hang in here a little while longer to visit, but if I yawn, I'm headed to bed."

After a half-hour of light conversation, Kathryn clapped her hands together. "I brought something for you." She opened a large handbag and lifted a hardcover book from its depths. She handed it to Rachel.

"What the heck?" Rachel asked.

"The author is . . ." her mother coaxed her.

Rachel examined the cover. *Nightmare* by Kathryn Douglas.

"I'm a published writer!"

"No way." Her daughter opened the book. She flipped through the pages, then closed it. A recent photo of her mother on the back cover stared at her.

"I never dreamed I'd write a book people would pay money to read. I haven't forgotten how much you love animals and wanted to become a vet since you were a little girl. This money can help pay for your certification here in Oregon." Her tone ended hopefully.

Rachel rubbed the cover several times in disbelief. "You never told me. What's the story about?"

"A *fiction* account about a family with an alcoholic, abusive husband and father. Sound familiar?"

Rachel stiffened. "Mom, how dare you write about such a nightmare, *our* nightmare?" She placed the book beside her on the couch and shoved it away.

Rachel's reaction surprised Kathryn. "I thought you'd be proud of me for having the guts to rehash our ordeal. It was excellent therapy. I've been writing off and on for years and finally completed the story. I hope you read it."

"Don't count on it. No way will I let you pay for veterinary school with proceeds from the book." Rachel rose and faked a yawn. "It's been a long day. I'm heading to bed."

"I regret the misery you and Cliff experienced. But I'm finally over the guilt for not protecting you and staying in such a horrendous environment." Kathryn wasn't about to let Rachel dismiss her. She parked herself in front of Rachel, blocking her escape. "And speaking of guilt. You're still not blaming yourself for Lee's death, are you?"

Rachel stepped around her mother. Kathryn grabbed Rachel's arm and turned her daughter to face her. "I don't want you to remain consumed with guilt."

Rachel glared at her mother.

"Sit." Kathryn pointed to the couch.

Rachel plopped her body against the couch's back, pressing her lips together. How dare her mother? Her guilt was genuine, an unwelcome, constant companion. It was like ice in her guts. She wanted Lee's forgiveness despite his broken marriage vows. She stared at the ceiling, tuning out her mother as Kathryn tried to convince Rachel she couldn't let guilt rule her life.

Rachel seethed with irritation, tapping her fingers on the couch. She was ready to explode. Finally, she interrupted Kathryn. "Okay, Mom, enough. Thanks for caring, but I am tired. I'm going to bed. Now." She walked to the front door and opened it.

Kathryn glanced at her watch. "You're right. It's almost eleven. I've had my say. Goodnight, my dear."

Locking the door after her mother's departure, Rachel moved toward the lamp to turn it off. Her eyes strayed toward the book. It lay on the couch, daring her to read it. She picked it up and hurled it across the room.

Chapter 11

E arly the next morning, Eddie ran into his
mother's bedroom. "An old man is outside."

Groggy, Rachel stretched. It took her
a few moments to comprehend she was at home in
Alder Creek.

Eddie hopped up and down next to the bed. "Hurry,
Mom! Come to the door."

She peered at the clock. *7:35. Who'd be here so early?*
Rachel donned her bathrobe and limped down the hall
to the living room. The sunshine glimmered through
the windows, promising another hot day.

Rachel opened the door. Gerald stood on the
porch grinning. He swung her around. Holding up her
bandaged foot, she said, "Put me down." Gerald obliged,
and she stepped back, balancing and supporting her
weight on one foot.

"Welcome home," Gerald said. "So sorry about Lee."

"Thank you," Rachel said, wrapping her arms
around his waist. She hugged him and pointed to her
foot, still wrapped in a stretch bandage. He raised his
eyes in question. "Later." She pulled him inside.

While Gerald introduced himself to Eddie, Rachel
eyed him. He hadn't changed an iota since she had

last seen him. His six-and-a-half-foot frame towered over her, and his gray hair was as wavy as ever. Years of carpentry and sculpting wood made his hands more callused. He wore his signature heavy work boots and long-sleeved khaki shirt.

Palm down, Gerald raised his hand to Eddie's height. "Gonna grow tall enough to dunk a basketball hoop."

Eddie tugged on Gerald's shirt, speaking at a rapid pace. "I can already dribble really good."

"Eddie, talk slower," Rachel said.

Gerald nodded and patted the boy's head. "Maybe I'll challenge you to a shooting contest."

"I'll beat you," Eddie predicted. "Hey, what're those things in your ears?"

"I don't hear well nowadays," Gerald answered, "so I need to wear these aids."

Eddie ran to awaken his siblings. Rachel heard him tell them. "Guess what? An old man is here that can't hear. He has small things in his ears."

"You want coffee?" Rachel asked.

"Sure."

Rachel tightened the belt around her robe and headed for the kitchen. Barry shuffled to where Gerald sat at the table. He walked around the man, scrutinizing him. Gerald pointed to Barry's stitches, frowning. Barry stopped next to Gerald's side, examining the small device in the man's right ear. "Does that thing hurt?"

"Not a bit." He pulled out one aid and let Barry hold it.

Barry squished his nose. "Yucky!"

"You don't need to yell." Rachel stood beside Gerald. "This is Barry. And meet my daughter, Gina."

Gerald pushed up his wire-rimmed eyeglasses then shook Barry's hand and winked at Gina.

"I feel sorry for you. Are you sad?" asked Gina.

"Not one bit. I'm a happy fella. I hope we can become acquainted. Right now, I'm here to help move furniture or whatever your Mom needs."

"I thought I'd paint first. We can start tomorrow after I buy several gallons."

After consuming the coffee, Gerald gave Rachel a bear hug, waved to the children, and departed. Rachel found clean clothes for the kids in the packed boxes. The family trooped next door to the café for a "home-cooked" breakfast. The aroma of sizzling bacon and freshly brewed coffee greeted them as they entered.

Rachel stared in disbelief as she surveyed the interior. It cried out for major improvements. The eight booths' frayed upholstery, the cracking linoleum, and the faded gingham curtains all needed replacement. Nicks and scratches marred the dozen tables. The wooden bar stools along the counter were candidates for firewood. The dreary walls begged for a bright coat of paint.

"Let me guess," Grandma Kathryn said, "pancakes for everyone."

Sliding into a booth, they answered, "Yeah!"

"With lots of syrup," Eddie said.

Ceiling fans blasted in the kitchen while Kathryn hustled to complete orders. The children gobbled down the buttermilk pancakes and scrambled eggs.

Rachel pitched in to wash dishes in the small kitchen, swallowing bites here and there.

When the breakfast rush thinned, the kids beat feet out the back door to play outside. The two women sat at a table where Rachel could watch them.

Rachel commented, hoping not to offend her mother. "This place needs a major overhaul."

"I mentioned to Aunt Regina the stove and cooler are ready for the appliance graveyard. And guess what? She said she'd been thinking about renovations. She and Gerald collaborated and he'll do most of the work. He'll start in a few weeks. It's going to cost a bundle, though."

Rachel patted Kathryn's shoulder. "But well worth it. Gerald hasn't changed one bit. Hard to believe he's seventy-one. Has he recovered from losing Poncho?"

"Four years have passed since his beloved dog disappeared on the hunting trip. He carved a wooden statue of Poncho. I've seen him sitting and staring at it. He keeps busy with his various projects and helps Aunt Regina maintain the café and her property."

"He built his cabin from scratch by himself, didn't he?" She sipped her coffee.

"Yep. Quite the carpenter. Did you notice the thirty-foot-high bear covered with ivy on the other side of this building? Gerald built it a few years ago. We call it the Ivy Bear. It's his pride and joy. The local paper did a write-up about it. Aunt Regina's been considering changing the café's name to *The Ivy Bear*."

Rachel rose and fetched the broom and dustpan. Sweeping up a pile of crumbs, Rachel said, "I've always wondered about the relationship between Aunt Regina and Gerald. What's the scoop, Mom?"

"They met at a grange dance years ago when they were in their late twenties. Rumors swirled they were lovers. After almost forty years, they're still completely devoted to one another. Gerald stayed in Aunt Regina's basement while he built his cabin on her property. And boy, did the tongues wag at the arrangement. Aunt Regina couldn't care less." She grinned, recalling the hullabaloo. "I don't know why they never married."

Leaning on the counter, chin resting on her hands, Rachel remarked, "I always thought they were so opposite . . . Aunt Regina so prim and proper and authoritative. Gerald, rough-and-ready, yet shy and gentle. How romantic in a weird sort of way. Kinda like *Lady and the Tramp*."

"Guess you could say that," Kathryn agreed.

"Speaking of Aunt Regina, I'm ready to head over to her place." Opening the back door, she shouted to the kids. "Come on, we're leaving."

"Where to?" Barry asked as he ran ahead of the others to the car. "Shotgun!"

Eddie ran at his heels and Gina wailed as she hobbled along. "I can't run."

"Oh, the life of a mother." Rachel shook her head and kissed her mother's cheek.

"You don't fool me, my dear. You love it."

"Kids, come back. We aren't taking the car. We're just going across the road."

Eddie made a quick detour to the cottage to fetch Leo.

Heatwaves rose from the asphalt. A construction crew working to extend the two-lane road to a four-lane highway paused often to gulp water from canteens. Perspiration rolled from the crews' foreheads and their sweat-soaked shirts clung to their skin. Exhaust fumes from the idling vehicles permeated the stagnant air.

The highway expansion troubled Rachel. She was certain it would generate an increase in speedy vehicles traveling to and from Mt. Hood. Standing at the road's edge, she waited for an opportunity to shepherd her family to the other side.

The flagger stopped all traffic and signaled for them to proceed. Another worker approached Gina and reached for the crutches. Gina raised one to defend herself from this stranger. The man addressed Rachel. "I want to carry her across the road. Is that okay with you?"

Rachel addressed Gina. "He wants to help you across the road."

"Oh."

"Here we go. Can't hold up all that traffic, can we? They don't know you're a princess in disguise." The strong worker handed Gina's crutches to a co-worker. He wiped his sweaty palms on his dirty jeans, then carried her to the edge of Aunt Regina's driveway.

Further back in the line of idling vehicles, Rachel could see heads leaning out of windows.

"Eddie, Barry, catch up."

The boys scurried behind the worker, followed by Rachel.

"I've got a daughter about the same age as yours. I would hope that any guy would help her out if she had a similar injury."

"Thanks. It was thoughtful of you to help." Looking past the man's shoulder, Rachel saw the stern expression of the crew leader. "Guess you'd better head back to work."

"Yeah." He saluted and returned to his post, pulling the walkie-talkie to his lips and shouting out orders. The flagger turned his sign and cars moved again.

Eddie pounded on the bright red door. Barking erupted, and a voice yelled over the racket, "Come in!"

The troop filed inside. Aunt Regina sprang to her feet. She hurried toward Rachel without her cane, arms outstretched. "*Mia cara, Rachel. Ancora bella.*"

Born and raised in Bologna, Italy, Regina Estelle Pagnini, a month shy of seventy-one, was striking with silver-gray hair, not one strand out of place. Make-up covered her wrinkle-free face, including her trademark passion-red lipstick. Her bright blue eyes sparkled behind her jewel-framed eyeglasses. She was slender and dressed in a sleeveless cotton dress. She exuded authority and confidence.

Gina ran her fingers along the three strands of faux pearls dangling from Regina's neck. "These are pretty." She also admired the glitzy bracelets adorning both wrists. "When I grow older, I'm going to wear jewelry like yours."

"You've all grown so much since I last saw you. Let me remember, four . . . five years ago? You were a toddler, Barry. Eddie, how tall you are! And," she waved her hand at Gina. "Looks like my namesake won't be dancing around for a while." She ended up making a tsking noise.

Gina pounded one crutch on the flowery carpet. "I hate these."

Eddie placed Leo on the floor. "This is our cat."

Aunt Regina's two dogs, Ming and Chang, darted toward the unsuspecting feline. They pounced on him, rolling him over before he could escape.

Gina raised one crutch. Aunt Regina stepped between the girl and the dogs. Her foot shoved the two Pekingese from the cat and she admonished them. Tails wagging, they retreated to their overstuffed doggie beds, eyeballing Leo.

"They're protective of me and their territory," she excused their behavior. "Hold your cat or better yet, put him outside." Aunt Regina acted unashamed at how much she loved her dogs and spoiled them rotten.

Rachel picked up the trembling Leo. She was aware of her great-aunt's devotion toward her "babies" and how she always defended Ming and Chang. She sat on the red velvet sofa and gazed out the room-length picture window. "You look marvelous as always," she complimented her great-aunt.

"Thank you, my darling," Aunt Regina said, sitting beside her great-niece. "You can't imagine how happy I am you've moved back." She placed her hand on Rachel's. "But sad about the circumstances that caused your return. I loved Lee and was shocked about his death. I regret I couldn't travel to the funeral."

Eddie piped up. "Daddy said he'd get me a basketball, and even a hoop when I turn eight. But now he can't 'cause he's dead."

Aunt Regina asked, "When is your birthday?"

"September seven."

"*Oh mio*, this Friday, only two days from now. We'll have to make sure you have a cake and ice cream."

"I'm going to be seven!" Barry announced.

"Barry's birthday is Monday," Rachel said.

"Well, that goes for you too, *mio caro bambino*. How about we celebrate both your birthdays on Saturday?"

"I don't wanna share my birthday with Barry," Eddie said. "We already did at Uncle Dom's."

Aunt Regina smiled. "Two parties coming up!"

"Yea," Eddie and Barry shouted in unison.

"Nice," Rachel said, "but one party is sufficient."

The boys' expressions changed from excited to disappointed. "On second thought," Rachel said, "two celebrations will be fun." She faced her sons. They looked at one another, high-fiving.

"All settled," Aunt Regina said. "Eddie's party on Friday; Barry's on Monday. I'll make two cakes."

"I want a chocolate cake," Eddie said.

"Me, too," Barry emphasized. "And with a dinosaur on it!"

Eddie pressed his nose against the picture window. He wiped the sweat from his forehead. "Can we play in the water? And Leo too."

Rachel gazed out the window. The fir trees were about six feet higher since her last visit. Overgrown morning glory covered the path leading down to the creek. Rachel's lips curved upward as she recalled the many times she and Cliff spent splashing each other on hot summer days. It was a welcome respite from their monster father.

"Maybe later. And you need Aunt Regina's permission."

"Don't be silly. You're welcome to play in the creek anytime."

"Why not now?" Eddie pouted. "It's hot."

"If you finish unpacking your clothes and toys, we'll come back later," Rachel promised. She embraced her great-aunt. "Thank you for letting us stay in the cottage." With her most convincing smile, she added, "And I plan to spruce it up, with your permission, of course. I'm going to paint first."

"By all means, go ahead. Why don't you leave the children with me and run to the store?"

Rachel liked the idea. "Are you sure you don't mind?"

"Of course not. It'll give us a chance to get to know one another and for me to start spoiling them."

"I'll bring Leo home, then head into Sandy. Should be back within a couple of hours if I'm able to get out of the driveway. The construction crew is holding up traffic right in front of our driveways."

When Rachel returned to her great-aunt's two hours later, the children were munching on hot dogs, baked beans, potato chips, and cold soda drinks.

When everyone finished eating, she pointed out to her aunt. "You've already spoiled us."

"My pleasure. Your children are enchanting. It's going to be wonderful having them so close."

Shaking the boys' hands goodbye, she extended her left hand to Gina.

"Wow!" The girl marveled at the huge gemstone gleaming on the woman's ring finger. Aunt Regina held up her hand, admiring her three-carat sapphire and diamond ring. "My one indulgence years ago. You like it?"

"Yeah."

"It must a cost a bazillion dollars," Barry said.

"Not quite, but it is north of four thousand. It matches your deep blue eyes, Gina, like mine." Removing the ring, she slipped it on Gina's small finger. The girl waved her hand like a princess on a parade float. The ring flew off and sailed across the room. Ming and Chang darted to it. "Stop!" Aunt Regina ordered. They lowered their heads and recoiled.

"Sorry," Gina said. "I didn't mean to."

Rachel retrieved the jewel and handed it to her aunt. Slipping the ring back on, the older woman winked at Gina. "Your finger's too small . . . for now."

The ring would pay for my tuition for veterinary school. But Rachel pushed the thought aside. It wasn't hers and that was that.

Chapter 12

Two days later, on Friday, thunder and lightning pierced the serene atmosphere. Raindrops hammered the roof and rapped the windows like pellets. The parched vegetation devoured the welcome downpour. By the time everyone gathered to celebrate Eddie's birthday, the deluge stopped. Patches of blue peeked through the clouds.

"Before you blow out the candles, make a wish," Rachel reminded Eddie.

The birthday boy inhaled, puckered his lips, and blew out all eight flames. "That means I'll get a basketball!"

Rachel put the used paper plates into a grocery bag and handed it to Eddie. She told him to deposit the trash into the garbage can.

"But it's my birthday."

Rachel pointed toward the door. "Go." As Eddie grasped the sack and dragged it outside, everyone followed him. He picked up the lid and dropped the garbage inside and turned away.

"Your new ball's in there!" Barry burst out, bending into the can, but unable to reach it.

Eddie yanked Barry away and peered inside. Lying on the bottom underneath the birthday clutter was a brand-new Spalding basketball.

"Yippee!" Eddie squealed. He pulled it out and dribbled around the driveway.

"Throw the ball through the basket," Grandma Kathryn said.

"There's no basket."

She pointed to the garage.

"Wow! A hoop too!" Eddie launched the ball toward the basket, hitting the rim. He rebounded the miss and moved closer. He shot again. Swish!

"A future basketball star," Gerald said.

"You can thank Aunt Regina for the ball and hoop and Gerald for installing it," Rachel said.

Eddie wrapped his arms around their waists, then resumed dribbling and shooting.

"Hey, Uncle Cliffy, would you play with me?"

"Nah, kid, gotta leave. Another time. And call me Cliff, not Cliffy."

Cliff half-heartedly hugged his mother and great-aunt and waved to Gerald. He hopped into his '54 Chevy and screeched away, radio blaring.

"How come he wouldn't play with me?" Eddie asked. "Uncle Vince always did."

Rachel refused to make excuses for her brother. "I guess he didn't want to."

"All he does is comb his greasy hair and smoke his nasty cigarettes," Gina said.

"And brag about winning pool all the time," added Eddie.

On Monday, the children attended school for the first time, and the family gathered once again for Barry's seventh birthday. By Friday, Gina discarded her crutches, and the doctor removed Barry's stitches. Rachel hoped the scar wouldn't bother him.

During the next three days, Rachel and Gerald completed the painting, unpacking, and furniture arrangement. Above the stone fireplace, she hung the last portrait of Lee dressed in his navy uniform. She positioned the folded flag and a framed photo of the entire family on the mantel. She stepped back, focusing on her late husband's smiling face. Sobs shook her body. Her heart withered. It hurt to breathe.

Gerald wrapped Rachel within his sturdy arms. She leaned her head against his chest, her teardrops blotting his shirt. The warmth of this gentle giant soothed her.

Releasing Rachel, Gerald said, "I wish I had the power to make your pain disappear."

She stroked the flag. *I'll regret until my dying breath that I threatened to leave him.*

With the completion of the cottage updates, Rachel decided Leo was overdue for a checkup. Aunt Regina steered her to Dr. Abbott, Ming's and Chang's vet. Virginia, the indispensable office manager, gave Rachel a few forms to complete. "The doctor will see Leo shortly." She petted the trembling cat.

Doc Abbott, the well-respected veterinarian in Sandy, resembled everyone's favorite grandpa. His engaging smile reassured Rachel. During the visit, he mentioned how short-staffed the clinic was and he was looking for help. Now that all the kids were in school full-time, Rachel's days were free, and it was time for her to get a job. "I'd like to apply. I'll volunteer for a month as a trial." She hoped she didn't sound desperate.

He asked her a few questions, then welcomed the idea. After only a week of volunteering, Rachel's rapport with animals impressed the doctor. He offered her a job as an assistant.

Rachel took to her job with gusto. She loved the animals most of the time. She made a point of learning the names of the beloved pets and their owners.

Rachel opened the door and led an Australian shepherd into the waiting area. "Here you go, Mr. Moody." Rachel handed the dog's leash to him. "She's checked out okay, but Dr. Abbott wants to increase her insulin dosage a little." She gave him the written instructions, asking if he had questions. "And Dolly's a tad overweight. Watch her diet."

He laughed. "Guess I'll cut out the leftovers. Gotta keep her healthy. She's a fabulous guard dog. Can hear a mouse pee on a cotton ball."

Virginia pushed aside a strand of her striking auburn hair, then handed him a receipt.

Rachel bent over and rubbed both hands on the dog's head. Dolly licked her face.

"Come on, girl," Mr. Moody said, grabbing the leash. "Let's go home to Mama." He waved to Rachel and Virginia, losing his balance as Dolly darted toward the door.

Virginia complimented Rachel. "You're the best assistant we've ever had. So glad you've been on board the past couple of months."

Rachel blew her a kiss. The relationship between the two co-workers was developing into more than business. Childless Virginia couldn't resist Gina, Eddie, and Barry. "I'll spoil them as though they were my grandchildren."

"What's in there?" Rachel asked, pointing to a cardboard box near the entrance.

"Little League uniforms for next spring. Doc sponsors the team. Coach DeLuca will pick them up later today. He's the high school basketball coach. Rumor has it he will also handle the eighth graders this season. Double duty, but he's up to the challenge. His life revolves around coaching kids."

The following morning, the box was gone. "I see the coach came for his box," Rachel noted to Virginia.

"He came a few minutes after you left. I wish you'd been here. He's a wonderful guy and not married. How about I introduce you?"

"Not interested." Rachel waved the comment aside and continued to the back of the clinic. She didn't need a man in her life or any outside interference. She gave a firm nod to confirm the thought.

Chapter 13

—◆—

Rachel hosted the Thanksgiving gathering. She hoped playing hostess would distract her from dwelling on her first major holiday without Lee. The meal exceeded her expectations. She relished her family's compliments. Even Cliff expressed his satisfaction after gobbling down three helpings of turkey. As was customary, each family member voiced what they were thankful for. When Rachel's turn came, words escaped her. She'd lost her husband forever. How could she be grateful? She glanced at all the eyes focused on her. "I'm home with the people I love the most."

Kathryn and Aunt Regina offered to help with the cleanup. Rachel shooed them home. She wrapped the leftovers in aluminum foil. The movements felt like a familiar dance. She'd done these many times over the years during happier times in Vineland with Lee's family. She'd helped her sisters-in-law and mother-in-law. They'd laughed and teased while tidying the kitchen. She'd glance into the living room where the men played poker, cigarette smoke permeating the air. Here there was no sound. The kids were in bed, and she was alone in the kitchen. It wasn't the same. It never would be.

Placing the dirty roasting pan into the warm, sudsy water, she scrubbed hard, then harder, as though she could wipe away her sorrow and Lee's infidelity. She threw the SOS pad into the water and leaned over the sink, resting her head on her wet hands. The tears streamed non-stop and her lips quivered.

Leaving the pan to soak, she flipped off the kitchen lights and dragged herself to the bedroom. She plopped onto the bed. Exhausted from the day's events, she closed her eyes. Her mind drifted to thoughts of Lee. Eight months after his passing, she still missed him. She would whisper sweet musings he'd never hear. She could only define her sorrow and guilt as death by a million paper cuts. Lee's affair was another cut to her injured psyche. Her breathing became soft and rhythmic, and she drifted to sleep.

The telephone's incessant ringing woke Rachel. She jerked up, shivering as she probed in the dark for the lamp's light switch. Hurrying into the living room, she stubbed her healed left toe against the coffee table. "Crap! Damn!" Lifting the earpiece, she said, "Who the hell is this? Better be important."

"It's Dominick."

Rachel regretted her outburst. "I'm sorry. What's up?" She rubbed her throbbing foot. She glanced at the clock. Nine fifteen.

"I've got good news. I have a full-price offer for the house." His voice raised a little with excitement.

The words sunk through the fog, and her heart rate increased. "Full price? Wonderful! When is closing?"

"So, you're accepting the offer?"

"Of course!"

"I'll call their realtor to prepare the paperwork and mail them as soon as they're ready. I suggest you have a lawyer read them. If the terms are satisfactory, sign the papers and mail them back. They are asking for a thirty-day closing if you're agreeable."

"Yes! The house is empty, so they can move in when the paperwork is complete." Tears of joy and relief leaked from the corners of her eyes.

"How are you and the kids?"

"We're all fine. Better now. How is everyone at your end of the world? Who hosted the dinner?"

"We did this year. Most of the family is still here, even though it's after midnight. The realtor was sorry to bother me on a holiday but his clients were insistent. I've got Vince here. He wants to chat with you."

Vince greeted Rachel and gave her updates about everyone.

"When are you coming for a visit?" Rachel asked. "The kids miss you." She felt the warmth of the family's love and concern in his voice. Her heart warmed.

"I thought I'd come at Christmas and surprise them. Is that okay with you?"

"Of course. The kids will be overjoyed. Eddie will be eager to show you his improved basketball skills."

He hesitated. "Rachel, how about you? Will you be glad to see me?"

"Why wouldn't I?" After a few more pleasantries, the conversation ended. Rachel turned down the thermostat and returned to her bedroom. Closing the curtains, she saw delicate snowflakes drifting downward, carpeting the backyard. "Time for the skiing season."

She pulled out her flannel nightgown from her bottom dresser drawer. A book fell to the floor. *Nightmare.* She'd put it there weeks ago with no intention to read it. Rachel picked up the book, ready to toss it inside the drawer. But this time, the picture on the cover of a silhouetted man with a raised fist roused her curiosity.

Leaning against the headboard, she opened to the first page. *He was a gem*, the story began. Intrigued, she continued reading. She read the paragraph describing the first time the husband's knuckles landed a severe blow on the wife's cheek. Rachel's muscles tensed as she recalled her father doing the same. To this day, Rachel blamed the almighty bottle for the demons controlling her father. She glared at the words daring her to continue reading. Through the blur in her eyes, she turned the page. After a while, her eyes closed, and the paperback slipped from her grasp.

"Mom, it snowed!" Eddie ran into the room, jumping on the bed. "Can I make a snowman?"

Almost eight! Everyone had slept in since there was no school the day after Thanksgiving. Her eyes saw *Nightmare* lying at her side. She wouldn't read anymore. Too painful. She arose and forced a cheerful face before flinging the book into the closet and kicking the door shut.

Barry entered the bedroom, wearing his hooded jacket over his pajamas. "I'm going outside and make snowballs!"

"I'm bringing Leo too," Eddie said.

"Hold on, boys. You'll eat breakfast first and get dressed. Beds made?"

Their heads lowered and turned side to side.

"Scoot."

Rachel cracked a contented grin as she stood in the doorway watching the children romp in the snow, throwing snowballs at one another. She laughed when Leo's paws touched this unfamiliar substance, and he made a beeline for the door.

Gerald appeared with a wheelbarrow full of wood for the fireplace and joined the snowball fight. He had become the children's surrogate grandfather. He visited them nearly every day, involving himself in their lives ... teaching the boys how to carve small wooden objects, playing H-O-R-S-E at the basketball hoop with Eddie. He bought three used bikes and spiffed them up. He presented them to the kids. He accompanied them on bike rides along the gravel road to the Sandy River. The children had grown fond of Gerald and started calling him grandpa.

Three days before Christmas, Gerald, Rachel, and the children traipsed through the nearby woods to find the perfect tree. That evening, Gerald secured it in the tree stand. He placed the six-foot Douglas fir near the window. Eddie picked up a strand of colorful Christmas lights and wrapped them around the branches. "Grandpa" Gerald strung the second strand on the upper half. Aunt Regina sat in the overstuffed chair, holding her spoiled pets on her lap.

Kathryn arrived with the makings for hot chocolate. She also brought a fresh batch of sugar cookies shaped like Santa, reindeer, stars, and Christmas trees to decorate.

Eddie and Barry followed their grandmother into the kitchen, eager to frost the goodies. Gina arranged the wooden nativity scene on a small table. When she finished, Aunt Regina pulled an ornate angel from the box sitting by her feet.

"Wow!" gasped Gina. "How pretty. Can I hold it?"

"I've had this since I was a child in Italy. I want you to have the angel, *mia cara nipote.*"

Gina's face lit up brighter than the tree lights. Gerald lifted her so she could place it on top. He then placed Gina on his shoulders and stepped back so the excited girl could admire the ornament. Watching Gina's joy, Aunt Regina reminisced how that angel had delighted her as a child.

There was a knock on the front door. Rachel poked her head outside, then opened her mouth to yell with glee. The unexpected visitor silenced her. He entered, tiptoed toward the tree, and reached for the unsuspecting girl. Rachel silently gestured to Gerald it was okay to let the man take Gina from him. During the exchange, Gina fell into the man's arms. Turning her head, she let out a high-pitched shriek. With the strength of a bodybuilder, she wrapped her arms and legs around her Uncle Vince.

Barry and Eddie appeared from the kitchen, frosted cookies in hand. When they saw their favorite uncle, they rushed to him with the intensity of raging bulls. They leaped toward him, the weight of their bodies causing Vince to tumble backward. His body cushioned Gina. The boys pounced on top of him, the cookies crumbling to the floor. Elated by their reception, he wrestled with the overjoyed children.

Heartened by this display of genuine affection, Gerald retreated to the kitchen. He patted his eyes with a napkin.

Vince asked Eddie how much his basketball skills improved.

"I'm getting better and better. I wish I had someone to play with. Gerald is ok, but he's too old. And Uncle Cliff doesn't play with me much. When he does, he hogs the ball. I don't like him. He's not nice like you." Eddie spoke the last part in a lower tone for Vince's benefit.

"Yeah," Gina agreed. "He's a meanie."

Barry picked up a hiding Leo from behind the couch and handed him to Vince. Ming and Chang yelped and wagged their tails.

"He's twice the size," Vince said. He lifted the cat and rocked him back and forth. "I heard how you lost him after the accident."

"Yeah, we were so sad, but a nice man found Leo and brought him to us in the hospital," Gina said.

"How long are you stayin'?" Eddie asked.

"Seven days." He looked at Rachel. "Okay with you?"

"Heck, yes."

"Yay! We can shoot baskets." Eddie jumped with delight. "I got a brand-new ball and hoop for my birthday."

Kathryn appeared and hugged Vince. "So happy you came. You're still as handsome as ever. Hard to believe some lucky gal hasn't lassoed you yet."

Vince stepped back, holding Kathryn's hands. "I'll say the same about you. If I were older, I'd be wining and dining you." And approaching Aunt Regina, he took her hand and kissed it. "Beauty runs in this family."

"*Grazie*, Vince. If I was younger and in better shape, I'd insist you take me dancing!"

Kathryn signaled for everyone to come and enjoy hot chocolate and cookies.

The kids grabbed Vince's hands and pulled him into the kitchen. Gerald was leaning against the stove, sipping coffee.

"That's Gerald," Eddie told his uncle.

Vince extended his hand. He saluted Gerald with his other arm, recalling meeting him at Rachel's wedding.

While choosing several cookies, Vince asked Rachel, "Hey, where's your brother?"

"Who knows? I invited him." Rachel shrugged the question away.

Around ten, Vince carried each child piggyback to the boys' bedroom. The boys yapped about their activities over the past few months. Eddie bragged about his developing basketball skills.

"I wish you lived closer," Gina said as Vince escorted her to her room. "I miss you."

Rachel tidied the sofa. She pulled two blankets from the linen closet and bent to arrange them for Vince.

Vince entered the living room. At the sight of Rachel's slim figure arranging blankets, he paused. He took several deep breaths to compose himself. He opened his overnight suitcase and pulled out an envelope.

"The kids are all tucked in," he said as he approached Rachel.

"Your accommodations are ready. I don't have an extra bed. Mom thinks you should sleep on her couch or at Aunt Regina's. Or," she shook her head, "at Cliff's."

"This is fine." Sitting down, he handed her the envelope.

Her eyes questioned him.

"Look inside."

She tore open the envelope and pulled out a check. "What?"

"The house closed, and the proceeds were available before I left. Dominick gave me the check and told me to deliver it to you. Nice timing for Christmas."

Rachel stared at the amount. "More than I expected. Now I can finish paying Steve."

"Steve?"

"The shop owner who repaired the car after the accident. He's the one who brought Leo to the hospital. He was so kind to us."

She put the check in her pocket and walked to the fireplace, touching the flag.

Vince followed her. "Nice display, Rach. I still miss Lee. The whole family does. We often talk about him.

And," he gazed straight into her sad eyes, "you too. Still wish you would have stayed in Philly or moved to Vineland."

He took her hand and led her back to the couch. "Any chance you'll ever return?"

"Only for visits. This is my home, Vince. I'm as content as I can be without Lee."

"How are ya coping?"

She sighed. "It's been nine months now. I miss him, and when I turn out the light each night, he's the last thought on my mind."

Vince drew her close.

"Little things remind me of him. Leo, for instance. Lee defied me and got the kitten against my wishes. But," she cracked a smile, "Leo's been a blessing. Except for causing the accident. Thank God he showed up the next day. The kids love that cat."

Vince shook his finger at her. "I wish you'd allowed me to go with you. I worried the entire time. When I heard about the accident, *after* you'd arrived home, I was hurt and disappointed you didn't call."

"Sorry, but everything's okay now."

"Yeah. Too bad about Barry's scar. Quite noticeable."

"He's adjusting. He'll no doubt style his hair to cover his forehead when he gets older. I try to be strong for the kids' sake. They miss their dad."

He lifted her left hand, stroking it. "I see you're still wearing your wedding ring. What did you do with Lee's?"

Lee's missing ring still baffled and troubled Rachel. She couldn't explain what happened, so she dodged the question. "In my heart, I'm still married. No one can take Lee's place."

"You can't be serious. You're what, thirty-two now? Too young and beautiful to remain single."

"I don't want anyone else."

Vince cupped her face in his hands. "Tell me straight. Do you want to stay a widow for the rest of your life?"

Rachel removed his hands from her chin. "I want Lee back."

"You know that's impossible. I know you loved Lee, but don't let your guilt stop you from remarrying. You're allowed to fall in love again. I know Lee is a hard act to follow. He loved you and the kids more than life itself. He was a perfect husband and father. Do you realize how lucky you were?"

Vince's words cut Rachel like a knife. She turned away from him and slid to the opposite end of the couch. In a raised voice, she said, "Lee wasn't the . . ." She stopped before the awful truth leaked from her mouth. As much as she wanted to confide to someone about Lee's affair, she wouldn't divulge his adultery. She still loved him enough to never reveal her secret to his family and friends. Let their respect for him remain intact. Nothing to gain.

Vince slid next to Rachel. Pursuing her seemed pointless but he wasn't yet ready to give up. "I want to be in your life. I admit I acted too soon to show my feelings for you before you left Philly."

Rachel didn't look at him. She loved him, but not romantically.

"I want to be more than a brother-in-law," he said. "I'd move here in a heartbeat if you gave me an inkling of encouragement. I love the kids and I'm sure they reciprocate." Pausing and clearing his throat, he blurted out before he lost his courage. "I'd be a fantastic stepfather. I'm positive Lee would approve. And," he chuckled, "your last name will still be Favretto!"

Surprised Vince's "proposal" flattered her, Rachel took his hand in hers and said one word. "No."

Vince's shoulders slumped and he sighed dejectedly.

"I owe it to Lee to never remarry, especially after I threatened to leave him. I'm sure I caused him emotional distress." She blinked back tears as Vince ran his left fingers up and down her arm. He pulled her close, running his lips along the nape of her neck, across her cheek, then onto her lips. His musky scent and soft touch aroused Rachel. Without permission, her lips responded, pressing hard against Vince's. They locked eyes as Vince discarded his shirt and shoes.

Sex isn't merely a fun activity, like playing cards or dancing. Rachel believed it is a strong union between two persons who love one another and are married. This wasn't the case with Vince. Her arousal disappeared as she knew she couldn't be a traitor to her morals. She pushed Vince away.

"Good night," she said and retreated to her bedroom. Poor Vince. She loved him, but not the way he wished.

Chapter 14

A unt Regina insisted she host the holiday celebration. After Christmas morning Mass, the family gathered in her spacious living room to open gifts. Vince acted as Santa, distributing the presents to the gleeful children. They ripped off the bright wrappings with gusto.

Cliff came in from the kitchen with another plate of appetizers and sat on the floor. He'd brought a couple of beers. He set his drink between him and Rachel. She sniffed and glared at Cliff while he smirked at her.

"Throw the beer away." She spoke between clenched teeth and in a low voice, so no one else would hear the exchange. She grabbed the beers and tossed them into the garbage.

"Go ahead, Rachie, make a scene." He munched on a raw carrot, emphasizing the crunching.

Rachel crossed her arms and clamped her lips together.

"Pajamas," Barry said, tossing them aside and tearing open the next present. "Oh boy! A set of dinosaurs!"

Gina stroked the doll's dark hair which matched her own. She looked at her mother, but Rachel shook her head in denial. Gina read the card. From Uncle Vince. She hugged him hard. "How did you know I wanted another doll?"

"I have an in with Santa," he whispered back with a wink.

Aunt Regina clapped her hands. "I have a couple of special gifts. Take a seat, everyone."

"I'll check on the turkey first." Kathryn stood to make her way to the kitchen.

Aunt Regina pointed to the sofa. "Sit," she ordered Kathryn.

Resembling a queen holding court, Aunt Regina sat erect in her overstuffed chair, Ming and Chang at her feet. "I'll be brief. I'm getting up in age and arthritis is having its way with my body. I no longer want the responsibility of the café. Kathryn, I'm giving it to you." She announced the gift with a flourish, holding out a fat envelope.

Kathryn's jaw dropped. She stared at her aunt. Her mouth moved, but no words came out. Recovering, she said, "Thank you, but at this stage in my life, I'm not sure I want to be tied down."

"Nonsense," Aunt Regina said. "I see how you thrive running the café, and you're a superb manager. The renovations are underway. You've built the business up, and the regulars love the food and you. You can hire a manager like I hired you and pursue other interests if you chose, like writing another book."

Kathryn gave her a slow handshake, still in a bit of a shock. "I appreciate this, Aunt Regina, but I can't accept your gift."

"I knew what your reaction would be, so I had my attorney prepare a bill of sale. It's yours for one dollar." Ignoring Kathryn's objections, she continued. "But there is one stipulation." Looking fondly at Gerald, she said, "Instead of *Regina's Café,* change the name to *The Ivy Bear.*"

"I don't know what to say. I–"

Aunt Regina waved her right hand, silencing her niece. "All settled." She turned her attention to Rachel. "*Mia cara,* I was sad when you left for Frisco and ended up in Philadelphia with Lee. But I'll confess I'm thrilled you've returned to Alder Creek along with my great-great niece and nephews. And for purely selfish reasons, I'm deeding the cottage to you. This way, you'll be close to me for the rest of my life. At least I hope so."

All eyes focused on Rachel. "I appreciate your gesture, but I'm considering moving to Sandy so the kids will be closer to school."

"You'll do no such thing. Subject closed." She took her cane and slowly stood up.

Cliff pulled his pack of Marlboros from his breast pocket. He lit one and blew several puffs of smoke right in front of his sister's face.

His mother approached him, removed the cigarette from his fingers, and extinguished it. "Not inside the house. Don't think about giving me any lip."

"What about me? I'm family." His tone bordered on belligerent.

Aunt Regina sighed. "When you clean up your act and show more respect, I'll consider something comparable. But in the season's spirit, I'll give you the old motorcycle in the garage. You're a talented mechanic. You can fix it."

"That's it?" Cliff asked in disbelief. "Not fair. You always liked Rachel better." His voice had risen to a whine.

"Take it or leave it. Stop bellyaching," Aunt Regina said, heading into the kitchen, followed by Kathryn.

Cliff lit another cigarette. "That old witch."

"She is not," Gina admonished her uncle.

"What do you know, kid?"

"Come on, Cliff," Vince said. "Let's step outside where you can smoke. Be respectful of your aunt." Vince slipped on his jacket.

"Hey!" yelled Eddie. "Let's go shoot some baskets!"

"Basketball. That is all you ever think about!" Cliff grabbed his leather jacket and stomped to the door, jerking it open and leaving it ajar.

Eddie's shoulders slouched as he slinked away.

"Eddie, don't mind him. He's a little touchy." Vince ruffled the boy's hair as he passed and followed Cliff, shutting the door. "Not cool, Cliff."

"Yeah, whatever." Cliff stood on the porch steps, lighting up.

Rachel opened the door and stepped outside.

Vince zipped his jacket and pulled up the collar. The nippy wind snuffed out Cliff's half-smoked Marlboro. He tossed the cigarette on the damp stone pathway and crushed it. "Crap!" Rachel pulled tighter the shawl she'd snagged off the chair.

"Why are you always in such a foul mood?" Vince asked.

"Everything bothers him when things don't go his way, right Cliff-ee?" Rachel stressed the last syllable.

Cliff glared at them as he attempted to light another cigarette. "What's it to ya, Mr. goody-two-shoes?"

"Your niece and nephews could use a father figure and a friendly male besides Gerald to play with them. They're still hurting from losing their dad."

"Kids aren't my thing."

"What are you going to do when you have children?" Vince challenged him.

"I'm not the marrying kind and don't want kids. Having too much fun playing the field." He grinned, running his hand through his greasy hair, leaving it spiked.

Vince pressed him. "You're missing out. Children are a blessing."

Rachel stepped forward to add to the conversation, but Vince gripped her arm and shook his head.

Cliff bent and threw a stone, then another, and another. "Yeah, wish someone had told my alcoholic father. He worshiped the almighty bottle. I remember all the beatings with a belt and the pain burning through my skin. My father used every ounce of his strength with each strike." He scooped a handful of rocks and hurled them toward the leafless maple tree. "He yelled at Rachel for something as simple as not drying the dishes thoroughly. He slapped Mom around. But she did nothing to help us. I hated him! I laughed when he died!"

Rachel reached out to comfort him, but Vince held her still. She tried to pull away, but he shook his head again.

"I'm sorry you and Rachel had such a terrible father. Instead of following in his footsteps, you might try to break the pattern and be the opposite."

Cliff swore, turning to Vince. "I don't need a therapist. You and Rachel can't hide—"

Vince's hand closed over the younger man's shoulder and spun him around, stopping the words. "Don't say another word. Our relationship is none of your business. I'm trying to help you see a better way." He released his hold and brushed Cliff's jacket in place.

Ever the macho guy, Cliff walked the length of the path, pretending to stare at the sky. "I need a beer." Cliff turned and raised a fist toward the house. "Mom, Rachel, and Aunt Regina don't allow beer of any kind in their houses. Period." He snickered. "You're craving a drink too, aren't you? Admit it."

"I'll be honest, I wouldn't mind one, but I don't need one. I choose to honor the house I'm in and the people I'm with."

"Self-righteous ass . . ." He stopped from finishing the word. "Rachel thought Lee, you, and Dominick drank too much," said Cliff. "She wanted Lee to retire from the Navy and move to Oregon, to get him away from you and Dom. That's why she came back to Alder Creek. She hated the drinking and didn't want Eddie and Barry influenced by you and all the other Favrettos when they got older."

"Cliff, knock it off. You're sore. I don't believe you. Go home and get a full night's sleep. You'll be better tomorrow," Vince said.

A smug Cliff said, "Ask her if you don't believe me!"

Vince turned toward Rachel. "True?"

Gina flung open the door. "Hey, uncles and Mom, time to eat."

Rachel ignored Vince's question. Yes, she'd mentioned to her brother she had considered trying to persuade Lee to move to Oregon. She'd set the record straight with Vince later. Also, discuss what almost happened between them. She didn't get the chance. Vince refused to discuss Cliff's accusation and focused his remaining time on the children. When his visit ended, he simply said "Goodbye, Rachel."

Chapter 15

The daffodils and crocus emerged from their winter hibernation. Gina planted marigold seeds in two window planters. "When they bloom, I'll make a bouquet for you, Mom." Barry mastered carving simple wooden objects with Gerald's guidance. Eddie worked at perfecting his free throw shots. Rachel reveled working at the clinic, endearing herself with both the human and animal clients.

Almost a year after Lee's death, Rachel's life centered on the kids' activities. Eddie and Barry were the only "men" she needed. Except, of course, Gerald. He became the kind, loving, helpful father she never had and was the children's surrogate grandfather. She loved him! If only Cliff would become a male presence for the kids.

Well into March, Cliff continued to express his annoyance with Aunt Regina.

"Enough. I'm tired of hearing you complain," Rachel said.

Cliff smoothed back his greased hair and lit a cigarette, blowing a few smoky rings into the air.

Rachel shoved Cliff, yelling, "You remind me of Dad! All you do is drink when you're not at work. You're disgusting, and I don't care to be around you."

Cliff couldn't resist. "You hate anyone drinking. Poor Lee. You had a fit if he drank one lousy beer, didn't you? Talk about stress. I'll bet you contributed to his heart attack."

Rachel's guilt was akin to gasoline swathing her body. She needed only a spark to set her ablaze. Her eyes burned toward her brother. Her fists balled, and she took a step in his direction.

He must have seen her reaction as he backed away from her. "Sis, I'm sorry. I meant nothing by that."

Rachel took a deep breath. Her heart slowed to its normal beats, and her blood drained from her flushed face.

"How come you don't engage with the kids? How about shooting baskets with Eddie or bike riding with Barry and Gina?" She kept her voice in an even tone.

"Don't have time."

"Yeah, right. You always find time to hang out at Calamity Jane's playing pool. Before we left Philly, Vince came to visit the kids at least twice a week. I was hoping you'd be a male presence in their lives like he was."

Cliff pulled out a chair from the kitchen table. He sat backward, draping his arm over the back, smirking. "I'm surprised Vince didn't move here. I noticed the way he undressed you with his eyes. He has the hots for you, dear sister. He probably pretended to care for the kids so he could be close to you."

Cliff's words rocked Rachel. She threw a spatula in his direction. "How dare you! Vince loves the children. The only person *you* love is the one staring back at you in the mirror!"

Cliff leaned closer to her, and his eyes narrowed. His lips thinned, and the words spewing out of his mouth sounded hard, like stones thrown at her. "Vince slept at your house. Now, who's talking about being an example to your kids? Did he leave your bed before they woke up?"

She charged at him with the frying pan she was drying. Before she reached him, a hand pulled the pan from her grasp. Powerful arms gripped her waist, lifting her off her feet.

Gerald.

He set her behind him and motioned for Cliff to leave. The order wasn't mistaken or arguable.

Cliff jumped up, trembling at what had happened. He shook his finger at his sister. "You're nuts. If you would've hit me, I'd have called the cops on you!"

"Leave my house!" She shouted at him, pointing to the door.

He grabbed his leather jacket and thrust open the door.

Rachel followed Gerald, who shut the door in her face. She stood where neither of them would see her and tried to hear the conversation. Gerald was the only one able to reason with Cliff. She suspected Cliff respected Gerald. The man had tried to be his friend over the years.

"You should go inside and apologize," Gerald said.

"Later," Cliff retorted and revved his cycle, roaring down the driveway.

Rachel finished drying the dishes as Gerald came into the kitchen. She turned to him. "I'm sorry. I shouldn't allow him to make me mad. He just does."

"Learn to control your reaction when he provokes you." Gerald patted her on the shoulder. His disappointment in her didn't sit well.

With the warmer March temperatures, Eddie dashed to the basketball hoop every day after school. He bragged to anyone who would listen that he was the best player in the third grade. He lost track of time too often, delaying the departure of the school bus. The driver complained to the principal, who summoned Rachel.

"Eddie," scolded his mother as she approached her son inside the school entrance. "No more shooting baskets after school. It's not fair to everybody else to hold up the bus waiting for you. Gina and Barry are never late." She stopped in front of him, her hand on her hip. "I had to leave the clinic early. The principal warned me if you're not on time, the driver will take off without you." Her voice changed pitch when she saw his apologetic expression. He glanced at the clock and then at his mother.

"I'm sorry, Mom. It won't happen again." He grabbed his book bag and headed past her to the door.

Gina and Barry joined them for the ride home. "Eddie, I can't leave work to run over here to pick you up and waste gas. I don't mind that you want to play with the other boys, but the bus is the only option and it's free. From now on, I expect you to go straight to the bus as soon as you're dismissed. Agreed?"

"Yeah." He slouched in the front seat, his chin resting on his chest.

Rachel hated to be the bad guy all the time, but she must enforce obedience.

The following day, Eddie calculated he could shoot a few shots and still board the bus in time. "Don't tattle to Mom," he said to Gina and Barry.

The interim eighth-grade coach observed Eddie, impressed. The ball got away from Eddie after a shot hit the rim and sailed toward the coach. He caught it and threw it at the youngster. "Here ya go," he said. "How would you like to–"

The bus driver honked the horn. Eddie rushed to the bus.

"Hey, do I know you?" The coach hollered after Eddie. Intent on reaching the bus before it took off left Eddie no time for a conversation. He jumped onto the first step just as the driver reached for the handle.

"Cutting it close, aren't you?"

Chapter 16

D r. Abbott stuck his head into an examination room. "Norm, I want you to head out to the Monzo farm. Their pregnant mare is due next week, and I want you to check on her. Herb's worried about the foal's birth. He's overreacting, but let's reassure him. Use the company pickup and take Rachel with you. By the time you return, it'll be after hours. Make sure everything's locked up before you head out."

Norm grinned at Rachel. "Let's go. Grab the gear and I'll bring the pickup around. The sooner we leave, the better."

She hastened to gather the medical bag and meet Norm at the truck.

The mid-August temperature climbed north of ninety degrees. The 1948 truck had no air conditioning. She rolled down the window and unbuttoned the top two buttons of her shirt. As soon as they arrived at the farm, she jumped from the sweltering pickup, her clothes clinging to her skin.

Herb Monzo greeted the duo and led them to the barn. Dr. Walsh examined the mare. Twenty minutes later, he said, "Everything is fine. Expect a normal birth."

Handing the instruments to Rachel, he continued. "My guess is she's going to give birth within a week."

Herb leaned against the fence, breathing a sigh of relief. "This is Tutti Frutti's first time and I'm nervous. I lost a foal a couple of years ago and I don't want to lose another one."

"From what the doctor said, she'll be fine." Rachel squeezed the older man's arm.

He patted her hand in response. "Thanks, Mrs. Favretto."

"Call anytime. Either Doc Abbott or I should be available." Norm and Rachel walked toward the barn's exit. He shook Herb's hand and joined Rachel. He puffed a few breaths on Rachel's neck as she reached to pull herself into the pickup.

"Mr. Monzo loves his animals, but he worries too much," she commented, fanning herself with Dr. Walsh's notebook.

"Yeah."

When they were a mile from town, Norm said, "I'm going to stop by my place and change out of these sweaty clothes."

Rachel glanced at her watch. It was almost quitting time. She wanted to go straight to the clinic, gather her purse, and head home.

"I've got a date. It'll save me time if I don't drop you off first and then backtrack home. I won't take long."

Rachel objected but had no choice. Norm parked the pickup in his driveway and jumped out. He walked to the passenger side and opened the door. He took Rachel's hand. "Come on."

"I'll stay here with the doors open. Hurry."

"Are you crazy? It's too hot." He pulled her out with a little more force than necessary. Rachel resisted, but he didn't let go of her arm and ushered her to the entrance. He unlocked the door and threw the key ring on the coffee table. Flipping on the air conditioning and heading to his bedroom, he pointed to the sofa. "Make yourself comfy. You'll be cooler in a moment."

Rachel didn't respond or sit, but surveyed the room. A few articles of clothing lay haphazardly over a lounge chair, and an empty beer bottle rested on an end table. Otherwise, the place was tidy. A small stack of *Playboy* magazines was piled on the floor near the sofa. *Hmmm.*

Rachel stood in front of the air conditioner, soaking in the coolness. Ten minutes elapsed before Norm appeared. He wore only a pair of shorts and carried two glasses of wine. He positioned himself close to Rachel.

Rachel backed away. "I don't drink. I want to go home." She headed to the coffee table for the keys. Norm cut her off. "Come on. Time to unwind."

"I said I don't drink, nor do I associate with anyone that does. You can stay here. I'm leaving."

He set the glasses down. He moved toward her, grabbing her arm before she could move.

"You're even more beautiful when you pretend to be mad," he smirked, pressing his body firmly against hers.

Rachel stepped away, but Norm pulled her to the sofa. "It's been a long time since you've had sex. I'm the guy to accommodate you. Don't deny you're interested. I've seen the subtle signals you've sent my way." Before Rachel could break away, Norm was on top of her, smothering her lips with his. He came up for air, shoving her shirt up and exposing her bra. Rachel pounded her boots against his butt as a revolting sensation crept throughout her body.

"Feisty," he laughed. "I like that. Relax. You'll enjoy it more." Holding her down with one arm, he unzipped her jeans.

Rachel couldn't believe this was happening. Norm was like a man possessed. Physically, she was no match for him. She schemed. *Maybe if I trick him.* "Okay, Norm, you're right. It has been quite a while. Why don't we go to the bedroom?"

He eyed her with suspicion but believed her smile. "Now you're talking." He stood and pulled her up, planting a fierce kiss on her lips. He bent to lift her.

Rachel pushed away, trying to remain calm. "Go ahead. I'm right behind you. I want to start undressing, so I'll be ready for you." As Norm turned away, she zipped up her pants, then pretended to unbutton her shirt.

When Norm had advanced halfway across the room, Rachel turned and hopped a little, pretending to remove her boot. He turned back toward the bedroom. She seized the keys from the coffee table and raced to the door. As she put her hand on the knob, Norm grabbed her ponytail and yanked her backward. "You stupid . . ." He turned Rachel around and gripped her shirt, ripping it.

Rachel rammed the keys into Norm's face several times. Blood trickled down his face. He screamed at her as his hand went to his cheek. Pulling away from him, she raised her right leg and thrust her boot into his groin. Norm staggered back and doubled over in pain. "Damn you!" He lunged at her, missing her, and falling to the floor.

Rachel reached the door and pulled it open. Norm chased her, holding his crotch. She had enough of a head start to jump inside the truck and lock the doors before Norm reached the pickup and pounded on the passenger window. With trembling hands, she fought to insert the key into the ignition. The motor roared, and she gunned the accelerator, backing out of the driveway without looking for oncoming traffic. She left Norm yelling at her as he retreated to the house, the hot asphalt scalding his bare feet.

Rachel's body shook during the three-mile drive to the clinic. She rubbed her blurred eyes with the back of her right hand. Her foot slammed on the brakes as she almost ran through a red light. She rested her forehead on the steering wheel, exhaling deep breaths. Oblivious to the changing traffic signal, Rachel didn't proceed. A blaring car horn jerked her into action.

Arriving at the clinic, Rachel parked behind Dr. Walsh's car, blocking it. She jumped out. Before entering, she turned and stared at Norm's '57 Ford. Impulsively, she scraped the key from the front bumper to the rear fender on the driver's side. She didn't regret what she'd done.

Darting to the office, she unlocked the door. She threw the keys on Virginia's desk and grabbed her purse. Walking backward, Rachel surveyed the interior she'd never step foot in again.

She flung the door open and peered outside. She ran to her car, fearful Dr. Walsh might appear. All the way home, tears flowed down her cheeks. She cried about quitting a job she loved and the friends she'd made. She shook as the memory of the assault played like a movie on a loop.

Chapter 17

——◆——

Rachel pulled into her driveway and opened the car door. She inhaled deep breaths, holding them for ten seconds, then exhaled.

When Rachel stepped inside the house, bubbly seventeen-year-old Betty Ann ran toward her. "You're later than usual. Gotta go. My girlfriend is waiting. We're practicing for the cheerleading tryouts next week. The kids are eating dinner. Bye." She opened the door, then stopped. "Pardon me, Mrs. Favretto, but your shirt's torn. And you look awful. Are you okay?"

"Yes," she lied. She shooed Betty Ann out the door.

Rachel poked her head into the kitchen. "Kids, I'm going to shower. Finish your dinner, then all of you please clean up the kitchen."

"But, Mom," said Barry. "It's Eddie's turn to wash dishes."

"Don't give me any sass! Just do it!" she shouted, stomping to the bathroom. The kids stared at each other, mouths open.

Rachel grabbed a lightweight cotton nightgown from the dresser, banging the drawer shut. Undressing in the bathroom, she hurled her clothes against the locked door. The nonstop tears flowing down her cheeks blended with the water streaming from the showerhead. She scrubbed the soapy washcloth over her entire body. Soothed by the warm water, and feeling cleansed from Dr. Walsh's touch, she stepped from the bathtub.

Donning the nightgown, she gathered the clothing and marched straight to the back door. She tossed the garments inside the garbage can.

Rachel called for the children to join her on the couch. "I had a bad day at work. I'm sorry for losing my temper. Group hug?"

"Did an animal make you mad?" asked Barry.

"You could say that," she answered.

Later, after she tucked the kids into bed, Rachel phoned her mother. "Mom, I need to talk. Please come over."

When Kathryn walked in, Rachel sat curled on the couch, the fan at top speed. As soon as Rachel saw her mother, her body trembled.

Kathryn rushed to her daughter's side, enfolding Rachel in her arms. Rachel rested her head on her mother's chest, unable to speak.

"What's wrong?" Kathryn asked.

"Rape."

"What?" Kathryn asked, pushing Rachel away, her jaw dropping.

"Dr. Walsh. He tried to rape me!"

It didn't matter that Rachel was a thirty-two-year-old adult. This distraught woman was her daughter. Kathryn wrapped her arms around Rachel and held her tight. When Rachel's trembling subsided, she said, "Tell me what happened." Rachel recounted the ordeal.

"That scumbag," Kathryn said, her face red hot. "Good thing you escaped."

"I'm glad I scratched his cheek with the keys and kicked him in his crotch. He doubled over in pain. That's when I ran outside and jumped into the pickup. I barely had time to lock the doors before he started pounding on the window. When I got back to the clinic, I keyed his car. He deserved it." She let out an unexpected, nervous laugh.

"I don't condone vandalism," Kathryn smirked, "but good for you." She put her hands on Rachel's shoulders. "You must press charges. He can't get away with this."

"Mom, I can't. Who'd believe me? It's his word against mine."

"You must tell Doc Abbott about this first thing tomorrow."

"I can't go back. No way on God's green earth will I step foot inside the clinic as long as that . . . that goddamn son-of-a-bitch is there!"

Kathryn widened her eyes. "Rachel! Your language."

"The thought of being anywhere near that brute sickens me." She shuddered. Leaning against the couch back, she plunked her feet on the coffee table. "Would you believe he thought I was interested in him? The very thought that I'd think of him other than a co-worker is absurd."

Kathryn patted her daughter's thigh, asking, "Are you going to be okay? Would you like me to stay?"

Sitting erect, Rachel said, "I'm calmer now." She hugged her mother, thanked her for listening, and added, "Guess I'm unemployed." She leaned against her mother's shoulder.

"You're serious about quitting?"

"Is a forty-pound robin fat?" She wanted to lighten the mood.

"You shouldn't be the one to quit a job you love," Kathryn said, heading toward the door. She stopped and turned to face Rachel. "If you don't tell Doctor Abbott, I will. What if Walsh does this to someone else? I'll bet this isn't his first time."

Rachel's hair flapped around her shoulders as her head shook. "Promise me you won't."

"All right, I won't, but I disagree." Kathryn added, "How about helping at the café?"

"Mom, thanks for the offer, but you're fully staffed."

"Think about it."

The next morning, Betty Ann arrived at 7:30 on the dot. "Mrs. Favretto, you're going to be late," she said, noticing Rachel was still in her nightgown.

"Sorry I didn't call you," Rachel said. "I'm not going in today."

"Why not?"

"Take the day off. In fact, I won't need you for the rest of the summer."

Betty Ann's eyes expressed disbelief. "How come?"

"I'm quitting. Look at it this way," she smiled, "you'll have a couple of weeks of vacation from babysitting before school starts."

The teenager frowned. "I've been saving to buy some new school clothes."

Rachel accompanied her outside. As Betty Ann hopped onto her bike, Rachel patted the girl's hand. "I'll pay you for all of August."

"Thanks! And don't forget, I'm available any time you need a babysitter, except on nights when I'm cheerleading if I make the squad."

Rachel encouraged the hopeful senior to be. "You're a shoo-in."

"I hope so." She turned the bike toward the driveway. "I've got extra time on my hands now, so I can practice my routine even more. And I'll bet Mom asks me to help her clean the living room today. She's hosting the book club tonight."

"Your mother pestered me to join, but I'm not interested."

Betty Ann raised herself off the bike seat. "Guess what book they're discussing this month?"

"No idea."

"*Nightmare!* Your mother's novel. Isn't that cool?" Unaware her remarks had mortified Rachel, Betty Ann waved and pedaled away.

The dread crept over Rachel like an icy chill. Her stomach locked up tight. *I don't want anyone reading that story!* She wished her mother hadn't written the book. Anyone who knew them would figure out it was a thinly disguised account of her family's dirty laundry.

She had to call Virginia. "It's short notice, but I'm resigning."

"Quit joking," Virginia said. "Oh, here's Dr. Walsh. Talk to him."

Rachel slammed down the earpiece.

The phone rang a few minutes later. "Rachel, what's this I hear you're quitting?" Dr. Abbott's voice stung Rachel's heart.

Chapter 18

By mid-September, Rachel took her mother up on her offer to help at the café on weekdays while the kids were in school. Dr. Abbott begged her to reconsider. Rachel stuck to her "personal reasons" excuse. Kathryn continued to encourage Rachel to press charges against Dr. Walsh.

"Mom, I want to put the incident behind me and move on. And don't you dare tell Dr. Abbott."

"Walsh tried to rape you! You're letting him get away with it," Kathryn said, "but I'll honor your request."

November arrived. Basketball practice began. Eddie often poked his head into the gym after dismissal. He yearned to join the eighth graders . . . dribbling, shooting, passing, catching.

The week before Thanksgiving, Eddie burst through the door.

"Hey, son, what's up? You haven't been this excited for a long time." Rachel sat on the sofa, massaging her feet after another shift waiting on café customers.

Eddie spewed a story that seemed to want to come faster than his mouth could form the words. "You said I could shoot hoops if I didn't miss the bus. I was dribbling and I heard loud clapping from the opposite end of the court. It was the coach. He dribbled with me. He asked me if my father taught me to dribble so well. I told him my dad died. Then guess what? He told me to ask you if I could become the ball boy for the eighth-grade team during their games! I can, can't I Mom? I want to do this." Eddie jumped up and down in excitement.

"I should meet this person. What's his name?"

"I don't know. Everyone calls him Coach. He reminds me of the guy who helped us after the accident. Maybe it's him."

"I doubt it," Rachel said.

"Hurry, Mom! I can't be late," Eddie yelled.

"Hold your horses, Son," Rachel said. "Gina, Barry, get your coats."

"I hate basketball," pouted Gina. "Can Leo and I go to Aunt Regina's instead?"

"Sure. Call her."

Moments later, Gina announced. "She wants me to come. Whew."

After dropping Gina off, Rachel and the boys headed to the school. Eddie bounced up and down, unable to contain his excitement. As soon as Rachel parked, Eddie opened the door and sprinted away.

"Wait for us!"

Eddie continued to run, disappearing into the gym.

The packed gymnasium surprised Rachel. She surveyed both sides of the gym, searching for seats on the bleachers.

"Mrs. Favretto!" Looking in the voice's direction, she saw Betty Ann standing and motioning for the duo to join her.

Rachel waved and climbed the bleacher steps to the fifth row, squeezing by seated fans. "Wow," Rachel said, removing her coat. "Is it always this crowded?"

"It's Friday. Folks like to support the basketball and football teams. Not much else to do. Tonight's more crowded than usual because the opponent is Gresham, Sandy's longtime rival. Everyone is here hoping for a win tonight. Hi, Barry."

He raised his hand, acknowledging her. "Who's that?" He pointed to her companion, a tall, beefy dude.

"Ted, my . . . friend. He's the center on the high school team."

Red-headed Ted reached and shook Barry's hand. "Nice to meet ya."

"What brings you to the game?" Betty Ann asked.

"Eddie." Rachel pointed to the home team bench. Her heart skipped a beat when she noticed how excited her son was. "The coach, whom I haven't met, let him be the ball boy." She figured the man attired in the suit holding a clipboard was the coach.

"How neat for him!"

"Did you make the cheerleading squad?" Rachel asked.

Betty Ann nodded, beaming. "The varsity team's game is tomorrow night. You can come and watch me tomorrow night at the high school."

"She's the prettiest cheerleader," Ted declared, giving her a peck on the cheek.

After the pep band belted out the national anthem, a referee threw the basketball straight up. The visiting Gresham Gophers, dressed in blue and white, snagged the first possession. The Sandy Pioneers, wearing new black and crimson uniforms, went on defense.

At halftime, Barry stood, grabbing his mother's hand. "Can we go now?"

"The game's not over. There's still another half."

Barry plopped onto the bleacher, bowing his head. "I'm bored."

"You'll survive."

Down by six points at halftime, the Pioneers emerged from the locker room and gathered around Coach. The players tied the game early in the fourth quarter but fell behind again. The crowd encouraged them . . . yelling, whistling, stomping feet, and clapping. The squad came within one point, with four seconds left. Coach called a time-out to draw up a play. Eddie offered the team water as they huddled.

Not one spectator remained seated. Even Barry, on his tiptoes on the bleacher seat for a better view, was jittery. Standing at mid-court, the referee handed the ball to number two. The player inbounded to the point guard. He dribbled once, then launched a desperation shot, hitting the rim. A teammate jumped up and secured the rebound, then slam-dunked the ball a split second before the final buzzer.

Cheers erupted. Fans' arms shot upward, and the bleachers rattled from the jumping up and down.

"I hope we have the same result tomorrow night with the high school varsity team," said Ted as the spectators exited the gym.

Rachel tapped her fingers on the steering wheel. The last of the team's parents herded their kids into their cars. *Where was Eddie? Why did it always take him so long?*

"Barry, run in and see what's keeping your brother."

"Do I have to?"

"Go," Rachel ordered. What was it about this coach that had her son so enthralled? She knew Eddie loved basketball, but this guy seemed to reach him like she couldn't. All he did was talk about Coach. *Was Eddie forgetting his father?*

The door opened, and the two boys rolled into the car.

"Mom, Coach asked me to come to the game tomorrow and help cheer the high schoolers. He said the crowd was like the sixth man on the team. Pleeease," he begged.

"Another game?" Barry piped up with newfound enthusiasm.

"Yes. Coach wants Barry to come too. He said we could sit with the team. Can we go?" Two pairs of eyes showing excitement about the same thing? Unheard of. She had nothing planned for the next evening. Not wanting to burst the common desire, she nodded.

Rachel put the car into gear and headed home, smiling. It was nice her sons agreed about something for a change. She'd thank the coach at some point.

Gina carried Leo next door to Grandma Kathryn's to spend the evening. "I don't want to go to a stupid basketball game."

The two boys took off running to the gym before Rachel could stop them. She saw the tall man with black hair pat the boys on the head and introduce them to the man he was talking to. Then he spoke to them. The boys' shoulders slumped, and they joined their mother. Much to Eddie's disappointment, they had to settle in seats two rows from the top in the visitors' section. The spectators rose, clapping for the players as they ran onto the court and began pre-game drills.

"Hey, look!" Barry yelled. "There's Betty Ann with her . . . what do you call those things?"

"Pom-poms."

During the third and fourth quarters, the teams traded baskets. Sandy, behind by two points, scored, tying the game. The referee blew his whistle as Ted fell to the floor from an obvious foul. A successful free throw would put Sandy ahead by one point, with two seconds remaining. Gresham called a time-out to ice the center. During the huddle, Coach instructed the team on what to do if Ted missed.

Visiting Gresham students yelled and stomped their feet, trying to rattle Ted. Betty Ann covered her face as he bent his knees, dribbled the ball several times, took a deep breath, and shot. The ball bounced off the rim into the hands of a leaping Sandy player. He dribbled once and threw up a desperation shot. Swish! Cheers exploded as the final buzzer blared. Coach hoisted his assistant and twirled him twice.

At last! It was his first varsity victory against rival Gresham during his five-year tenure. For Coach, this win was comparable to a state championship title. Elated fans swarmed onto the court. They jumped up and down, giving Coach bear hugs, slapping his back, and shaking his hand. They basked in the glory of back-to-back victories against Sandy's rival.

An impatient Eddie started descending by stepping on the bleachers.

"Young man," Rachel ordered, "wait till the steps are clear."

When the family finally approached the crowd, Coach didn't see them. Fans still surrounded and congratulated him. Eddie began muscling his way through the throng.

Rachel grabbed Eddie's arm. "We're leaving. I'll meet him some other time." Her son protested, trying to pull from her grasp. Rachel tightened her grip and proceeded toward the exit.

"Coach!" a desperate Eddie shouted.

"Wait!" Rachel heard a deep voice calling as she reached for the door.

"Allow me." Coach pushed the door, holding it open as the family filed past him.

Eddie smiled up at the man as if he were a god. "Coach, this is my mom."

Rachel turned to the man her son worshiped. When his eyes met hers, his brows raised and he cocked his head.

"What?" she asked. "Is there popcorn in my hair?" She gave a nervous giggle at his studied attention.

Clearing his throat, Coach blurted out. "All this time I thought both boys appeared familiar. I think it's clear now. Were you in a car wreck outside of Missoula, Montana over a year ago? With two boys, a daughter distraught over a missing cat, and a flag that you insisted on getting from your damaged car?"

Rachel backed several steps away, staring at the man.

"That's when I got my scar," Barry pronounced, pointing to his forehead.

Rachel asked, "How do you know about the accident?"

"You don't recognize me, do you?" His forehead creased as he smiled down at her.

Eddie suddenly had a spark in his memory. "Hey! I was right! I told Mom you looked like the guy who brought us to the hospital!"

"Yes, that was me."

Rachel studied Coach. Her hands covered her mouth. "I remember you now. You live in Sandy? What are the odds?"

Coach tousled Eddie's hair. "If it weren't for Eddie's basketball passion, we may never have encountered each other a second time and discovered we lived so close." Looking at Rachel, he said. "I wondered how everything turned out."

"And I felt bad that I didn't offer my heartfelt thank you. No one got any info from you." Extending her hand, Rachel said, "Please accept my overdue gratitude."

"Unnecessary."

"I appreciate you letting Eddie help. He's been so excited."

"My pleasure." He smiled and asked, "I'm curious how your family's life has been since the accident. How about joining me at *Dea's In and Out*? My treat."

Rachel glanced at her watch. "It's late, already past their bedtime."

"Please, Mom." Eddie's smile was identical to his father's. It tore at her heart.

"Well, it is Saturday. We can go to Mass later tomorrow."

"I'll say a few words to the team. See you at Dea's." He waved as he jogged toward the locker room.

Addressing the Favretto boys, he asked, "What'll it be?"

"A sundae with gobs of chocolate!" Barry said.

"Me, too," said Eddie.

"And you?" Coach asked Rachel.

"A cup of coffee."

"Nonsense. There's a special on holiday peppermint milkshakes."

Rachel's taste buds came alive at the mention of *Dea's* shakes. "Okay, but make it strawberry. My favorite."

Coach waited at the counter for the order. When it was complete, he carried the tray to the table and slipped into the booth beside Eddie. "Now tell me. Did you find your cat?"

"Yeah," Eddie answered.

"Great. And how's your sister? Jenna? Jeanie? What about her foot?"

"Gina sprained her ankle. She used crutches for a while, and you can see Barry's scar. Eddie had a few bruises, and I broke my big toe," Rachel explained. "We spent a couple of days in the hospital while a wonderful man repaired the Frazer. He found Leo under the car while he hooked it up for towing."

"He was terrified," Eddie interjected.

"He brought the cat to the hospital?" Coach asked.

"Yeah. We'll never know what happened, but we're thankful the garage owner found him, especially Gina. I'm still driving the same car."

"Where do you live?"

"By the Ivy Bear," Barry said.

"In Alder Creek?" Coach leaned against the seat. "By the café?"

"Right next door. My mother owns it, and she lives above it."

"I've stopped there several times. I always order the meatloaf. It's to die for."

"How come your mom and dad named you Coach?" asked Barry.

Grinning, he said, "That's my nickname. It stuck with me when I began coaching over ten years ago. My real name is Philip DeLuca."

"Sounds Italian," Rachel observed. "Favretto is too."

"Yep, my parents immigrated from Treviso, a small town about an hour north of Venice."

"Wow! Aunt Regina is from Bologna."

"And your name?" Coach asked.

"Rachel."

"I'm going to play for you when I'm in eighth grade," declared Eddie.

"Varsity is my main coaching job. I'm only filling in this season for the eighth graders."

"How come?" a disappointed Eddie asked.

"The principal tugged at my heart by playing the guilt card. Said he'd be forced to cancel the eighth-grade team if I didn't step in." He chuckled. "Glad I'm single. Too much time away from home. But I'm not complaining."

Barry wiped chocolate syrup from his lips with his shirt sleeve. Rachel reached for a napkin. "Use this." She gathered her coat and purse. "Time to get going. Thank you for the treat, Mr. DeLuca. It was a pleasure meeting you again under more pleasant circumstances."

"I can't wait till the next eighth-grade game," Eddie said.

"Me, too," Barry stated.

"Only one more game before the first week of January."

Rachel smiled the whole time she put the boys to bed. What was causing this smile? She sobered and frowned at the figure in the mirror, but the frown didn't last. Ok, she would permit herself only this once to enjoy the company of the man Eddie idolized and who had rescued their family. She hummed as she dressed for bed.

Chapter 19

———✦———

Aweek before Christmas, Rachel pushed her grocery cart down the cereal aisle at Meinig's. As she reached for a box of Rice Krispies, a familiar voice called her name. She turned and saw Virginia standing at the end of the aisle, waving. The two met halfway and embraced.

"How are you and the children?" Virginia asked.

"Fine. Kids are busy with school and Eddie, of course, is still obsessed with basketball. The interim eighth-grade coach invited him to be the ball boy. He's thrilled. Why aren't you at work?"

"Doc told me to take a day off. No argument from me." Patting her striking auburn hair and flashing her manicured fingers, she said, "Fran worked her magic on me. Do I appear a few years younger than my fifty-four?" She chuckled.

"You're always lovely."

Virginia positioned her grocery cart close to the shelves. "It's not the same without you. Many regulars have said as much." She leaned against the cereal shelf. "Remember Dolly, Mr. Moody's dog? She's lost weight. Looks better, and her blood sugar is now where it should be. Herb's daughter named Tutti Frutti's foal Aurora."

"I like the name."

Virginia's tone turned serious. "Rachel, why did you leave without warning?"

Rachel sighed. "I had to." Four months after the assault, it still troubled her, but she tried not to dwell on the attack. She vowed to never let her guard down again. Hugging Virginia, she said, "Gotta finish shopping. Merry Christmas." She pushed the cart around to the next aisle.

The women ended up in the same checkout line. "Rachel, how 'bout I treat you to a cup of coffee?"

To her surprise, Rachel welcomed the invitation. The fragrance of fresh cedar garland greeted them as they entered the diner after depositing the groceries in their car trunks. Holiday shoppers and office workers popping in for a quick bite packed the cafe. They seated themselves in a corner booth. Rachel ordered tea and lemon meringue pie; Virginia, black coffee and pumpkin pie. "With whipped cream," she told the waitress.

Rachel shivered as she removed her coat and wool scarf. "Hope the winter is mild."

"Did you put your tree up yet?"

"Heck, yes!" Rachel grinned. "The kids made sure we chopped down a tall one. It's decorated, and Gina made a major production of placing her antique angel on the treetop. She keeps it in her room the rest of the year."

The two engaged in small talk, avoiding the topic of Rachel's abrupt resignation. Virginia placed her hand on Rachel's. "Tell me why you quit. Maybe I can help. I'm a first-rate listener."

I can trust this woman. Rachel surveyed the room, concerned about unintentional eavesdroppers. In a subdued voice, she made Virginia promise not to repeat to anyone what she was going to recount.

"Okay. Scout's honor." She raised three fingers, giving the scout salute.

Rachel described in graphic detail the attempted rape by Dr. Walsh. "When I got home, I took a shower, then threw my clothes into the garbage."

Virginia's eyes widened, and her mouth gaped open. She hugged Rachel for an eternity. "I'm so sorry. I don't blame you for quitting. You okay now?"

"I'm not letting it control my life."

"Hard to believe Walsh attacked you in such a vicious manner. He's so caring with animals. It'll be difficult working with him now."

Rachel devoured every morsel of the pie. "Lemon meringue's my favorite. Thanks for the treat and listening." She smiled and leaned close to Virginia's face. "You're the only person besides my mother I've told. Please keep my secret."

"You should tell Doc Abbott. I'll bet he will fire Walsh. He deserves it." Virginia signaled the waitress for the bill. She ran her fingers over her lips, pretending to zip them shut. "I won't tell a single soul. It'll be hard not to confront Walsh. I've lost all respect for him." As the pair stepped outside, Virginia waved at a familiar figure driving by in his black Chevy. The driver honked and waved back, almost running a stop sign as he stared at Rachel.

"That was Coach. Have you met him?"

"Yes."

Virginia nudged Rachel. "He's single."

Rachel rolled her eyes.

Chapter 20

─◈◆◈─

The second Friday in January, Rachel sat in the stands watching her sons hobnobbing with the eighth-grade team. Barry was now the official "assistant" water boy, joining Eddie on the sidelines during games.

"I like basketball now," Barry declared.

Rachel marveled at the bond developing between her sons and the coach. She hadn't seen Mr. DeLuca since he waved at her the day she exited the diner with Virginia. From her seat several rows up, she focused on him. She thought he was good looking . . . muscular, tan, coal-black crew cut, clean-shaven. In his mid-thirties? And what a rapport with the team. She could tell the players would walk barefooted on a bed of sharp nails for him. He wore a suit and tie required of coaches during formal games. She sensed he was uncomfortable in such attire.

Another nail-biter game finished with a buzzer-beating basket by the Sandy Pioneers. Rachel descended the bleachers. She congratulated Coach.

"Thanks," he said, loosening his tie. "My ticker can't take much more of these close games. Need to play better defense. We should have won by a wide margin.

So far this season Centennial is in last place. But a win is a win."

Barry pulled on Coach's coattail. "Can we go to *Dea's* again?" Barry asked. "I want another chocolate sundae."

Embarrassed, Rachel said, "Not tonight. We're going straight home. Put on your coats."

"Shucks. So long, Coach."

As they walked toward the car, Rachel scolded Barry for asking Coach to take them to *Dea's*.

"He wouldn't mind."

Rachel placed items from her purse onto the hood, trying to locate the key ring. She wished she had her gloves. She noticed the boys' bodies shivering. "Put on your hoods."

"Uh oh," Eddie said, pointing inside the vehicle. "I see the keys on the car seat."

"Shoot." Rachel snapped her fingers. "How careless."

"Coach'll help." Eddie ran back to the gym before his mother could stop him. Barry followed.

Rachel covered her head with the coat hood. Across the parking lot, she saw her sons sprinting alongside Coach.

"The spare key is at the house," Rachel said.

"Come on. I'll drive you there and back. Everyone pile in. Alder Creek, here we come!" They were on their way before Rachel protested. Did she want to?

Kathryn volunteered to stay with the kids when Rachel explained how stupid she'd been. "So, you're the 'cool' guy my grandsons can't stop talking about. Pleased to meet you." Extending her hand to Coach, she asked, "Do your children attend Sandy Elementary or high school?"

"No children. Not married."

"Oh? Take your time. Stop for a cup of coffee," Kathryn suggested, crossing her fingers behind her back.

Gina approached Coach. "Remember me? I hurt my foot."

Coach grinned. "Of course. You were, shall we say, uncooperative that night."

Gina held up Leo. "This is our pet that ran off."

Coach reached for the furry feline. Leo snuggled against Coach's chest, purring contentedly.

"He likes you!" Gina said.

"Most animals sense I'm an animal lover, and they respond with affection." He stroked Leo. "The heart shape on his fur is unique. Never seen anything like it." He handed him back to Gina.

Coach opened the passenger door and held it open as Rachel seated herself. She glanced toward the house. She stifled a laugh as her family peered out the window. Her arm shot them a "gotcha" wave. Kathryn closed the curtains.

When was the last time anyone held the door for her? Not her husband. The thought leaked out, and she slammed the thought back to where it belonged. She wouldn't allow demeaning thoughts about Lee to surface.

"So sorry," Rachel apologized to Coach as he backed out of the driveway.

"No need to be. These things happen."

"Still have the truck we rode to the hospital?"

"Traded it for this Chevy last year." Arriving back in town, he turned off the main drag and turned into his driveway.

"Why'd you stop here?" Rachel asked, sitting erect.

"I'm gonna change out of this suit. Won't take long. You can wait inside the house where it's warm."

Oh no! Not again. Rachel would not get caught in that trap. She sensed Coach wasn't another Dr. Walsh, but she wouldn't take that chance. She grabbed her purse and stepped out. A frosty cloud formed with her breath. She buttoned her coat and covered her head with the hood. She started walking the two miles toward the high school.

Coach ran after Rachel, placing his hand on her shoulder. "What are you taking off for?"

"I want to get to my car. Thanks for the ride." She resumed walking.

"You'll freeze." He took her hand. "We'll head straight to the school."

Minutes later, Coach parked to the left of Rachel's Frazer. Wrapping her right fingers around the door handle, she turned toward Coach. "Thank you. I appreciate your help," her tone clipped and formal.

"Is something bothering you?"

"No. I need to return home so Mom can leave."

"Rachel–may I call you by your first name?–you seem nervous."

"I have trouble trusting men since Lee died."

"Your husband?"

"Yes." She bowed her head.

"Feel like talking?"

157

"You wouldn't be interested."

Coach turned and rested his right leg on the seat. "Try me."

She paused. His caring expression made her comfortable confiding in him. "A co-worker assaulted me five months ago. On the way back from checking a pregnant horse, he said he wanted to stop at his place to change clothes. He changed all right, into nothing more than shorts, and then attacked me. When you said the same thing, I thought it was happening again."

"Whew," Coach said, turning on the ignition and blasting the heat full force. "A lot on your plate. Now I understand why you took off. I'm not the suit and tie type. I wanted to get out of this suit and into my sweats." He held up his hands. "Honest."

Rachel believed his explanation. "Forgive me for judging you." She took the key from her purse and exited the Chevy.

Coach came to Rachel's side, helping her into the car. Looking up at him, she smiled. "Thank you for helping me tonight. I appreciate what you're doing for my sons. Hope you don't regret it."

"Not for a moment." Coach bent over and gazed into her eyes. "Eddie has basketball skills I'd like to help develop. Barry mentioned playing Little League baseball this spring. Happens I'm the coach. I wouldn't mind spending time with them. A male influence would benefit them."

Pressing her fingers to her smiling lips, Rachel said, "Those two rascals can be a handful. Sure you want to tackle the job?"

He saluted Rachel. "Reporting for duty."

"All right." She turned on the motor.

"I'm curious. How can you stand working with that lowlife?"

"I quit. I miss the job, though."

"Consider returning to the clinic."

"You think so?"

"Of course. You said you loved working there. Go back."

"As long as Walsh is still there, I won't step foot in that place." She gave him a little wave and backed out. Looking in the rear-view mirror, she saw him staring at her as she pulled out of the parking lot. She felt comfortable confiding in him, and he hadn't judged her. A warm sensation flowed throughout her body.

Chapter 21

The sun's warmth on the last Tuesday of March provided the incentive for Gerald to trim the ivy bear. He secured his thirty-foot ladder against the statue. Before ascending, he trimmed the stray ivy around the bear's base. Fatigue seized him, and he wiped the sweat from his forehead. He climbed the ladder, stopping on the fifth rung to catch his breath as sharp pains shot through his left arm. A young couple, regular café patrons, waved to him at the moment Gerald clutched his chest, then fell to the ground.

Running to an unresponsive Gerald, the husband felt for a pulse. "Go inside the café and call an ambulance!" he yelled to his wife. Recalling his high school first aid course, he administered CPR.

The wife ran inside shouting to Kathryn that Gerald had collapsed. Kathryn pointed to the phone and rushed to Gerald. Fear gripped her body as she knelt and took over CPR. Rachel was right behind her mother. A small crowd gathered, and a middle-aged gentleman stepped up to relieve Kathryn.

The paramedics arrived and stabilized Gerald. They loaded him into the ambulance and sped to Oregon City Hospital.

Dread at the outcome crept over Rachel like an icy chill. Gerald was her rock, always there for her and the kids.

Kathryn forced herself to act, directing her staff to handle the afternoon customers or close. She didn't care. All that mattered was Gerald. She untied her apron, tossing it on a chair.

Rachel rubbed her clammy palms together. "Mom, I'll pick up the kids from school and meet you at the hospital."

Kathryn gunned her car across the highway to Aunt Regina's. Leaving the motor running, she dashed into the house.

"Aunt Regina, we're going to the hospital."

Her aunt was removing a loaf of zucchini bread from the oven. "What?"

Kathryn turned off the oven and got her aunt's coat and cane. "Gerald is in an ambulance. I think he had a heart attack!"

Leaning against the drainboard for support, Aunt Regina wailed, "*Oh mio Dio!*" Chang wagged his tail and yelped, sensing something troubled Aunt Regina. Ming ran circles around her. She picked up her pets, rubbing their noses together. "Don't worry."

Handing her aunt the cane, Kathryn said, "Let's go."

Inside the café, Rachel grabbed her purse and ran to her car. She arrived at Sandy Elementary a few minutes before the closing bell. She sped to the office and explained the circumstance to Mrs. Bloomington.

The secretary reached from behind the counter and patted Rachel's hand. "So sorry, Mrs. Favretto."

"Mom, what're you doing here?" Gina asked.

"Gerald is in an ambulance on the way to the hospital in Oregon City. We're going there."

On the almost thirty-mile drive, Rachel thumped her thumbs on the steering wheel every time a slow vehicle or a stoplight delayed the trip. *Damn!* Thankfully, the children sat subdued. Not a sound, except for sniveling from Gina. They finally drove into the hospital parking lot. The family sprinted inside, heading to the emergency area.

The receptionist tried to stop them, but they ignored her. The children followed their mother down the hallway and around the corner.

"Mom!" Rachel shouted when she saw her mother slumped next to Aunt Regina. "Any news?"

"Nothing yet."

Gina sat beside her great-great-aunt. "I love Gerald," she said.

The downcast elderly woman, holding her rosary beads, patted the girl's hand.

"Is he going to die like Daddy?" Barry asked.

"It's in God's hands, *mio caro*."

Rachel paced back and forth, annoyed by the boys' nonsensical arguing about whom Gerald liked better. Her thoughts drifted to the many fun times she and Cliff had spent with Gerald. He provided an oasis of relief from their drunken father. A smile appeared as she recalled the time he served a stew featuring snake meat. She had commented on how good it tasted. When he told her it was rattlesnake, she dumped the bowl's contents into the sink and spit out her mouthful.

Cliff laughed till Rachel thought he'd burst his guts. Oh, Gerald . . .

A nurse came through the ER double doors. Kathryn rushed to her, followed by Rachel. The family bombarded her with questions.

"Gerald Whitcomb. How is he?"

"How much longer?"

"Is he going to be okay?"

"Can we see him?"

Accustomed to this kind of anxiety from worried families, she answered with empathy. "I'm not working with the doctors who are caring for Mr. Whitcomb. I can assure you, the staff is doing its best. A doctor will talk with you as soon as possible." She gave an understanding smile to the adults, then disappeared down the hall.

Rachel continued to pace. Kathryn sat with her arms wrapped around her body while Aunt Regina prayed.

Coach appeared. The three children ran to him.

"Grandpa Gerald is sick," Barry said.

Rachel approached Coach. "How did you find out what happened?"

"The school secretary told me you'd taken the kids to the hospital and were quite distraught. I thought I'd come to give you support or perhaps take the kids out to *Dea's* or my house."

Her heart grew at his kindness. "Thank you." She contemplated what would be best for the worried children.

He addressed Kathryn. "How is he?"

"No word," Kathryn answered. "The waiting is nerve-racking."

A doctor wearing sweat-soaked scrubs emerged from behind the double doors. He pulled down his surgical mask, so it hung by its strings. He wore a grim expression as he approached the family. "I'm sorry," the doctor said.

The rosary beads slipped from Aunt Regina's hands onto the floor. Her cries were gentle, but the agony of her aunt's grief twisted Kathryn's stomach. She wrapped her arms around her aunt and pulled her close.

"Grandpa Gerald. He's dead?" Gina asked.

The doctor nodded. "He had a massive heart attack."

The harsh sounds of the children's sobbing poured from their mouths.

Rachel's knees buckled. Coach grabbed her, supporting her while she leaned against him, her tears soaking his shirt.

Aunt Regina arranged a simple service for Gerald, what he would have wanted. The entire Alder Creek community gathered in the shadow of the ivy bear to pay their respects to the gentle giant of a man. She was heartened so many folks attended. She swore Cliff's eyes appeared puffy and red. Struggling to maintain her composure, Aunt Regina delivered the eulogy. "In conclusion," she said, "Gerald was, I mean is, my best friend, my soul mate, and he will remain in my heart forever. The ivy bear will be a constant tribute to him, along with all his wooden carvings many of you received as gifts. His legacy is how he treated young and old alike. He loved and respected everyone. No doubt we all reciprocated." Many heads nodded.

Guests shared memories. After many heartfelt anecdotes, Eddie and Barry released five white balloons. "Now grandpa Gerald is in heaven with Daddy, Poncho, and our Favretto grandparents," Gina said. Rachel wouldn't allow a balloon launched in memory of her monster father. Besides, her children never knew him. Thank God.

Long after the mourners departed for the reception at the cafe, Aunt Regina remained behind. Death had ripped away a part of her. She hugged close to her chest the hand-carved wooden urn Gerald had crafted for this inevitable day.

Rachel used an entire box of tissues that night as she lay in bed. She loved Gerald. He meant more to her than her father. First Lee, now Gerald. Gone forever.

Chapter 22

—◆—

"Y ahoo!" Barry shouted as he and Eddie darted off the bench, flinging themselves onto the dogpile. Bodies buried the batter who'd scored the winning run after four extra innings. Coach squatted, bowing his head, and wiping sweat from his face. A one-run victory to end the season! Whew!

Rachel watched the enthusiasm of her sons and their coach. He had told her he was taking the team for sundaes after the game, then he'd bring them home, so she didn't wait for them.

She stopped by *The Ivy Bear* when she saw the lights on in the kitchen. Kathryn was finishing a food inventory as Rachel entered.

"The boys win?"

"Yep. Extra innings. Coach is bringing the team to *Dea's* for sundaes. He'll bring the boys home."

"You don't call him by his name." She used her pencil to count the boxes on the shelf. "When are you going to see him as a man, not a job?"

"What are you talking about? His whole life is coaching. Everyone calls him Coach," Rachel protested.

"Everyone isn't a woman and the mother of his favorite boys. I'll bet he'd like you to address him by his first name. What is it, by the way?" Kathryn gave Rachel a sideways glance.

Rachel ignored the question and counted plates.

"Do you even know what his name is?"

"Yes." She drew out the answer. "Phil." The word sounded odd on her tongue. Too intimate and personal. It put him on a different plane. She wanted him kept at a distance. *Or did she?*

"Rachel, Lee has been gone over two years. Do you think he would want you to stay tied to his memory? To a relationship you were thinking about leaving? It's time to move on. The boys will always remember their dad but the memories will weaken, replaced with new ones. What are you going to do with the rest of your life?"

"You didn't marry again," Rachel shot back.

"My story is different. I will welcome finding love again, but I haven't found someone that made me feel like he's the one. If that ever happens, I won't let it pass by." Kathryn shook the pencil at her daughter. "I didn't give up on love and you shouldn't either."

Rachel's shoulders slumped. "I loved Lee, but I didn't understand why he didn't respect my wish that he not drink beer. I tried to be a good wife." *Apparently, my efforts weren't enough to keep him from straying.*

"You wanted to control Lee by putting restraints on him about drinking. I get that, but Lee wasn't your father. He was a loving husband and an amazing parent. You wouldn't listen to me when I explained you needed to let up on the chokehold you had on him."

"You're probably right. That's why I blame myself for his passing."

"Stop blaming yourself. You might consider counseling." She broached the subject again. "I wish you would read *Nightmare*. There are things in there that could help you get through your guilt feelings. Go home and think about it. The boys will be here soon. Gina's upstairs."

Banging open the door, Barry hollered, "Guess what? Coach is—"

"…taking us camping!" Eddie finished the sentence.

Rachel placed a bookmark inside *Gone with the Wind*. Surprised to see the boys pulling Coach into the house, she ran her fingers through her hair and smoothed her clothing.

"And we can fish, too!" Barry shouted.

Coach approached Rachel. "I hope I didn't overstep any boundaries, but I'd like to take everyone on a camping trip this weekend. An end-of-school-year getaway."

"Aw, Gina too?" Barry asked.

"Of course," Coach answered. "And," looking at Rachel, "your mother also."

"Oh no. Count me out. And as for the kids …" She wasn't keen on this trip.

Coach rubbed his palms together. "Campfire, fishing, hiking, beautiful scenery," he tried to entice Rachel. "And *I'll* do all the cooking. I guarantee you'll enjoy yourself. You deserve a getaway."

Eddie knelt, lacing his hands, projecting his most persuasive smile. "Pleeeeease, Mom."

Rachel stood, surveying four eager faces. Outnumbered, she flung her arms upward. "Oh, what the heck! I'm game." Their enthusiasm rubbed off on her. "There's a tent stored in the garage."

Rachel lost her balance when the thrilled children bowled her over as they rushed to her. As Coach's hands caught her, a sensation overcame her. *Pleasure? Awkwardness?* She backed away, clearing her throat.

"Not to worry," Coach said. "I've got all the necessities except sleeping bags. But I know where I can borrow what we need."

"Can I bring Leo?" Gina asked. "Wouldn't leave without him. Keep track of him. Don't forget the carrier." Phil wagged his finger at her nodding head.

Phil? Was she beginning to think of him as Phil?

They arrived at Timothy Lake the following Friday. The boys bugged Coach to teach them *right now* how to fish. "First things first," he said, handing each boy a box containing a tent. With the "help" of Eddie and Barry, Coach pitched the tents – "one for boys and one for girls" – Barry pointed out. The group finished setting up camp for the weekend. Eddie and Barry raced to the lake's edge. Gina joined them. Coach taught them the basics of fishing . . . baiting, casting, reeling.

Rachel stood at the water's edge, soaking in the strong fragrance of the pine trees circling the lake. Gentle waves lapped at her bare feet. She raised her face skyward, basking in the sun's warmth. The rocks she threw caused ripples across the smooth, glass-like water, a perfect mirror for Mt. Hood. Rachel slipped into her sandals and relaxed against a fallen log, Leo purring on her lap. Her lips cracked a smile as she watched her children's clumsy attempts to secure the worms onto the fishhooks.

After welcome relaxation, Rachel strolled back to the campsite to unpack the dinner supplies. The sound of the returning kids told her they'd been successful.

"Mom! You won't believe what we caught!" Eddie held up his large fish as he ran toward her.

Gina, right behind him, held up her smaller fish. "I got three. Eddie only caught one."

"Yeah, but mine is the biggest. Right Coach?" He didn't wait for an answer but slapped his gutted fish on the plastic tablecloth covering the picnic table.

"Hold on there, Son." Coach picked up the trout. "We're going to eat at this table." He handed Eddie his catch, while Gina paraded around holding her trout for approval.

After everyone finished dinner and cleaned the mess, they sat around the campfire. The flames cackled and danced in the moonlight. Rachel smiled as the kids carried on about the day's fishing experience.

Coach reached into his duffel bag. He pulled out one package each of jumbo marshmallows, graham crackers, and Hershey's chocolate bars. "We're going to make s'mores!"

The children squinted their faces. "Huh?" Eddie asked.

"Never eaten s'mores before? Let me introduce you to a gourmet delight." He placed a piece of chocolate between two graham crackers, then stabbed a marshmallow with a stick. Holding it over the campfire flames, he rotated the twig. "Don't want it too white or burnt black. Should be light brown." When the marshmallow was just right, he put it inside the cracker sandwich and pulled out the stick. "All done!" Winking, he handed each child their fighting tools.

Barry plunged his stick right into the flames. Too late, he withdrew it and threw the smoking black mass onto the ground. "Shucks."

Coach handed him another marshmallow. "Try again."

"Mmmm. This tastes yummy," Gina said, licking her lips. She wrapped her arms around Coach's waist. "Thanks for this neat treat and for taking us camping."

"My pleasure."

Barry leaned closer to Coach. His head rested on the man's arm. "I wish you could live with us."

"Me, too," Eddie concurred.

Rachel's face turned a bright red. She grinned with motherly affection at her kids. And when her tender gaze rested on Coach, it was filled with warmth. It wasn't a look like a mother would shower on a child, but an expression of what? Surely not a look of love. Coach winked, then turned his attention back to the children.

"Tomorrow we'll hike along the trail that leads to an area where you can see a spectacular view of Mt. Hood," Coach said.

Jumping up, Rachel announced, "Bedtime." She put an arm around Gina's shoulders and held Barry's hand as she escorted her tribe to their respective tents. Coach sat staring at the few red coals flickering under the black ashes.

Rachel sauntered back to the campfire and sat next to Coach. She leaned against the rough log and stared upward at the clear sky illuminated by a plethora of stars. Her face expressed a faraway stare of sadness.

"You okay?"

"Ah, sure. Why do you ask?"

"You seem deep in thought."

"I was thinking about . . . never mind." Rachel reached out to touch Coach's arm and say thanks for all he'd done today. And how sorry she was about what the boys said about him living with them.

Coach leaped up. He ran to the car's glove box. He presented Rachel with a cribbage board and a deck of cards. "Okay, deal!"

After her fourth defeat, Rachel displayed a phony pout and tossed the cards onto the ground. "I'm no match for you."

Coach shot her a smug grin. "What can I say?"

Removing the rubber band from her ponytail, Rachel shook her head, allowing her hair to fall loose below her shoulders. "Thank you for suggesting this outing. The kids are having a blast."

"And you?"

"Me, too," Rachel admitted, rubbing her goosebumps. Coach stoked the dying embers. They cackled back to life, the orange and yellow flames emanating renewed heat.

Coach slid next to Rachel, draping his jacket around her. Face to face, their eyes locked on one another. Coach massaged her arms. The warmth from his fingers crept into Rachel's consciousness. The urge to allow him to continue was strong but she pulled away, her body no longer chilled.

"Tell me about yourself," Coach said. "I know you love animals. What else makes you tick? Besides your three rascals."

She looked upward, admiring the twinkling stars. "Not much to tell. I hoped to one day become a veterinarian. But that's only a pipe dream now. The kids are my priority, and I couldn't afford it. Besides, I'm getting too old. No school would accept me. Folks are still reluctant to trust a female vet with their precious pets."

"Don't sell yourself short." He adjusted the jacket on her shoulders as it slipped off. "Are you glad you returned to Alder Creek?"

"Yes. I love Lee's family, but this is my home."

He lifted her left hand. "You still wear your wedding ring. Why?"

Rachel stared at the full moon glistening on the calm lake. She'd been tempted to remove it when she grasped the extent of Lee's transgression. In her heart and mind, however, removing the symbol of their marriage would erase everything they'd shared for almost ten years. Her love for Lee hadn't died with his death. She rubbed her index finger and thumb over the ring several times. Phil wouldn't understand her reasoning.

"I shouldn't have pried about such a personal decision. You'll know when it's time." He gathered the pile of cards and secured them with a rubber band. "You aren't into sports, are you?"

"No, except for watching the boys."

"Eddie's becoming quite the basketball player. No doubt he'll make the eighth-grade team."

"He's obsessed," Rachel said. Her eyes shot a thankful gaze at him. "I can't thank you enough for everything you do for Eddie and Barry."

"Since Gerald died, I don't mind filling the role of a male figure. I want to believe I'm a positive influence."

Rachel turned her body toward Coach. "Enough about me. What makes *you* tick, besides sports?"

"Sports are my whole life. I've been involved one way or another since I can remember. My father gave me my first basketball on my seventh birthday."

Rachel laughed. "I can relate. Eddie got his first basketball for his eighth birthday. Tell me about your family. Any brothers or sisters?"

"Only child, much to my mother's disappointment. Couldn't have any more after me. Mom kept bugging me to get married. She wanted grandkids. She's been gone five years now. I still miss her and her Italian cooking. She cooked delicious lasagna and ravioli meals. We ate Italian food four or five times a week. She tried to teach me the basics of cooking, but I had little interest. My specialty is Swanson TV dinners, except for my scrumptious spaghetti."

"The kids' favorite."

"Maybe you'd like to come with the kids to my house and I'll make spaghetti and garlic bread." He added for good measure. "It's lonely eating alone."

"Name the date and time." Then, surprising herself, she said, "You strike me as the perfect guy. No flaws whatsoever. How come you're not married with a ton of children? You'd make a wonderful father. What are you thirty-four? Thirty-five?"

His answer was quick and to the point. "Thirty-four. Haven't met Miss Right yet." His eyes said otherwise as he stared at Rachel. "You've pegged me wrong. I'm not a picture of perfection." Coach dipped his chin down and a flush crept across his cheeks. "I confess I use to gamble to excess. An addiction. That's why I'm so adept at cards. Lost and won quite a sum of money."

Rachel's mouth fell open. Phil a gambler? No way. "Do you still–"

"My gambling bothered my mother. She begged me to quit. When I came home one night with a sizeable win and handed her the cash, she threw it on the floor and told me how ashamed she was of me. She said I disgraced her. I still remember the slamming of her bedroom door."

"Wow!" said Rachel. "I would never guess you had a problem of that nature."

"I didn't have a clue to the extent I hurt Mom. I quit cold turkey. Only play for fun now, like tonight."

Standing, Rachel faked a yawn. "Guess I'll hit the sack." Rachel handed Phil his jacket. Their hands touched.

Wrapping his fingers around her hand, he asked, "Did my gambling confession sour your impression of me? I hope not."

"No," Rachel said, removing her hand from his hold. "Goodnight." She walked away, turning her head in his direction. Her eyes pulled to Phil like a magnet. His expression captivated her. She was powerless to remove her stare from him. When she stumbled on a mound of dirt and fell to her knees, Phil raced to her. He pulled her up but didn't release her.

His touch gave her a sensation she hadn't felt since Lee. She scurried to the tent. Her breathing became more rapid, but the smile on her face was as soft as the morning light. Her breath warmed the pillow.

Chapter 23

⸺◦✦◦⸺

The Thursday evening after the camping trip, the doorbell rang. Barry ran to the door and swung it open. "Hey, Mom!" he yelled, "the doc is here. And Virginia too!" He greeted Virginia with a quick hug.

"Who?" Rachel asked, appearing from the kitchen, drying her wet hands on a dishtowel.

"Good evening, Rachel. May we come in?" Dr. Abbott asked.

"Yeah," said Barry, grabbing the doctor's hand and pulling him into the house.

Virginia's expression spoke volumes. Rachel guessed the nature of their visit. She did not welcome this intrusion. "Now is not the best time."

"We need to talk," said Doc Abbott, his voice firm.

Virginia's eyes implored her.

Rachel caved. "Kids, the doctor and I are going to discuss adult stuff. Go outside and play." She gave them an expression that meant it wasn't a choice.

"Do we have to?" Eddie sulked. "Can we watch TV? *Leave it to Beaver* is on."

Barry jumped up. "Yeah! Can we? Can we?"

Dr. Abbott interjected. "Let them, Rachel. We can talk in the kitchen."

"All right," Rachel agreed. The three adults pulled out chairs. Rachel offered them a glass of iced tea.

Hoping to redeem herself, Virginia wiped her clammy hands on her pants and blurted out. "Rachel, please forgive me for breaking my promise. Doc Abbott told me he was retiring next year and decided to turn over the clinic to Dr. Walsh. I couldn't remain silent. Working in Walsh's presence since you told me what he did has been a challenge."

Rachel slumped, lowering her head. Virginia put her hand on Rachel's.

"Tell me what happened," Dr. Abbott said.

Virginia's touch empowered Rachel. She wasted no words. "He tried to rape me! I fought back and barely escaped."

Dr. Abbott jerked back. "Go on."

Rachel recounted the assault.

The doctor removed his eyeglasses and rose from the chair. He paced back and forth, gathering his thoughts. "So that explains the cut on his cheek. Not the lie he told me." His next words surprised both women. "Thank you, Virginia, for telling me." Sitting, he leaned toward Rachel. "I believe you. You aren't the type to concoct such an accusation. I understand why you quit. I only wish you'd revealed what happened."

"I figured he'd deny it. His word against mine."

"I can't have Norm working for me. He might do it to a client. It would ruin the clinic's reputation."

"Any chance you'll consider coming back?" he asked.

"I won't step foot in the clinic as long as that brute is there," she answered, her voice strong with conviction.

"I'm going to fire him and notify the police."

Rachel noted the determined expression on his face. Dr. Walsh deserved what he got, but she didn't want to involve the cops.

"Please don't contact the police."

Dr. Abbott shook his head. "I disagree. What if he attacks again?"

"I don't want to relive the ordeal if the law intervenes. Besides, it's he said, she said."

A deep sigh escaped. "Okay. I'll warn him to stay away from the clinic or I'll be visiting the police."

Virginia asked, "Am I forgiven?"

Rachel gave Virginia a gigantic bear hug.

"So, can we plan on you returning?" Dr. Abbott asked.

"I'll be in touch."

For the next few days, Rachel pondered whether to resume the job she loved and missed. Working at the café helped supplement the reduced income. But she preferred her animal friends. She showed up at the clinic on Monday morning. Although Dr. Abbott had asked her to return, she hoped he meant it.

She pulled the door open like she was there for a visit. Patients she remembered sat in the waiting area. They smiled at her.

"Are you back?" one asked.

Her tone was noncommittal, and her face gave nothing away.

A delighted Virginia whispered, "Have you come to your senses and decided you can't live without this job?"

"Yeah, if it's still available."

Virginia pulled Rachel along the hallway into Dr. Abbott's office. "Look who's back!"

Dr. Abbott stood looking at Rachel, smiling. "What are you waiting for?"

"I'm not wearing a uniform."

"That's no excuse. Your attire is suitable for today." Virginia pushed her toward the back.

Rachel was glad she'd told her mother what she was planning. Kathryn wouldn't worry if she didn't show up for her shift. A call at noon would set things right.

Walking down the hall, Dr. Abbott stepped from his office. "Fantastic you're back, Rachel." Handing her a chart, he said, "Room Three. A pregnant Cocker Spaniel awaits."

She saluted the doctor. "Yes, sir. Right away."

Virginia squeezed Rachel so hard she gasped for air. "I'm thrilled!"

"Me, too! But are you sure Dr. Walsh will never again set foot in here?" Rachel had been apprehensive she'd encounter him around town.

"Unlikely," Virginia assured her. "He got a job in Laramie, Wyoming. We gave him his last paycheck on Friday. He said he was leaving the next day. Good riddance."

As far as Rachel was concerned, Mars wouldn't be enough distance away. But she now considered Dr. Walsh a footnote from her past.

Chapter 24

On the third Sunday of July, Rachel stood in the crowded parking lot of Madeline School. Thanks to Aunt Regina's generosity, the kids waited to board school buses for a week-long adventure at Camp Howard. Unlike a few anxious campers, her children exhibited enthusiasm.

"Hope there's a basketball hoop," Eddie said.

The teenage counselors loaded the luggage and sleeping bags, then blew their whistles. The rowdy group silenced and listened for their assigned bus. Gina, Eddie, and Barry climbed inside without saying goodbye to their mother. As the drivers steered the convoy of buses out of the lot, Rachel ran beside the bus, pounding on it. Barry stuck his head out the window, waving and yelling, "Bye, Mom!" Rachel stopped, bending for a moment to catch her breath. She blew kisses until every bus disappeared around the corner.

Rachel glanced at the illuminated clock. 1:27. She kicked off the sheet and turned the fan up a notch. This was the first separation from all three kids. She thought she'd welcome the break and solitude. Instead, they occupied her thoughts non-stop. Would they enjoy camp? Be homesick? She missed them after less than twelve hours.

Rachel took the week off to tackle the neglected yard work. Before going outside, she paused to gaze at Lee's framed picture. Her threat continued to haunt her and take her down the familiar path of guilt. It was like an ugly scar, destined to remain for life. Had her inflexible stance toward drinking beer played a role in his infidelity? She struggled between blaming herself and putting the entire fault on her husband. *Will I ever come to terms with Lee's affair?*

A bout of tears overtook her as she toiled in the flower garden, yanking weeds and digging small holes in the soil. As noon approached, she wiped the sweat from her forehead. She wouldn't quit until she finished planting a flat of pansies. The bright yellow and purple blossoms lifted her spirits. Leo lounged under the shade of the maple tree. He appeared forlorn without the kids.

When she pressed the dirt around the last pansy, she aimed the hose at the flowerbed. She stood back, admiring the assortment of colorful flowers. "Does this meet with your approval, Leo?" she asked.

"Yep! Pleasing arrangement!"

Rachel spun around, drenching Phil's lower body with the hose. "You startled me!"

"Didn't mean to." He turned off the water spigot. Approaching Rachel, he ran his fingers along her cheek, wiping away a smudge of dirt. "Are you okay? Your eyes appear bloodshot."

"Hay fever," she lied. "Sorry about your wet shorts, but that's what you get for sneaking up on me."

"Not to worry. They'll dry in this heat," he said.

Rachel sat on the picnic bench, removing her gardening gloves and gulping down a torrent of water. She focused on the pansies to avoid staring at Phil's shirtless body. "What brings you here?"

"I dropped by to see how you're coping without those three kiddos."

Kiddos? That was Lee's endearing name for the kids. "No one except me has called them that since Lee died."

Phil shrugged. "A coincidence. Are you bothered?"

"No. I miss them. Thought I'd enjoy a week of tranquility, but I can't wait for their return. Cooking for one is foreign to me, and the house is too quiet. I can't believe I miss the noise."

Phil snapped his fingers. "Hey, no kids. How 'bout dinner tonight at Lido's in Gresham? It's not crowded on Mondays."

"Like a date?" She nearly choked saying the word.

He suggestively wiggled his eyebrows.

Rachel hesitated. "I appreciate the invitation and it sounds better than an evening by myself, but I'll pass."

"You have to eat, right?"

"Yeah, I suppose so."

"You can relax and let someone else do the cooking."

"I'm tempted," Rachel said, folding her arms and tapping her foot. "Oh, why not?"

"Not an enthusiastic response, but I'll take it. Pick you up at six." Rachel caught herself staring at his muscular physique as he walked toward the car. There was a bounce in his gait and a smile on his face.

Rachel took extra time to apply makeup and snorted when she noted the glow on her face. "You'd think this was a romantic date," she said to her reflection in the mirror.

Rachel tried on four outfits before she settled on a pink skirt and print blouse. She needed some new clothes. She hadn't changed her wardrobe since she moved here. Kathryn bought her a few things she'd found at a thrift store in Portland, but she hadn't shopped for herself.

Opening the door to Phil's knock, Rachel's heart hammered against her chest as he eyeballed her. "Wow! All dolled up. Come, your chariot awaits."

Rachel laughed at the compliment. "This 'ol thang?" She exaggerated a southern drawl and took the offered arm.

The maître'd seated the couple and placed menus on the red and white checkered tablecloth. Rachel surveyed Lido's. There was soft lighting, mood music, and grapevines painted on the walls. A Chianti wine bottle coated with melted wax from the candle stood in the center of the table. Rachel inhaled the fragrance of the deep red single rose in a glass bud vase. "Aunt Regina would enjoy coming here. It would remind her of Bologna."

The waitress placed a basket containing breadsticks and an antipasto platter on the table. "Ready to order?"

"May I order for you?" asked Phil. "Or at least make a recommendation? I'd like you to have a wonderful dining experience tonight."

Rachel nodded.

Phil ordered the entrees. "Also, two iced teas."

"We have an extensive selection of wines."

"No thanks." He passed a salad plate to Rachel. Eyeing the assortment on the antipasto platter, he said, "Dig in. Quite an assortment of cheeses. And I love marinated olives! An Italian meal should be an experience to savor."

"Oooh. Provolone cheese. One of my favorites." They relished every bite and chatted about a variety of topics. Rachel mentioned she was looking forward to the upcoming visit of Jo, Lee's niece.

"Joe? Isn't that a male name?"

"Jo grew up a tomboy. That nickname fit her instead of Joanne, her given name. She's finally accepted she's a female, but the family is used to calling her Jo." Rachel warned, chuckling. "Don't mess with her. She's not intimidated by any guy."

The candle burned low. The waitress offered *dolce* and after-dinner *espresso*. Rachel sat back in her chair, rubbing her stomach. "Ate too much. Bet I gained a couple of pounds. Thanks a lot," she pouted.

Phil reached across the table and placed his hand over Rachel's. She liked the feel, the way she did when Lee touched her like this. But Lee's hold on her surfaced and she withdrew her hand.

"So, you think you can survive till Friday without the kiddos?" Phil asked.

The word *kiddos* again. Maybe it did bother her that Phil referred to the children using Lee's pet name for them. She closed her eyes, picturing Lee in the living room horsing around with the kids. If only she could undo what she'd done to him and he the same.

Phil noticed Rachel's saddened expression. "You still miss him."

That simple statement struck a raw nerve. Rachel slouched.

As they rose to leave, he hugged her. "I'll be here for you when you're ready to talk or whatever."

Rachel leaned into him for a moment . . . so close she could feel each beat of his heart. A long time had passed since she experienced this kind of embrace. It felt pleasant and safe. She didn't fear what would come next. It was merely a friendly hug.

Chapter 25

⟞⟐◆⟐⟝

J o bounced on Gina's bed. "Mattress is softer than I'm used to, but I'll survive. You sure you don't mind bunking with Gina while I'm here?"

"Of course not." Rachel stood an arm's length from Jo. "You've outgrown your tomboy tendencies. You're looking feminine and attractive. I'm so excited you're here! And I'm glad the kids got home yesterday from camp to greet you."

"Same here," Jo said, squeezing Rachel. "I'm the farthest I've been from Vineland. Uncle Vince warned me I may fall for the natural beauty of Oregon and the recreational activities. You remember how I adore the outdoors."

"Yeah, Miss Former Tomboy. You'll love it here."

Barry entered the room and tugged on Jo's blouse. "Wanna go play in the creek?"

"I didn't bring a swimsuit."

"Barry, slow down," Rachel ordered. "Jo only arrived a couple of hours ago. Give her a chance to settle in."

Jo liked the idea. "Why not? I can wear a pair of shorts and a sleeveless blouse."

The group ran across the highway. They traipsed past Aunt Regina's picture window, heading downward along the path to the creek. Jo paused, drawn to a shiny red motorcycle. "Whose bike is this?"

"My brother's," Rachel answered. "Don't touch it. He might go ballistic. I'm surprised he's here 'cause he rarely visits. Come inside for a few minutes. I'll introduce you to my aunt."

"Hi, Aunt Regina," Rachel said, hastening to hug her. She acknowledged Cliff. "What are you doing here?"

"I'm visiting Aunt Regina. What's it to ya?"

Rachel aimed her tongue at Cliff.

"We're having a discussion right now," Aunt Regina said.

"Gotcha." She winked. "Before I join the kids, I want you to meet Joanne, but call her Jo. She's the kids' cousin from Vineland. She's visiting for a couple of weeks."

Jo extended her hand. "Pleased to meet you."

"And I, you," Aunt Regina said, touching Jo's fingers.

Rachel pointed to her brother. "That's Cliff."

"Hi," Jo said, waving her arm. "Cool Harley."

Cliff's eyes almost bulged out of their sockets. He rose and wiped his clammy palm on his jeans, then shook Jo's hand. "You like motorcycles?"

"Sure do."

Rachel pulled Jo toward the door. "Let's go. I need to keep an eye on the kids while they're playing in the creek. We'll be back tomorrow." She blew her aunt a kiss.

Before long, Rachel heard pounding shoes on the path. Cliff appeared and sat on a huge boulder beside his sister, focusing on the visitor from back East. "So, what's the scoop on Jo? Married? Boyfriend? Age?"

Rachel elbowed her brother. "You don't remember her? She was at my wedding. She's my sister-in-law Sophia's daughter. That makes her my niece, even though I'm only a few years older than her. She's twenty-eight and was a diehard tomboy, but seems she's outgrown that phase." Rachel tapped her fingers against her chin, pondering. "Maybe not, though. She liked your motorcycle."

Cliff studied Jo. "She must've changed or I would remember her. She's easy on the eyes. I'm gonna get to know her better."

Rachel's fist pushed into her brother's shoulder. "Forget it. She's not your type, buddy boy. She's a class act and I would rather you steer clear of her."

"Ah, come on. I won't corrupt her."

Cliff pulled off his shirt and shoes, then blasted into the creek. He splashed his nephews with gusto. The boys, along with Gina and Jo, all ganged up on him.

"I surrender!" he said, hopping out of the water and dropping onto the creek bank.

"What fun, Uncle Cliff," Eddie said. "Let's do it again."

"I'll pass."

Jo started toward the water's edge but lost her balance when she stepped on a slippery rock. "Whoa!" she yelled, as she plummeted backward into the water. Cliff jumped up and pulled her upright. He stood by her side as she wrung the dripping water from her shoulder-length hair.

"You okay?"

She raised her arms and twirled around. "Heck, yeah. It'll take more than a measly rock to derail me." Jo's soaked blouse clung to her skin, accentuating her slender form and ample breasts.

A little while later, the group trudged up the path and headed home. Jo lingered, admiring Cliff's bike. "May I sit on it?"

Cliff allowed no one on his pride and joy. But for this intriguing woman, he didn't hesitate to make an exception. "Sure." The response surprised Rachel.

Jo positioned herself on the seat and pretended she was zooming down the highway. "Vroooom!"

"How about going for a spin?"

"Thought you'd never ask," Jo grinned. "But not now. I want to put on dry clothes."

"This evening then. Sevenish?"

"I'll be waiting," she said with a playful snicker.

The smile on Cliff's face pleased Rachel. This was a side of Cliff she hadn't seen in a long time.

Jo came in behind the kids. "How about I make my scrumptious spaghetti and meatballs? I remember this is the kids' favorite meal."

"No doubt always will be," said Rachel. "Lucky for you, I've got all the ingredients."

"I'll start preparing the meal as soon as I've changed into something dry."

Rachel positioned herself on a stool while Jo updated Rachel on the Favrettos. "Carmela's trying to get PG. The family business is thriving thanks to Dom's and Vince's management. And Mom, bless her soul, teaches Religious Ed at St. Michael's. Dad's going to retire next year, and Neil's stationed in Okinawa." She turned toward Rachel wearing an enormous smile. "Guess what? Vince is engaged!"

"Are you kidding?" Since his Christmas visit when she rebuffed his romantic sentiments, their contact was minimal. During infrequent phone conversations, he didn't once mention a girlfriend.

"Heck, no. He's so happy. When he came home from visiting you that first Christmas after you left Philly, he was quite depressed. Moped around for months. Do you know he considered becoming a priest? The family wondered what in the world happened here that caused him to be so unhappy."

Rachel didn't reveal she had squashed any possibility of romance between them when Vince had proposed marriage in a roundabout way. And that Cliff had upset Vince with his remarks regarding Lee and his brothers' drinking. "Beats me. He had a fantastic time with the kids. Now tell me about his fiancée."

"Vince hit the jackpot. Maggie is a gem. Petite, mid-thirties, an angel. Works for an attorney. The family loves her. They met literally by accident. Maggie drove into the back of his car and caused extensive damage to her front end. Vince got out, intending to give the driver a piece of his mind. But when he saw her sitting there with her make-up streaked from an avalanche of tears, he mellowed. They laugh about it now."

"When's the wedding?"

"No date set. I suspect they're going to elope next June, then have a reception later. Maggie doesn't want a huge ceremony. She'd rather spend the money on a dream honeymoon to Italy." Standing near the warm stove stirring the simmering sauce, Jo wiped the perspiration that dotted her skin. She reached over the sink and closed the cotton curtains, blocking the early evening sun rays. "You and the kids better come for the reception. You haven't visited since you left. The family will love seeing you and the children." Jo noted it was almost six. "Gotta hurry. Your brother is coming in an hour to take me for a ride on his bike."

Rachel jumped from the stool. "I wish you wouldn't go."

"Why not?"

"Cliff isn't your type. He drinks too much and his attitude on most things stinks. He's unpleasant to be around and seldom plays with the kids or helps. Since Gerald died, he hasn't lifted a finger to help Aunt Regina. Coach stepped in and does a lot of outside maintenance for us."

"Coach? Who is he?"

Rachel ignored the question. "You shouldn't hang around with a loser. I'm warning you, Jo. You'll regret it."

"Trust me. I can handle him," Jo assured her. "I don't think he's the hard-nosed guy everyone thinks. He's kind of handsome." She drained the noodles and combined them with the meatballs and sauce. "Tell me about this dude you call Coach."

"His name is Phil DeLuca, but everyone calls him Coach. He's a PE teacher and coaches high school basketball and Little League baseball. Eddie and Barry are the team ball boys. You won't believe this. He's the guy who rescued us when we had our accident in Missoula. Literally, an accidental encounter. Thanks to Eddie's basketball obsession, we encountered him again. Turns out he lives less than ten miles from us. Quite unbelievable."

"I'll say." Jo tasted a bite of spaghetti. "Ready. Time to eat, everybody!"

"This spaghetti tastes better than Mom's," Barry said as he sprinkled a ton of Parmesan cheese on the noodles.

Gina admonished her brother. "You hurt Mom's feelings."

"Not to worry," Rachel said. "It *is* better."

A short while later, the doorbell rang. Jo glanced at the clock. Quarter to seven. "Your brother's a tad early," she said, rising and rushing to the bathroom. "Tell him I'll be right out."

Eddie opened the door. "Coach!"

Rachel hadn't spoken to Phil since their "date" at Lido's. Her heart skipped a beat when she heard Eddie greet him and ask, "Want some spaghetti?"

"My favorite meal. But I can't stay."

Jo entered the kitchen, expecting to see Cliff. Rachel rose and introduced her to Coach. "This is my niece, Jo. Remember I told you at Lido's she was coming for a visit? Cliff should be here any time now. He's taking her for a motorcycle ride."

"You sure you want to go anywhere with him? I don't think he's your type."

"Rachel said the same thing. Is this a conspiracy against him?"

193

"He has a reputation, and it's not flattering," Rachel pointed out.

"I'll be fine." She waved off their concerns.

With a mouthful of food, Eddie asked Coach, "Want to shoot baskets? Bet I'll beat ya."

"Can't stay. I dropped by on my way home from Timberline Lodge to invite you kids to go hiking tomorrow. You too, Rachel." Coach studied her, waiting for a response.

"We had fun hiking at camp!" Barry yelled. "Yeah, we'll go!"

"Can we bring Leo?" Gina asked.

"Not this time."

"Shucks." She joined her brothers as they focused on their mother for an answer. Rachel concealed her enthusiasm. "Looks like we've got plans for tomorrow afternoon."

"Yahoo!" Barry and Eddie raised their arms in victory.

Cliff appeared, eyeballing Jo. "Ready?"

Rachel noticed her brother's improved appearance. He wore a new pair of Levi's, a navy blue short-sleeved shirt, and had shaved his stubble. A slight aftershave fragrance hung in the air. *Hmmm . . .* She shot him a silent expression. *Better be on your best behavior!*

"Cool your jets, Rach. I'll have her back safe and sound. See ya." All three kids pushed back their chairs, abandoning their meal. They followed the pair outside, teasing them.

"Are you gonna be polite to Jo?" Gina asked. Her voice sounded like Rachel's and she stifled a giggle.

Cliff ignored his niece and motioned for Jo to sit in the passenger seat.

Inside the kitchen, Rachel glanced at Phil, seeking reassurance. "Please tell me everything will be okay."

He approached her. "Jo'll be fine."

"You're right. She's a transformed tomboy. Males never intimated her. You sure you don't want some spaghetti?"

Phil glanced at his watch. "Tempting, but gotta go." He took several steps to leave the kitchen, but then stopped, turning to face Rachel. Reaching for her hands, he raised them to his lips. Rachel's heart fluttered and a wave of heat swept from head to toe.

The door opened late that night. She listened to the soft tones of conversation and then the sound of tiptoeing down the hall.

"Jo?" she called out.

"You still awake, Rach?" Jo pushed open the door and peeked inside.

"Everything all right?" Rachel asked, propping herself up on her elbows.

Jo sat on the edge of the bed. "Yes, I saw his attitude when we met. He tries to be a hardnose." She leaned toward Rachel and whispered. "He's not."

Rachel raised her eyebrows in disbelief.

"I'm sure around you he acts the way he's always acted, the way you expect him to act. Tonight, he was like a different person. He acted like a perfect gentleman, polite and respectable. Almost like a little boy trying to behave for once."

Jo slid to her feet. "If you talk to him the way you talk to Eddie or Gina, you'd get a different reaction. 'Nite, Rach."

"By the way. We're going hiking with Coach . . . ah, Phil. Do you want to join us?"

"Nope. Cliff is taking me on a long ride."

Rachel rested her head on her hands, her knees bent upward. Her mind wandered deep in thought about Cliff. It was true he seemed to have a chip on his shoulder. She didn't approve of his choices, but had she ever talked to him like they did when they were kids? Free of judgment. *I'll work on that.*

Chapter 26

⁙

The next day at noon, Phil arrived, loaded with water and lunch items. He invited Jo to join them, but she declined. "Cliff's taking me for a motorcycle ride up to some camp."

"Government Camp. A popular ski area in winter," Rachel said. "I wish you'd come with us instead. I'm still down on Cliff's behavior." Her negative outlook toward Cliff wouldn't disappear overnight.

"Something about him interests me. And I enjoy riding motorcycles." Jo dismissed Rachel's concern.

Phil commented, "Did he cast a spell over you or vice versa?"

With a little laugh and a shrug of her shoulders, Jo said, "Beats me. But I can tell he's not as bad as he wants everyone to believe."

As the troop piled into Phil's car, Cliff arrived and turned off his motorcycle.

Barry leaned his head out the window, singing, "Cliffy likes Jo. Cliffy likes Jo."

Gina pulled him back inside, scolding him. "You shouldn't say that. Uncle Cliff will get mad."

Rachel rolled her eyes. "Till later, Jo. I told you where the key is hidden if you return before us." Phil backed out of the driveway and headed toward the Columbia Gorge scenic area.

"Where are we going hiking?" Rachel asked.

"I'm taking you to Multnomah Falls, then to Rooster Rock Park to swim in the Columbia River. Did you bring swimsuits?"

"Mom! Did you pack swimsuits?" Eddie asked.

"And towels?" Gina added.

"Yes. While you were eating breakfast, I put in some buckets and shovels for you to play in the sand at Rooster Rock. It'll take over an hour to drive to Multnomah Falls. Try to spot small falls coming out of the cliffs along the way."

The children peered out the backseat window, jockeying for the best position.

Rachel leaned her head against the window, trying to ignore the arguing in the backseat. "They're fine. They'll settle down." Phil reached over and touched her hand. "Relax. Enjoy the scenery."

Rachel sighed and stared at the azure sky, admiring the variety of trees jutting from the cliffside. She swore she saw a couple of mountain goats standing majestically high atop the cliffs.

"Are we almost there? When will we see the biggest fall?" Barry asked.

"Yeah, when can we?"

"It's yes, not yeah," Rachel corrected Eddie.

"It means the same thing."

"Not to me. You will say yes, not yeah." Her tone meant no argument. Eddie resumed staring out the window looking for the mighty falls.

Barry shouted. "There it is! Wow!"

After parking, the group crossed under the highway via the tunnel. They walked to the stone building that housed a gift shop and snack bar.

"I want an ice cream cone," Barry said.

"On the way back," Phil said. "Everyone, take a bathroom break."

The dirt trail led upward to the bridge overlooking the breathtaking waterfall. They felt spray spewing from the water on their bodies. Refreshing.

"Go to the rail." Phil motioned them to stand together, and he took a few pictures. The boys made funny faces just as he pressed the button. "Stop it!" Rachel ordered. "Give Coach a smile."

Walking in a single file, they left the bridge and ascended further. Within twenty minutes of uphill climbing, Rachel became exhausted and the kids complained. "We've had enough hiking. Let's head to Rooster Rock."

Barry ran ahead.

"Wait for us," Rachel shouted.

Barry turned to face the others but lost his footing when he stepped too close to the edge of the trail. The earth gave way, and he slid downward.

"Barry!" Both Rachel and Gina screamed, rushing toward the edge.

"Stay back!" Phil commanded, his voice booming above their shouting. "The ground isn't stable."

Rachel breathed quick, shallow breaths. "Barry, say something!" she called as Phil crawled to the edge, testing the ground in front of him.

"I'm scared," a feeble voice whimpered from below.

"Stay still, Barry," Phil said in a calm voice. "I'm coming for you. Remember how brave you were after the accident in Missoula? You can do it again." Phil peered downhill and then turned to Rachel. "He's clinging onto a small fir tree about ten feet down." With trembling lips, Rachel asked in a shrill voice, "What if you slide further down the bluff? There are gobs of huge rocks on the way down and a pool of water at the bottom." Her voice raised as dread gripped her.

"Stay back and try to remain calm for the kids' sake."

Calm? Being petrified is normal in such a situation. That's my child! Rachel watched helplessly as Phil considered a plan of rescue. Eddie stood rooted to one spot. Gina's anguished yell reverberated through the towering trees. "Help!" A small crowd gathered. Two twenty-something male hikers sprang into action.

"We'll form a human chain," one of the men addressed Phil. "You lower yourself and grab the boy's arm."

"Sounds like a plan. Be aware the ground is unstable."

Four males securely gripped their hands together. Phil slithered over the edge. The lead man lowered himself. A minor avalanche of loose dirt rolled downhill, spewing dust particles onto Barry's face. His grasp on the tree loosened as he rubbed his eyes. Phil grabbed him and pushed him toward the lead fella's extended hand. He clasped his strong hand around Barry's.

He smiled at Barry. "Okay, Buddy, here we go!"

When Barry and the men stood safely on solid ground, Rachel ran to Barry, squeezing him tight. Barry clung to his mother.

Phil crawled upward, grabbing the hand of a rescuer. He sat, bending his head between his knees, and exhaled deep breaths to calm his racing heart. After brushing off the excess dirt from his clothing and hands, he stood and addressed the men. "Thank you. I shudder to think what might have happened without your help."

The rescuers and onlookers cheered the successful outcome.

One man ruffled Barry's hair. "You were a real trooper."

Barry stared at the man. "What does trooper mean?"

"You made the rescue easier because you acted bravely," said Phil.

Barry perked up, swelling his chest.

The crowd dispersed. Phil and the family finished the descent. Rachel warned everyone to stay clear of the edge.

"Do you still want to go to Rooster Rock?" Phil asked when they reached the car.

"I've had enough excitement for the day. Let's eat our lunch, then head home. I saw a grassy picnic area next to the gift shop."

After devouring the sandwiches and fruit, Coach clapped his hands. "Okay, kiddos, how about an ice cream cone?"

Eddie jumped up. "I want chocolate."

"I'm going to order raspberry," Gina said.

"How about you, Mr. Brave?" Coach asked Barry.

"I don't want one."

Phil squatted at eye level with the youngster. "You deserve a treat for being so brave once again."

A grin appeared. "Do they have chocolate swirl?"

"Let's find out."

Exiting the parking lot, Phil said to Rachel, "I'm sorry. This wasn't the outing I'd hoped for."

"No need to apologize." She turned her head to observe the children in the back seat. Gina leaned against the locked car door and Eddie did the same on the opposite side. Barry conked out in the front seat, his head resting on Rachel's lap. She glanced at Phil, a genuine smile building on her face. She was grateful for the risk he took without hesitation to rescue Barry. No wonder the boys were drawn to him. His bond with them and Gina reminded her of what an awesome father Lee was. Sigh.

Phil carried Barry on his shoulders into the house and placed him on the lounge chair. Gina and Eddie sat on either side of Jo.

"Barry fell over a cliff and almost rolled down to the bottom. He could have drowned in the water below. But Coach saved him," Eddie said.

Jo shot a worried expression at Rachel.

"Everything turned out okay thanks to Phil." Rachel recapped the incident. She stared at Jo's bandaged ankle. "What happened?"

"You hurt your foot as I did," Gina said, touching the swollen ankle. "Does it hurt? Hey, you can use my crutches! You can make them fit ya."

"Thanks. I'll need them. And," she announced, "I'll be staying for an extra week if it's okay with you."

"Of course," Rachel answered.

Jo described her tumble down the porch stairs, sugar-coating her injury. "An unfortunate accident." She added, "Your aunt loaned Cliff her car." She grinned. "More suitable than his motorcycle."

"Where is he now?"

"Next door at the café getting ice cream. I had a craving."

The inquisitive expression on Rachel's face brought a hardy laugh from Jo. "No, I'm not PG."

Phil brought in the cooler, and Rachel sent Eddie to fetch the rest of the bags.

Rachel glanced at Phil, reassuring him the outing wasn't a complete bust. "We had a pleasant day, despite Barry's accident."

"You won't hold that against me, will you?" he asked in a serious tone.

Rachel put her hand on his arm. "Of course not. It wasn't your fault. Thank God for you. No wonder the kids worship you. Their hero. Thank you." She hugged him.

Phil slid his arm around her waist and dipped his face toward her.

Rachel stepped back before her pounding heart burst.

Cliff arrived, carrying two containers of ice cream. "Hey! Cliff brought ice cream. I hope it's chocolate," said Eddie.

Rachel noticed Cliff whistling as he stood at the table dishing up bowls of the frozen treat for everyone. She remembered what Jo had said the night before and what she had promised to do.

"Thank you, Cliff, for the treat. It was a good thing you were here with Jo to help her." She gave him a quick hug. He smiled back.

Cliff took vacation time for Jo's last week before her return home. He was a fixture at the house. He arrived early in the morning and stayed well after Rachel returned from work. He paid attention to the kids, taking them to wade and splash in the creek, and shooting baskets with Eddie. Rachel suspected his voluntary babysitting stemmed from his desire to hang around Jo. No matter. She welcomed Cliff's improved attitude.

When it was time for Jo's departure, Cliff insisted he bring her to the airport. "She's going to need someone to carry her suitcase and help her to the gate."

Rachel eyed Jo's grinning face. "All right. You have a champion, so I'll say goodbye here." She hugged her niece. "Come back for Christmas. I'm sure Cliff won't object," she whispered.

Chapter 27

---❖---

Aunt Regina spent the Friday before Labor Day dealing with Gerald's belongings. She sat on the well-worn couch, rummaging through several boxes of his wood carvings. Holding up a majestic elk, she marveled at the intricate detail of his handiwork. She nestled it against her chest, her eyes moist. "Oh, how I miss him."

"We all do, Auntie." Rachel reached across the cushions to pat Regina's shoulder. "I cherish all my memories."

"I'm glad you stopped by today, Mr. DeLuca," said Aunt Regina.

"Please call me Phil."

"Phil it is." Pointing to a box resting on a shelf, she said. "Please bring it to me. I want to go through the items before I donate them."

Phil increased the fan's speed. He brought the box down and set it next to her feet. He removed the lid. "Gobs of cups and glasses."

Aunt Regina stroked a mug stained with coffee. "He sure loved his morning cup of Joe." Her lips quivered. "Touching his belongings allows me to stay close to him."

"He's in your heart." Phil watched as she fondled the items.

Rachel observed the interaction between the two. Phil had a way about him that people gravitated toward. Her children sure did. The boys couldn't stop singing his praises. Now he'd won over Aunt Regina and her mother.

Rachel picked up a box. "I'll carry this out to the car."

"Let me. Looks heavy." Phil reached for the box.

Rachel's lips formed a smile. "No thanks, I can do it. You stay and talk to Auntie." Turning on her heel, she marched out the open door.

She put the box into the trunk and returned to the porch. Wanting to take a short break, she sat on the steps. The conversation between Aunt Regina and Phil didn't filter into her conscience until she heard her name.

"What are the odds your encounter after the car accident in Missoula would result in another unexpected meeting a year and a half later?"

"Thanks to Eddie's basketball passion," Phil said.

"Fate."

"I wish fate would intervene on my behalf with Rachel. She keeps me at a distance. It seems she can't trust or allow any man to get close to her."

Rachel's muscles tensed as a long pause passed before her aunt spoke. She prayed her aunt would keep her opinions to herself. The next words caused her heart to sink to her stomach. She considered interrupting the monologue, but curiosity prevailed.

"Let me explain Rachel's childhood so you'll understand her attitude about alcohol. Almost everyone living in Alder Creek knew her father was a drunk and an abuser. Cliff and Rachel grew up in that environment. Their father's drinking scarred both of them. Rachel developed a hatred for the beverage and Cliff imbibes too much. When Rachel married Lee, he drank a few beers a week, but not in her presence. When the Navy stationed him in Philadelphia, the new assignment overjoyed Lee. They now lived only an hour from Vineland where his family lived. He played cards nearly every Friday night with his navy friends. His brothers joined them once or twice a month. Lee wasn't an alcoholic. He consumed a beer or two each week, but to Rachel, that was one too many. No matter what Lee did for her and the kids, she held that minor deviation over his head."

"Doesn't sound like much drinking. Is there more?"

"Yes, and I wish she'd tell you. You should know the full story. It might help you understand her mindset. Obvious to me you're attracted to her and want more than friendship. It's not my place to disclose what she did and why guilt consumes her. However," she cleared her throat, "Rachel threatened to . . ." Aunt Regina paused.

Rachel buried her head in her arms. Despite Lee's infidelity, tears leaked through her lids as she recalled what she'd done to Lee. If Aunt Regina continued, she would seem like an awful person. She would not allow her aunt to talk anymore. Wiping away the tears, she entered the room. "I heard my name. Are you talking about me behind my back?" she asked, half-joking, half-annoyed.

"I thought if Phil knew about your threat, he'd understand your guilt and why you're having a problem overcoming it."

"You have no business telling him anything about me!"

Phil stood inches in front of Rachel. "Don't blame your aunt. I asked her a question and she was answering."

"About me, right?"

"Yes." Phil's muscles stiffened.

Rachel's eyes narrowed at the man standing oh so close to her. His handsome face would not get him out of this. "I'd appreciate it if you didn't talk about me." Her icy stare pierced into him.

Phil put distance between them, shaking his head and massaging his temples.

Aunt Regina stood, taking control to ease the tension. "Phil, since you won't let me pay you, I want to give you a memento from Gerald's collection." She walked to a pile of boxes and pointed to a wooden case with an attached lid. It had a detailed carving of Poncho. "Take this one. It was his favorite creation."

"I couldn't."

"You have no choice," Aunt Regina said. She picked up the case. "Here. Take it."

Rachel spit out the words. "Cliff wanted that carving. You're giving it to Phil?"

"Yes. You object?" A spasm of irritation crossed Aunt Regina's face. "Phil stepped in to help us since Gerald died. Cliff hasn't."

Phil handed the carving to Aunt Regina. "Thanks, but I can't accept this. I don't want to cause any problems."

She shoved the figure back into his hand.

Rachel turned a cold eye on her aunt.

Gina bounded into the room ahead of her grandmother. "Here we are!"

Kathryn surveyed the room. "Whew! I thought there'd still be a mountain of stuff left to pack." Addressing Phil, she thanked him. "You accomplished more than I imagined."

"Nothing remains except Gerald's wooden carvings and a few odds and ends. I'll be by tomorrow to move them into Miss Regina's house. Then I'll shoot baskets with the boys."

Spotting the carving in Phil's arms, Gina said, "That was grandpa Gerald's best one. Are you taking it?"

"I guess so."

"I'm glad." Gina smiled up at him.

Phil patted Gina on the head. "I'm done for the day. I'll head home." He glanced at Rachel.

"Wait," said Kathryn. She reached into her oversized purse and pulled out *Nightmare*. "Here's the book I told you about. If you read it, it'll help you understand what we all endured and how their father affected Rachel and Cliff."

Rachel shot a scorching glare at her mother. Her voice turned thin and cruel, rising hysterically. "So, you and Phil also talked about me?" She grabbed the book, shaking it at her mother. "You know my objection to anyone reading this trash!" She shot a harsh stare at

Phil. There was a thread of warning in her voice. "Don't you dare read the story."

"You're overreacting," Aunt Regina said. "Calm down."

"You're all ganging up on me!" She hurled *Nightmare* across the room and stomped outside.

Chapter 28

◆◆◆

The next day when Phil arrived to shoot baskets with the boys, Rachel avoided him. She regretted her shameful outburst. Phil didn't deserve her verbal attack, nor did her aunt and mother. Apologizing to her mother and Aunt Regina was one thing, but Phil . . .

Conflict enveloped her. *I'm attracted to him, but I'm not ready to see him regularly without defining what exactly he means to me.* She convinced herself no man could replace Lee in her heart. She still missed him, but she couldn't overcome the pain of his affair and the child he may have fathered. But of more importance, she had the children to consider. They'd lost their father. She didn't want them becoming attached to another man if he wouldn't be around long term.

Eddie validated her concern a few days later when he wished Coach lived with them. He suggested another idea. "Hey, Mom! If you and Coach married, we could shoot baskets every day."

Barry jumped in, excited. "Yeah, he'll take me to scouts and help me build my car for the derby like Grandpa Gerald did."

Rachel's mouth became tight and grim. She hated to burst their bubble. "Boys, two people don't marry just to share a house. I will not wed Phil or anyone else so you'll have someone to play basketball with you."

"You shared our house with Daddy," Eddie pointed out.

"Your Dad and I loved each other. We wanted to be together. When you three kids were born, we became a family and raised you with more love than you can imagine. It's different with Coach. He's like your Uncle Vince."

"Can't you fall in love with him?" Eddie asked. "Jessie's mom married again and now he has a stepfather."

"How about we ask Uncle Cliff to move in with us? He'll play with you."

Barry pretended to gag, and Eddie crinkled his nose.

The conversation ended unresolved. They ran outside to the basketball hoop.

When the new school year began, Aunt Regina volunteered to babysit the children after school. "I'll make sure they complete any homework before they watch TV or play." The arrangement pleased Rachel.

"Guess what, Mom!" Eddie shouted, running up to his frazzled mother when she arrived to pick them up. She had assisted in emergency surgery at the clinic that day. A frantic family brought in their injured cat after a car hit it. The cat reminded her of Leo. She shed a few tears that Dr. Abbott's heroic efforts were unsuccessful.

"Hold on, Eddie. I've had a rough day. Can this wait till we get home?"

"No." He held up his right foot. "Coach gave me a brand-new basketball for my birthday and a new pair of tennis shoes."

"Me, too," Barry showed off his Converse sneakers and new baseball bat! He swung it around, barely missing an heirloom lamp. Aunt Regina suppressed a gasp.

Phil included Gina. She held up a collection of Laura Ingalls Wilder's *Little House on the Prairie* books.

"I hope he comes this Saturday for cake and ice cream," Barry said.

Phil's kindness touched Rachel. But the kids were becoming too attached to him. She'd have to consider the ramifications of Phil's continued presence in the kids' lives. She wouldn't allow him to replace Lee.

After the kids' bedtime, Kathryn showed up to discuss birthday gifts for her two grandsons.

"It's a simple decision what Eddie would want. Anything basketball," Kathryn chuckled. "I'm considering a new ball. The one Vince gave him last year is already wearing out."

"Don't bother. Phil gave him one, and Barry a bat. Gina books." Her tone projected disapproval.

"How thoughtful," Kathryn said. "Since Gerald's gone, Phil provides a male figure in their lives, and I notice a strong bond developing. We can't count on Cliff, although I've seen an improvement. Because of Jo, I suspect."

Rachel massaged her temples, complaining. "I believe they've forgotten their father. I don't like that."

"Lee was the perfect father, but the children have put their grief behind them and moved on. You should as well."

"I can't, Mom. I blame myself for Lee's death," Rachel said with the certainty of someone who would never overcome her guilt. "They need to remember their father and all the countless things he did for them and how much he loved them."

"Then what prompted you to consider leaving him and separating him from his children?" Kathryn rose and left, leaving her daughter to think about her remarks.

Kathryn's words stung Rachel. She flopped backward on the sofa, running her hands through her hair. *Lee was an awesome father, but he failed me as a husband. An adulterer.* She pondered how she would have reacted if she discovered his affair before his death. One thing was certain, however. She could never undo her threat. She'd wrapped herself within her guilt and couldn't escape its clutches. And involving herself with another man? No way. She decided to cut ties with Phil and only allow the children to see him at school when necessary.

"You're unfair!" shouted Eddie when Rachel told them of her decision. He stomped his feet. "Barry and I won't be able to be the ball boys!"

"How come Coach doesn't want to play with us anymore?" Barry stared at his mother.

"I made the choice, not Coach. I haven't told him."

Gina curled her lips. She glared at her mother and retreated to her room, slamming the door.

"But we want to see him! We like him!" Eddie screamed. "You're mean!" His tongue aimed at his mother.

The negative reactions surprised Rachel. She acknowledged Phil was already entrenched in the kids' lives. Nonetheless, she would not change her mind. *Was this a sensible decision benefiting the whole family? You seem to want everyone miserable.* The words came to her as if Lee spoke them. What would he want for his family?

Chapter 29

Rachel remained firm, prohibiting any extra contact with Coach. The children protested their mother's edict. Their attitudes and behavior changed for the worse. They displayed a united front against their mother.

"Eddie, clean Leo's litter box," Rachel said one day.

"I don't want to," he replied. "You can't make me."

This kind of response was a daily occurrence. Rachel's irritation reached the boiling point. She had to quell this mini-rebellion. Allowing Coach back into their lives, of course, was the solution.

Rachel picked up the kids the day before their two-week Christmas break began. Aunt Regina ordered Rachel to come back tomorrow, alone.

"What for?"

Aunt Regina's blank expression gave no hint. "Be here."

Aunt Regina pointed to a small platter filled with Christmas sugar cookies. "Gina made them all by herself. Quite tasty. Try one."

"Yum, yum." Rachel smacked her lips.

"Now sit."

Rachel detected her aunt's cold and disapproving tone. She noted the absence of Ming and Chang from their usual position by her side. Rachel braced herself. Aunt Regina minced no words. "You're being selfish."

Rachel did not expect such a scathing statement. The harsh words stung her. She crossed her arms over her chest. "What?"

"You're only thinking about yourself. Because you're having a problem with guilt, you don't need to slap down the boys and Gina by telling them they can't see Phil. You're punishing them for your irrational reasons."

"But–"

"Don't interrupt. Phil mentioned he bought gifts for the children and you refused to allow him to deliver them. You crushed him, Rachel."

Rachel's breathing grew thin and ragged.

"Take a hard assessment of yourself and how you're treating your family. If you want to wrap yourself in a cloak of guilt, leave the kids out of it. I've invited Phil over for Christmas dinner. If you can't be civil to him, stay home. The rest of us are fond of him. We don't want anyone with a poor attitude to spoil the day."

"You want him over me?" Rachel asked, swallowing hard.

"Your choice. Phil's a wholesome individual and an amazing male figure for the children. We want him to share the day with us. So, consider what I said." She rose and opened her bedroom door. Ming and Chang scampered out. Aunt Regina turned her attention to her spoiled pets.

"Hey, Eddie," Barry shouted. "It snowed!" The white Christmas the children hoped for had materialized. Barry put on his clothes and slipped on his boots. He ran outdoors and imprinted his footprints in the snow. Eddie wasn't far behind. Leo followed.

"Leo's pawprints are cute," Eddie pointed out.

Rachel stretched. Seven forty-five the illuminated clock numbers glared. Christmas. Dread overtook Rachel. She didn't want to endure the festivities at Aunt Regina's. She couldn't face Phil. For the children's sake, she would put on an Academy Award performance pretending to enjoy the day.

Before noon, Phil walked into Aunt Regina's, house carrying a bag. The children flocked to him, their sheer delight clear. They all clambered for his attention. Phil picked up Barry and swung him around.

"Guess what, Coach?" Eddie asked, his smile as wide as the Columbia River. "The PE teacher said I dribble and shoot the basketball so well he's positive I'll make the team when I'm in eighth grade!"

"No doubt." He reached into the bag and pulled out gifts for each child. They ripped off the haphazard wrapping.

Rachel sat across the room, watching the reunion. A twinge of remorse surfaced when she saw the joy on display between Phil and her children. He wandered to Rachel. "Merry Christmas." As he handed her a card, his fingers touched her. Her heart fluttered and a river of warmth flowed throughout her entire body. Her emotions betrayed her. She wouldn't succumb. She rose, face to face with him. Her deliberate icy stare bored into Phil. He backed away. "Excuse me," Rachel said, heading to the opposite side of the room.

Aunt Regina hugged Phil, welcoming him, then directed Rachel into the kitchen. Kathryn engaged Phil in a conversation about the snow and the daily parade of skiers headed to Mt. Hood.

"Slice up the cheese and arrange it on this platter," Aunt Regina ordered Rachel. Then she got right to the point. "I noticed your indifferent response to Phil. I'm warning you. Change your attitude now. It will affect the kids. They don't understand your thinking. Put a smile on your face and act as though Phil is the most fantastic person to enter your life. Or you can go home. I'm not joking."

Rachel nodded, forced to choose between her kids and home. It was a simple decision. "Okay, fine. I'll try."

After everyone filled their bellies, Gina bragged, "I helped Mom make the sweet potato dish. I put lots of brown sugar on them."

"Along with the turkey, it was my favorite," Phil complimented Gina. "I ate two helpings."

"Okay, ladies, let's get busy clearing the table before we bring out the desserts," Aunt Regina said.

Phil stacked the plates. "I'll bet Eddie and Barry won't mind lending helping hands." He winked at the pair and glanced at Cliff. He took the hint and reached for several items.

Eddie balked. "Okay, but can we shoot baskets when we're done?"

Phil pointed to the picture window, reminding the youngster snow covered the ground.

"So?"

Kathryn clapped. "I have a terrific idea. Why don't you kids go outside and build a snowman? Cliff and Phil can assist."

"Rachel, too," Aunt Regina said.

"Yeah!" Eddie welcomed the suggestion. The boys wasted no time putting on their coats and boots.

Aunt Regina handed a wool scarf to Rachel. "Wrap this around Mr. Snowman's neck."

Cliff threw a snowball in Rachel's direction. She retaliated. She compacted a handful of snow and hurled it with all her strength at Cliff, missing by several feet. Instead, it smacked Phil upside the head, knocking his baseball cap off. "This means war!" He aimed a volley of balls at Rachel, as did Eddie and Barry. Gina stood by, clapping and rooting for Phil.

"Okay, I surrender!" Rachel declared after losing her balance and ending up on her butt, legs spread. Phil reached for her arm, pulling her up. Their faces were so close, his breath warmed Rachel's face. She turned away. Cliff noted Rachel's blush.

"I'm headed back inside," Rachel stated, blowing warm breath on her fingers.

"Me, too," Gina said. The troupe traipsed into the mudroom, discarding their wet boots, soaked gloves, hats, and coats. An assortment of desserts awaited them. Eddie and Barry wasted no time grabbing a piece of pumpkin pie with whipped cream they piled sky-high. Aunt Regina's legendary mincemeat pie caught Phil's eye.

"Haven't eaten mincemeat since Mom died. And that's been over five years." Phil rubbed his hands together and cut himself a hefty slice. "It's my second favorite after lemon meringue." He licked his upper lip and swallowed a bite. "Can't determine which is better, Miss Regina's or Mom's."

"Doesn't matter," Aunt Regina commented. "Rachel, cut him another piece."

Phil declined, rubbing his stomach. "Enough for now, but I'll take a piece to go if you don't mind."

"Done."

Kathryn pulled out a deck of cards from a desk drawer. "We're going to play *Go Fish*. That's a game everyone knows."

Cliff and Phil declined. They retreated to the opposite side of the room, discussing male topics. Rachel snuck a few quick glances in their direction.

A while later. "Ha, ha," Gina raised her arms in triumphant. "I win!"

"I don't care," Eddie said.

Aunt Regina relished her family enjoying themselves. She didn't want the day to end. She had one more activity to prolong the festive atmosphere.

"Cliff, choose a record. Then you can teach the kids how to dance." Besides skill playing pool, Cliff excelled at dancing during high school.

Cliff fingered through the collection of records. Opera, Glenn Miller, The Andrews Sisters. Yuck. He spotted an Elvis Presley album among the 33 1/3 rpm records. He held it up. "An Elvis record? Surprising. Didn't think his style appealed to you."

A smile appeared. "It doesn't. Gerald gave it to me. I played it one time to please him."

Cliff put on the album and adjusted the volume. *Jailhouse Rock* vibrated throughout the room. The kids and Phil gathered in the middle of the room, engaging in all manner of silly dance movements.

Rachel couldn't stifle a smile as her kids danced with Phil. Watching the glee they showed sent a stab to her heart. The kids still harbored resentment toward her. Phil didn't ignore her, but he kept his distance. *Of course, he would after her chilly greeting.*

Love Me Tender was the last song on side one. The kids plopped onto the floor. Their hearts pounded from the physicality of their crazy dancing.

"I'm pooped," Eddie proclaimed.

"This is a perfect slow song for grownups who like each other," commented Cliff, glancing at his sister and Phil. He moved the needle to the beginning of the song.

Gina reached for her mother's hand and pulled her to Phil.

Before Rachel could move away, she found herself wrapped in Phil's embrace. When he gazed into her eyes, she didn't know what overcame her. The sensation was nothing like she'd felt before. It took her by surprise. Her legs became noodles. She clung to Phil for support.

The applause and silly cheers of her children at the song's end embarrassed her. In a flustered hush, she backed away from Phil, stammering, "I . . . I need to use the bathroom."

When she emerged, Cliff was leaning against the wall. "You're letting your guard down. It's about time you get over your guilt and accept Phil. Jo made me realize I was punishing myself and everyone around me. For what? Because my father was an alcoholic mad man I hated? I'm trying, Sis, to put our nightmare childhood behind me. You might start doing the same thing about your feelings toward Lee's drinking. He's gone. Why are you punishing the kids for your self-imposed guilt? Who cares anymore? Admit it. You enjoyed today." He brushed past her. "Merry Christmas. I'm headed home to call Jo, but not before I cut a slice of pumpkin pie for the road."

Cliff, of all people, was dead on. She had indeed let her guard down. But was that a bad thing? Rachel glanced down the hall, listening to the playful laughter of Phil and the children. She admitted he would be an amazing father. She rubbed her chest as the pain cut through her heart, thinking about the father they'd lost. If she had come straight home from shopping instead of stopping at the park the day he died, Lee might still be alive. *Or not. The autopsy confirmed a completely blocked artery.*

The next day, Rachel helped her aunt clean up the mess. With a hint of humility, Rachel thanked her aunt for insisting she attended the festivities. She wouldn't disclose that last night as she fought insomnia, Phil occupied her thoughts. There'd been a slight curve to her lips.

Aunt Regina patted Rachel's shoulder.

"Not surprised there's no dessert left except the mincemeat pie. Seems only you and Phil like it. He forgot to take a piece home," Rachel said.

Aunt Regina couldn't resist suggesting. "Why don't you take the leftover pie to him?"

Aunt Regina's motive didn't fool Rachel. "I'll pass."

"Speaking of Phil," Aunt Regina kept him front and center, "you saw the fantastic time he and the kids enjoyed. I'm hoping you've relented and will allow them to resume seeing each other."

Selfish and punishing the children. Her aunt made that clear a few days ago. It bothered Rachel that her aunt referred to her in those terms. She loved and admired her aunt, but those words hurt. How could she explain her anxiety that Phil might replace Lee in their lives? She couldn't let that happen. "I'm thinking about it," Rachel said.

Aunt Regina sat, lifting Ming onto her lap. She tried to stay calm. "They've lost their father and Gerald. Cliff's getting better, but they need a constant father figure. After yesterday's fun, how do you think the kids will react if you continue to cut Phil out of their world?"

Rachel could feel her heart in her throat. She didn't have a reasonable answer. She played with her ponytail, her eyes wandering around the room.

"Well?"

"I'm afraid they'll forget their father and replace him with Phil."

"They've moved on, Rachel. You should too. I don't expect you to forget Lee, but he wouldn't want you to keep dwelling on the past. Life is for the living. It's time for you to change your attitude." Pointing to Rachel's ring finger, she said, "It's time you stopped wearing your wedding ring."

Rachel ignored her aunt's comment. "I suppose Phil could take the kids for an outing now and then, and of course, he'll coach Little League this spring."

In a stern tone, Aunt Regina said, "I'm warning you. The kids will develop resentment toward you if you continue to prohibit them from seeing Phil."

Rachel considered her aunt's warning an exaggeration. "I doubt it."

Aunt Regina wagged her index finger. "When are you going to lift the barrier you've erected around your heart? It'll be three years this April since Lee died." She plowed ahead. "Your mother told me about your threat. It helps me understand why you're consumed with guilt. But you deserve another chance at love and marriage. Even if you don't want to marry again, the kids need a father figure. Phil fits the bill. Of course, no one should thrust you at Phil. He deserves a woman who will love him with all her heart."

"I'm not ready."

"Poppycock. Your feelings for Phil go deeper than friendship. Do something about it."

"Look who's talking. Everyone knew you and Gerald loved each other, but you never married. Why not?"

The pain of losing Gerald was still raw, and she could relate to Rachel. But she wasn't about to allow Rachel to steer the conversation in another direction. She dodged the question. She lifted Ming close to her bosom, paused, then continued. "Invite Phil to spend New Year's Eve with you and the children. You can play games, roast marshmallows, or pop popcorn. Whatever."

"Forget it."

Aunt Regina shrugged.

Chapter 30

———✦———

T he dreary winter weather stepped aside. Purple crocus and yellow daffodils dotted the landscape. Rachel sat in the living room reading a book from the library.

"Why can't we see Coach?" Barry demanded, putting his hands on his hips.

"Yeah, why not?" Eddie asked. "You're still being mean."

"You are unfair," Gina said.

Three sets of eyes glared at Rachel. She recalled the words of Aunt Regina. *The kids will develop resentment toward you.* The verbal attacks pained Rachel. She attempted to defend herself. "I don't want you to forget your father or replace him."

"Coach plays with us as Daddy did and he shoots baskets with me. And he lets me and Barry be ball boys. We like him!" Eddie said.

"Mom! We haven't forgotten Daddy. But he's gone forever. We wouldn't mind having a new dad. All the other kids have a father. It's not fair."

The matter-of-fact statement by eleven-year-old Gina surprised Rachel. Her words pierced Rachel's heart like an arrow. She rubbed the nape of her neck, unable to respond. Tears gushed. Her distress didn't bother the children.

"I'm glad you're crying," Eddie said, crossing his arms.

Three days later, on Friday, Rachel walked into Aunt Regina's after work to gather the kids. The clinic had two emergencies, and an uncooperative male cat scratched her right thumb. She wanted to soak in a hot bubble bath and shut out the world. Forget about cooking dinner. She'd serve canned chicken noodle soup and Kathryn's homemade applesauce.

Rachel pecked her Aunt Regina's cheek. "Everyone finish their homework?"

"Of course," Aunt Regina said. "I always make sure they do."

"Okay, kiddos, let's head home." Rachel hadn't addressed the children's concerns discussed a few days ago. The tension lingered. She felt like the enemy.

Gina and Barry gathered their textbooks. "Where's Eddie?"

"He stayed after school," Barry said.

"What for?"

Aunt Regina said, "I thought you knew, so I wasn't concerned."

Rachel addressed Gina. "Did he say anything to you?"

"Nope."

"Barry?"

"He said something about basketball."

Aunt Regina wrapped her arm around Rachel's shoulder. "I'm sure he's fine."

An exasperated sigh escaped Rachel. "He didn't have permission. How's he going to get home?" Rachel glanced at her watch. Five-thirty. She inhaled a deep breath.

An hour later, when Eddie still hadn't shown up, worry overtook Rachel. *Where is he?* She phoned Cliff. "Eddie didn't come home today. I'm worried. Would you please drive to the school and see if he's still there?"

Within fifteen minutes, Cliff phoned. Rachel's muscles stiffened when Cliff told her he saw no sign of Eddie. "The school is locked. No lights on. I'll drive around Sandy and search for him."

"Thanks." Rachel paced the room, her heart hammering against her chest.

Seven-twenty and still no Eddie. Silent panic built like a rolling snowball in the pit of her stomach. The chaos of her thoughts kept coming like waves on the beach. She would have upchucked her dinner if she'd been able to eat.

"I'll bet Eddie's with Coach," Barry said.

Rachel wished that was true. Although she still forbade the children from seeing Phil, she decided Eddie might be with him. She didn't want to involve him, but desperation prevailed. After a dozen rings, she slammed the phone into the cradle and wiped her clammy hands on her shirt.

Minutes after eight o'clock, she heard a knock on the door. Barry ran to open it. Phil stood on the porch with his palms resting on Eddie's shoulders. "Coach!" Barry shouted.

Phil gently shoved Eddie inside. Eddie dragged his feet, his head bent downward.

"Eddie!" Rachel ran to him, dropping to her knees and hugging him. "You worried me sick."

Eddie stepped away. He crossed his arms and refused to make eye contact or speak.

Rachel's relief turned to irritation. With a raised voice, she spewed questions at him. "Where have you been? Why didn't you come home? Do you know what you put me through?"

Phil encouraged Eddie to explain what happened.

Eddie remained silent.

Phil whispered into the boy's ear.

"I walked to the store and stole some candy. The clerk caught me and called the cops."

Rachel gasped. She couldn't believe her son would steal. "Phil, is this true?"

He nodded.

Barry and Gina stepped closer. "You two go to your rooms. This isn't for you."

"Why? We want to hear what happened," Gina said, her fists on her hips.

"Are you going to spank Eddie?" Barry asked.

Rachel gripped the two children's shoulders and marched them down the hall to their bedrooms and closed the doors. Within seconds, both children opened their doors, sticking out their heads.

"Why did you steal?" Rachel asked.

"I just did."

Phil spoke. "When the police officer approached Eddie, he gave his correct name but told the officer he didn't want to go home. He said he wanted to go to my place instead. The officer, a friend of mine, brought Eddie to my house. He told me what happened and let me handle the situation. We hung out at my house and then I took him to *Dea's*." He shot an apologetic stare at Rachel. "Sorry I didn't call you."

"Damn right," Rachel blurted out. "How dare you reward him at *Dea's* for stealing."

"I want to live with Coach! You're mean!" Rachel put her hand on her chest, taken aback by Eddie's sudden outburst. He ran past her to his room.

"Yeah! Me, too!" Barry shouted from the hallway. Gina expressed mutual agreement before they slammed their doors.

Phil guided her to the sofa. He embraced her. She leaned against his chest, unable to stop the flood of tears. Her voice cracked. "Aunt Regina was right. She predicted they'd hold a grudge against me." She lifted her head, staring into Phil's eyes.

Phil reached for a tissue. "Your mascara isn't waterproof." He chuckled, trying to lighten the mood as he wiped away the black streaks. He put out his hands to comfort her, but she waved them away. She needed to work this out. "I kept you and the kids apart and clung tight to the image of Lee as their father. I didn't want another man in the picture taking his place in their hearts and minds. That's the reason I justified prohibiting them from seeing you. They were becoming too attached to you. It upset me." She shook her head.

"I've been so wrong. And I can't shake the guilt about what I did to Lee."

"So, I'm clear on this. What exactly did you do that resulted in your guilt complex?"

She paused. "Didn't Aunt Regina tell you?"

"I want to hear it from you."

"I threatened to leave him and move back to Oregon with the children."

"What was so horrible that you decided you had no choice other than to dump your husband and break up your family?" He stood and leaned against the fireplace.

"He drank beer."

"Half the country drinks. Some more than they should. Did his brothers drink with him?"

"Yes, on many Saturdays he drove to his brother Dominick's in Vineland. They drank and played cards. Every Friday, he also played poker at his best friend Howie's. I know they had beer there." The anger she'd always felt came back and her face heated. "I didn't want him drinking. He knew about my rotten childhood and how much I hated alcohol of any kind." She jumped off the sofa to face Phil. Her fists clenched as she hugged her waist. "He promised to quit. But didn't. He kept a supply in the garage." Her voice raised and broke. She looked at the ceiling. "He promised," she repeated. The sound ended in a soft cry.

Phil didn't reach out to her. His voice had a steady tone as he spoke. "So, what you're saying is, all those years you punished him because he drank a beer or two each week?" His eyebrows raised in question as he waited for her answer.

She walked to the window, then turned back to him. "Maybe you're right, but I was afraid he'd turn into an alcoholic like my father. I would not live that nightmare again."

"What kind of man was he? Did he love you? Treat you with disrespect in front of the kids? Drag you around by the hair and treat you like a servant?"

"Of course not! You're not funny."

"I didn't intend to be. I was curious to know the type of man you hated."

"I didn't hate him. I loved him." *Despite his affair and possible fourth child.*

"Odd way to show it. I would stay away as often as I could if my wife treated me like I was an alcoholic bum."

"I did not!" She stomped to stand in front of him. "I cleaned his house, raised his kids, washed and ironed his clothes, and fed him. I was a wonderful wife to him!"

"Any housekeeper or maid could do what you did."

The reality of what he said engulfed her with anger. Her head was like a volcano, ready to explode. She shook, tears flowed again and she couldn't stop them. "We were arguing, and he told me he didn't need me for sex. He could satisfy his needs elsewhere." *How true, as it turned out.*

Phil approached her, but she batted his arm away and stepped across the room.

"After everything I did for him, he didn't want me."

"I'm sure he didn't mean those words. He no doubt said them in the heat of the moment."

Rachel directed the anger in her eyes toward Phil. Perhaps her obsession with alcohol had driven Lee to the arms of another woman. But she refused to accept the blame for the ultimate betrayal. "You don't know what Lee did to me. I'm tired of everyone believing he was a saint. He had an . . . never mind. I'm through talking. Please leave." She opened the front door.

Gina appeared, followed by her brothers. "Why are you yelling at Coach and telling him to go?"

Rachel denied raising her voice. "Bedtime. No arguing."

"I'm hungry," Eddie said. "I didn't eat dinner."

"That's because you stole a candy bar and almost went to jail," Barry said.

Phil glanced at Rachel. "Tell you what, kiddos. Follow me into the kitchen. I'll fix my super-duper spaghetti if I find all the ingredients."

"Yea!" Eddie said.

The kids and Coach headed to the kitchen, ignoring Rachel. She got up to challenge Coach's audacity to cook a meal in *her* kitchen but knew rebellion would reign. She remained in the living room. Her heart died a thousand deaths as the laughter and camaraderie drifted into her ears. By ten o'clock, the meal was over, and the kitchen spic and span. Phil herded the kids to bed then put on his jacket and walked toward the door. He disregarded Rachel.

"They all hate me! What have I done?" Rachel blurted out as Phil's hand turned the doorknob. He paused.

"They don't hate you. They are rebelling against your decisions."

"I'm a horrible mother and was a terrible wife. No matter what I do, it's wrong." Her voice broke as she eyed him for reassurance.

"You're an exceptional mother. You need a little mind adjustment and encouragement to make different choices."

Phil sat beside Rachel, then leaned oh so close to her to make a point. This time, when he touched her, she didn't push him away. "In my estimation, you punished your husband for all the things your father did to your mother, you, and Cliff. All that time, you used your perceived notion that Lee was an alcoholic as an excuse to continue lashing out. If he so much as mentioned beer, he'd never win. Right?" His voice trailed to a whisper. "If you don't choose to forgive your father, you will never be the mother or wife you want to be."

Phil's words formed a truth she'd never thought about. She used her fear and anger toward her father to punish Lee. He went to his grave with her threat hanging over him, which started the guilt she couldn't overcome. She wished she could re-live the day she threatened Lee and ask for his forgiveness. She also acknowledged there was no justification for forbidding Phil from the children.

His embrace was more than friendly. He kissed the tip of her nose. "Now that we've had this chat and I've read *Nightmare*, I understand your attitude toward alcohol. You can reach inner peace if you practice forgiveness. Can you forgive your father?"

All these years, Rachel allowed the monster's alcoholism and abuse to dictate her outlook on alcohol. She punished Lee because of her hatred for the beverage. Perhaps Phil was right. Forgiving her father might bring inner peace. "I can choose to remember the pleasant times. There were a few."

"That's all we can ask. And you should read *Nightmare*. It's enlightening. Writing helped your mother come to terms with your father. She's positive reading the story will help you, too."

"Humph."

"Last of all, can you forgive yourself?"

"I don't know."

"Repeat after me. I, Rachel, admit I made choices that hurt my husband and children. I promise to think twice about how my decisions may affect others." His serious manner kept any smart remarks from coming out of her mouth. "I will put the past behind me and focus on a future that will benefit myself and my family."

"Easier said than done."

Phil lifted Rachel's chin with his fingers, coaxing her to say the words.

She raised her left hand and stared at her wedding ring. She slipped it off, threw it across the room, and ran outside.

Chapter 31

———◦◦◦◦◦———

P hil sat speechless for a moment before dashing to join her.

Rachel leaned against the porch railing, her body trembling, but not from the late-night chill.

Phil asked. "Are you okay?"

She raised her voice and stomped her foot. "Of course not. The children resent me! My husband is dead! And I discovered he committed . . ."The "A"word refused to surface from deep within her throat.

Phil shot her a questioning expression.

"Adultery! He had an affair and may have fathered a fourth child!" She revealed her long-kept secret, not to her mother or Aunt Regina, but to this man standing inches from her. The man her children worshiped, the man who affected her emotions whenever she was in his presence.

"What the hell?"

"He betrayed me! His remark about satisfying his sexual needs elsewhere turned out to be true!"

Phil paced back and forth on the porch. "Are you sure?"

"Wait here." She went to her bedroom and pulled out the note from Lee's wallet. "Read."

My Dearest,

I live for the few hours I can spend with you on Friday evenings. Every day I dream I'm wrapped in your warm embrace. I'm not sure how you'll react, but I may be pregnant. What if I am? Will you acknowledge the child? What about your wife and children? We'll need to discuss this situation Friday. Till then . . . Love, DK

Phil folded the paper. He bent his head and rubbed his forehead over and over. "Hard to make sense of this revelation. Are you positive the woman wrote the note to Lee? Where did you find it?"

"In his wallet. Why else would Lee have the note?"

Phil exhaled a deep breath. "You still love him and are letting guilt consume you even after you found out about his affair?" He waved the devastating piece of paper back and forth.

She turned her back to him, her body still shaking.

"Come inside," Phil said. "It's getting chilly."

"Not yet, in case the kids might hear our conversation."

Phil removed his jacket and draped it around Rachel's shoulders. "I'm so sorry for you. I wish I could make things better."

"Another thing. His wedding ring is missing. He never removed it unless he worked on cars. I don't remember if he was wearing it when I found him."

Phil took her left hand in his, touching the bare ring finger. "It'll be a challenge to forgive Lee for what he did to you. Of course, there could be some innocent explanation."

"I'd like to believe that. But what?"

"Whatever the case, you need to forgive yourself and get rid of the guilt."

Rachel perched on the railing, pondering Phil's words. She clasped his forearm. "Thanks for helping me realize forgiving my father and myself is necessary to achieve inner peace and healing. I'm sincerely going to try." She stared into his eyes seeking an answer. "But how do I forgive Lee? How? How?" she repeated.

Phil ran his hands through his hair. "I don't know."

A yawn escaped. Rachel handed Phil's jacket to him. "Thanks for the pep talk. While we're on this topic, I'm sorry for my rotten attitude and for keeping you and the kids apart. Am I forgiven?"

Phil squeezed her hand.

The next morning, Rachel gathered the children.

"Can we see Coach?" Eddie asked in a soft tone, unsure of her reaction.

"Yes. I asked Coach for his forgiveness for mistreating him and keeping you from him. He forgave me. Can you all do the same?"

"Yes." Gina flung herself at her mother in tears. Barry followed with his brand of hugs and kisses.

Rachel peered at Eddie. She worried most about him. "And you?" Rachel held an arm out to him. Eddie hesitated for a moment before hurling his body toward the group and hugging his mother and siblings.

The atmosphere in the Favretto household returned to an easy routine. All was well between Rachel and her children. They forgave her, and she promised to be a better mother.

The boys and Gina relished Phil's attention. Rachel enjoyed attending Little League and cheering for her sons. During the games, she eyeballed Phil. When he shot a glance her way, a slight rush of excitement rippled through her body. She became more comfortable in his presence. They got along like best friends, and Rachel was fine with that. *Or am I?* The barrier she erected around her heart and Lee's grip on her emotions remained intact, albeit not as strong.

Aunt Regina didn't miss any opportunity to encourage her to spend time *alone* with Phil. "I see how you act in Phil's presence. You don't fool me. Stop resisting."

Rachel's coming to terms with her father's effect on her pleased Kathryn. "It took me a long time to get there, too."

"I still think you should finish reading *Nightmare*. It might help you with any other residual issues."

"I don't want to. And I don't have any issues, Mom." She added, "Phil also told me I need to read it. He said it's enlightening. Hard to believe."

Two nights before Memorial Day, Rachel pulled out a lightweight cotton nightgown from the bottom drawer. Underneath the gown lay *Nightmare,* placed out of sight all these months. She reached for the book and tossed it on the nightstand. She flipped on the fan and climbed into bed. Curiosity overtook her. Where had she left off? Oh yeah, in chapter twelve, where the father beat the son with a belt.

Rachel blinked awake. Four twenty. Her right hand rested on an open page of *Nightmare*. She had conked out with only two chapters left. She leaned against the headboard and read until the last word.

Rachel contemplated the narrative. Kathryn skillfully conveyed things happen beyond one's control. Her father *chose* to consume alcohol, and Lee's death happened. It was not her fault. One must move on; stop allowing the past to dictate the rest of your life. She couldn't yet reconcile the painful knowledge of Lee's infidelity and possible child. Did the children have a half-sibling? And what happened to Lee's wedding ring?

Chapter 32

—◦◦◦—

"Aunt Regina," Rachel said, "I'm headed to Meing's to pick up a few items for tomorrow's barbecue." She took a whiff of the potato salad Gina was making with minimal help from her great-great aunt. "The boys are in the backyard practicing their batting. Be back as soon as I can."

Tasting an enormous bite, Gina declared, "Mmmm. It tastes delicious."

Aunt Regina scraped a teaspoonful from the mixture. "Yep. I agree. I'll add a smidgeon of salt and how about a few diced dill pickles?"

"Ah, okay," Gina said.

"No onions," Rachel reminded her aunt as she exited the kitchen. She rolled down the car window and turned the key in the ignition. The unwelcome clicking sound of the battery gasping for life frustrated her. She rested her forehead on the steering wheel, yelling. "Crap! Damn!"

"Did I hear less than ladylike words spouting from your mouth?" a familiar voice asked.

Rachel jerked up. Phil bent over beside the open window, his face eye-level with hers. "You startled me," she said. A heatwave of embarrassment cruised throughout her body.

"Sorry. I brought Barry's mitt. He left it in my car last night. So, why the outburst?"

"The battery's dead."

"How 'bout I jump it for you?"

"Forget it. It's ready for the graveyard. I shouldn't have waited so long to replace it." She pounded the dashboard. "The old Frazer is starting to nickel and dime me."

"I'll drive you to Schwab's for a new battery." He raised the hood and disconnected the old one. "We'll bring it with us so we get the right model."

"I was headed to the store to buy a few things for tomorrow's barbecue," she said, exiting the car.

"Phil's taxi at your service." He bowed and gestured toward his Chevy.

"An offer I won't refuse." She ran back to the house to tell her aunt about the dead battery and Phil driving her to Schwab's. She rushed into the bathroom to run a brush through her hair and powder her nose. And spray a small trace of perfume. She stared at her image in the mirror. She ignored the smirking reflection and headed out the door.

"Take your time," Aunt Regina said. "The kids and I'll be fine. Invite Phil to the barbeque. And get some paper plates!"

When Rachel emerged from the house, Barry and Eddie were wrestling with Phil on the lawn. "Ready?"

Eddie and Barry stood, triumphant. "Pinned ya!" Eddie barked.

"Unfair. Two against one," Phil pointed out, wiping blades of grass from his T-shirt.

"Where are you going?" Eddie asked. Barry jumped up and down like a pogo stick beside them.

"I'm heading to Meing's to grab a few groceries. The car battery died, so Phil offered to drive me." She spoke to her sons as Phil held the door for her.

The boys dashed to the car. Eddie gripped the back door handle.

"You're not going. I'm making a quick run and I don't want you two begging me to buy everything you see." She shook her finger at them.

They looked at Phil to interfere on their behalf. "Your mother spoke."

When the Schwab employee presented Rachel with the bill, her eyes bulged. She needed the cash she had for the groceries.

Phil pulled out his wallet and handed the man a crumpled twenty-dollar bill.

"No, Phil. This isn't your car."

"Consider it a loan."

Rachel leaned against the building, ready to argue. "I won't let–"

Phil stepped closer than a finger's length in front of her. "You can pay me back by inviting me to the barbecue and putting a smile on your lovely face."

She couldn't refuse his self-invite. "Fine. The kids and Aunt Regina will enjoy your company."

"And you?"

I will too! Her silent voice screamed. *Calm yourself.*

On the way to Meing's, Phil switched on the radio. He tapped his fingers on the steering wheel in rhythm with Del Shannon's latest hit, *Runaway.* "This is my favorite station. It plays current and oldies hits."

Rachel rested her head on the seatback, closing her eyes and soaking in the songs' melodies. As Phil pulled into Meing's parking lot, Frank Sinatra's rendition of *You Make Me Feel So Young* floated through the speaker. Phil increased the volume. "One of my favorites."

Rachel's eyes popped open and she sat erect. She switched off the radio. Her hand covered her mouth.

Phil turned the motor off, puzzled by her sudden move. "Hey," he said, chuckling. "You hate the song that much?"

Rachel stared out the window.

"Rachel, you can tell me what's wrong."

"That song reminded me of Lee. He was thirteen years older than me. It became our special song." She let the memory linger but didn't allow it to bring tears. "Sorry for my emotional reaction."

"You're fine. Memories are what we have." He put his arm around her shoulders and pulled her into a hug. "Let's make some fresh ones."

Rachel rested her head on his shoulder. When Phil's fingers lifted her chin, their eyes met before his mouth covered her lips. Rachel felt her face flush warm, but not because of the stifling heat. It had been so long since such an intense craving for physical fulfillment overcame her. When he deepened the kiss, she responded with fervor but abruptly disengaged.

"We're in public and broad daylight. Not the place to make out." She admonished him with a smile.

"So, you're saying if we were alone and at my house, you'd let me continue? I can fix that in a heartbeat." His eyes projected hope.

She surveyed the area. No one took notice of them. She kissed his cheek. "I guess we'll never know." She pulled on the handle and swung her feet out the door. "You coming?"

"In a few minutes. Go ahead."

She grinned at him and shut the door. She swung her hips a little, as she knew Phil would be watching. Her skirt blew around her legs. Her lips spread into a huge smile as she approached the store's entrance.

After paying for her groceries, she declined help from the box boy and pushed the grocery cart to the parking lot.

Standing by his car, Phil hugged an attractive woman at least ten years younger. Blonde, *perky breasts* that seemed to want to push into Phil's chest. She talked in animated gestures. He lifted her and twirled her around. He nodded to whatever she'd said and she stood on her tiptoes and kissed his forehead before darting to her car. She blew him a kiss as she backed out of the parking spot.

A honk broke Rachel's stare. She pressed her lips flat and crossed her arms in front of her chest.

"Sorry, I got sidetracked. I'll load the bags."

Rachel wanted to refuse his help. She didn't speak while Phil drove to her house. She sensed Phil glancing at her.

"Did something happen inside the store? Your mood has changed."

She shook her head and stared out the window.

"Rachel. Don't hold it in. Talk to me. That's what friends are for."

She knew she was acting childish. She couldn't help herself. "I'm fine," she answered and smoothed the skirt of her dress.

The sun's rays beamed on Alder Creek at first light, promising another day of high temperatures

At one o'clock, Phil arrived at Aunt Regina's to escort her across the highway. She wore one of her colorful sleeveless dresses. Her signature assortment of costume jewelry adorned her ears and wrists and dangled from her neck. Rachel stared as the pair advanced toward her house. Aunt Regina chatted non-stop, her cane periodically tapping Phil on the arm.

At the end of the driveway, they stopped. Phil continued the conversation. Rachel couldn't hear the words, but she noted her aunt's annoyed reaction. Before they reached the porch, Rachel hurried back to the kitchen.

Phil approached Rachel, but she moved away. "I need to carry the food outside." She rebuffed his help. Phil turned his attention to wrestling with the boys.

Phil's disregard for her miffed Rachel. Her subconscious chided her. *So, it's okay for you to snub him, but not when he does it. Shame on you.* She cringed as she took ownership of her attitude. Maybe the embrace was innocent, and she jumped to an erroneous conclusion. The young woman could be an acquaintance or a co-worker.

Rachel argued with herself. *I was not jealous! Yes, you were. No way. You should tell him you're sorry and explain yourself.* She eyed Phil, laughing and joking with her entire family, including Cliff. *All right, I admit I was jealous.* She didn't want him paying attention to any woman but her. *Apologize.*

Rachel approached Phil at the same time Eddie and Barry pulled him away to play catch.

Chapter 33

—◦❖◦—

Three days after the barbecue, Aunt Regina invited–no, summoned–her great-niece. Her patience wore thin, and she got right to the point. "It's obvious Phil loves you and you're attracted to him. Don't deny it. Now tomorrow evening after work, I expect you to tell him your true feelings."

Rachel sat on the velvet sofa, staring at the ceiling. *How dare she!* She gathered the courage to defy her great-aunt. "I respect you, but I'll do no such thing. Phil is a decent, caring man, so wonderful to the children. But I still love Lee." The usual excuse rolled off her tongue before she could recall it.

Aunt Regina thumped her cane on the carpet. "Stop this nonsense!" She walked across the room and sat next to her great-niece. "I'm going to tell you something I've told no one, including your mother."

Rachel faced her aunt. "What?"

Aunt Regina shooed Ming and Chang away. "In our late twenties, Gerald and I met at a grange dance. The mutual attraction was immediate." She grinned, recalling that first meeting. "We were inseparable. In due time, I became pregnant. Quite scandalous back in the 1920s. Gerald wanted to marry me at once. I had a horrific miscarriage and almost died. I couldn't have children after that." Aunt Regina paused, her eyes moistening. She pulled her lace-edged handkerchief from her skirt pocket and removed her eyeglasses. Rachel slid near her aunt and squeezed her tight. She tried to envision what her aunt experienced. "How awful for you. I can't imagine being unable to give birth. I'm so thankful for my three. But I don't understand why you're telling me this."

Removing herself from Rachel's embrace, Aunt Regina proceeded. "My marriage refusals did not deter Gerald. He begged me over and over to marry him. But I kept refusing."

"Why?"

"Because I didn't want to deprive him of fatherhood. You witnessed how marvelous he was with the children. But he said it didn't matter." She tilted her head upward, mouthing Gerald's name. "*Mia cara*, I developed an irrational guilt complex because I couldn't bless him with children. I figured eventually he'd resent me. So, I denied him the one thing he wanted most . . . to be my husband. He never left me, even when I encouraged him to find someone else. I was his one and only love forever."

"But the miscarriage wasn't your fault. Why not adopt? You loved him too, so why not marry him?"

"Foolishness! Pure stupidity. I let guilt dictate the course of our lives and prevent me from marrying the only man I ever loved. Gerald stopped asking. He built the cabin to always be nearby. He wanted everything as respectable as possible so the self-righteous gossips wouldn't wag their tongues about our immorality." She grinned. "We were married in every sense of the word, just not legally. My point, Rachel, is you're choosing to let guilt stop you from allowing Phil into your heart. I refuse to let you make the same mistake I did." Aunt Regina paused. "I know how much you loved Lee. You had a wonderful ten years together. But that doesn't mean you should cheat yourself from another chance at happiness. Let Phil be in your world now. And the children's." She wrapped Rachel's hands within her wrinkled ones. "Go to him tomorrow."

Rachel leaped from the sofa and walked to the picture window. She stared at the potted geraniums on the patio. Speaking in a whisper, she said, "I read *Nightmare*. I'm working on getting over my guilt and forgiving myself for what I did to Lee."

"Speak up."

Rachel spun around, raising her voice several decibels. "I said I'm trying to forgive myself and move on. It's not happening overnight, but I believe I'm making progress." She paused. "I think there's another woman in Phil's life. She was at Meing's when we went for the food for the barbecue. She kissed him and he seemed to enjoy it. I don't want him to feel obligated to me because my children think the sun rises and sets on his head."

Patting the sofa, Aunt Regina said, "Come here."

Rachel plopped down, stretched her legs, and put her hands on her head.

"You're making a troublesome choice, Rachel. You're clinging to the notion you don't deserve another man's love. The consequence is you will never again experience what you and Lee had, and that would be a shame."

Rachel considered disclosing Lee's affair. *No, never. I will not ruin his stellar reputation, especially for the children's sake.* "Lee is still a part of me. Please tell me why it's so hard to let go."

"No one expects you to forget Lee. But love isn't a bus, a train, or a plane. It doesn't run on a schedule. It's unexpected, even ill-timed. When it comes, grab it and hold on tight."

Aunt Regina directed Rachel's head onto her bosom. She remained silent while Rachel's tears dotted her silk blouse.

After a bit, Rachel blew her nose and rubbed her eyes. "Are they red? Don't want the kids to see me like this."

"You're fine," Aunt Regina assured her, moving a stray hair from Rachel's forehead. She switched on her best authoritative voice. "Phil means more to you than a friend. You're in love with him. Now tell him!"

"What do I say? What if this other woman is whom he wants?"

"Listen, my dear. Cliff's a changed man after meeting Jo. The children have adjusted well, and I'm positive will grow up making you and yes, Lee, proud. Kathryn is free of *her* guilt for not protecting you and Cliff. If I die before Ming and Chang, your family will provide a loving home for them. I'm a content woman, at peace, ready to join my beloved Gerald whenever God calls me. I need to know you're settled with a man who loves you. No doubt the woman is an acquaintance. Did you ask about her?"

"No. He said nothing, so I didn't either."

Regina leaned back in her chair. "Phil's coming tomorrow afternoon to trim around the ivy bear's eyes and nose. He won't finish before you get home from work. Go to him. Tell him you saw him kissing another woman. Ask him who she is and if he loves her. I'll bet my entire jewelry collection, including my sapphire, he doesn't."

"Wow! Talk about a firm belief. But if I reach out to Phil, I want to be ready to open my heart to him. I'm not sure I'm there yet. What if he rejects me and only wants to be my friend?"

"Then so be it. He'll still be a male figure in the children's lives unless you banish him again. And you better not." Aunt Regina ended the discussion. "This conversation will be our secret."

Rachel ran two fingers across her lips. "They're sealed."

Aunt Regina raised Rachel's left hand. "You're not wearing your wedding ring. About time."

She didn't disclose she'd hurled it across the living room in Phil's presence. "It's stashed away in my top dresser drawer." She hugged her aunt. "Thanks for caring." Backing toward the door, she said, "And you will not die anytime soon. You're too pigheaded."

Rachel tossed and turned into the wee hours of the night. Her mind focused on Aunt Regina's surprising revelation. She turned on the lamp then walked to the living room, reflecting on the astute words Aunt Regina had spoken. In the time since their conversation, she concluded her aunt was right. She couldn't continue to let guilt govern her life.

Rachel flipped on a light and advanced to the fireplace mantel. She took down the framed family picture and sat on the sofa, staring at the smiling faces. *I was so happy then. I want to feel that way again.* She closed her eyes, exhaling a deep sigh. *Lee, I think I'm in love again. Please give me a sign I have your blessing, so I can open my heart to Phil.*

Rachel lay her head on the armrest, caressing the picture. As she drifted to sleep, Phil was the last thought on her mind.

Chapter 34

——◆◆◆◆——

The next evening, Rachel turned into Aunt Regina's driveway and honked for the kids. Thankful it was Friday, she anticipated a relaxing weekend. As she stepped from the car, she noticed the thirty-foot ladder wedged against the ivy bear. Clippings piled up at the bear's base, but no sign of Phil. She entered the house and plopped her tired body onto the couch. Kicking off her shoes, she placed her feet on the coffee table and closed her eyes.

"Mom, you've got to tell Coach you love him." Gina grabbed her mother's hand and pulled her up.

"What're you talking about?"

"Aunt Regina told us to make sure you go talk with Coach when you got home," Eddie said.

"And tell him we want him to be our dad," added Barry in a stage whisper.

"What the hell–I mean heck–is going on?"

The children surrounded her and pushed her into the bedroom. "You need to change into something *sexy*."

Gina's casual utterance of that taboo word shocked Rachel.

Rachel continued to resist the kids' efforts until Kathryn arrived and took charge. She ordered her daughter to change out of her grubby work clothes.

"Is this a conspiracy?" Rachel asked, surrendering. She put on her favorite pair of khaki capris and a bright pink blouse, leaving the top button unfastened. She applied a touch of makeup and let her hair hang freely instead of her customary ponytail. When she emerged, Barry complimented his mother. "You're pretty."

"Thank you. But," she feigned irritation, "I don't understand why you're insisting I bother Phil while he's busy."

"We want you to marry him," Eddie said.

"He hasn't asked me. Also, we're a package deal. Phil would be stuck with three lively rascals."

Kathryn tilted her head back, smirking. "Are you kidding? He'll be happier than a kid in a candy shop. Invite him to dinner."

"Do you suppose he's there now? I didn't see him when I got home," Rachel said.

"He took a break in the cafe." She spotted him through the window. "He's back."

"Wait!" yelled Gina, running to her mother. She held a perfume bottle and squirted two puffs on Rachel. "Now you're ready."

No, I'm not. She picked up Leo from the sofa. "I'm taking him with me." *To help calm me.* Kathryn pushed Rachel out the door. "Go! Don't come back till you've told him how you feel about him!"

Rachel sauntered toward the ivy bear. Goosebumps surfaced along the length of her arms. Approaching

Phil busy clipping ivy around the bear's eyes, she didn't want to disturb him. She turned to leave.

Leo leaped from her grasp and scampered up the ladder rungs. He rubbed his fur against Phil's leg, startling him. His right foot slipped. His body slid halfway down the teetering ladder. His shout pierced the peaceful evening as he lost his grip. Rachel's screech reached the upper stratosphere as she helplessly watched Phil plummet to the ground. Kneeling beside Phil's battered body, her face grew white and her eyes horror-stricken. Phil tried to raise his head. He mumbled a few garbled words before his bloody head sagged, and he became unresponsive. What was he trying to say? *Love? Forever? Day?*

Kathryn and the kids dashed to the stricken man along with café customers.

"Someone call an ambulance!" Kathryn shouted.

Barry pulled on Rachel's blouse. "Is he gonna die like daddy did?"

Kathryn knelt and wrapped her arms around Barry. "Let's say a prayer." Barry closed his eyes and laced his hands together. Gina sat beside Phil, urging him to wake up and telling him she loved him. Eddie turned his back to the crowd so no one would see him wipe away his tears.

The ambulance arrived and the EMTs worked on Phil. They placed a splint on his right leg.

Every nerve in Rachel's body prickled as the men loaded the stretcher into the ambulance.

Kathryn yelled at Rachel to get the car keys and head to Gresham General. "I'll stay with the kids."

Rachel was thankful this recently opened hospital was closer than Oregon City.

It didn't matter Rachel drove over the speed limit trying to keep pace with the ambulance. She struggled to focus on the highway through streaming tears. She had no doubt now she loved Phil. *Please, God, I couldn't bear for a second time the loss of a man I love. To hell with the stupid sign from Lee! I've got to tell Phil I love him.* She couldn't imagine life without him.

In her haste, Rachel parked two feet beyond the yellow line into the adjacent parking spot. She headed to the ER and ran toward the swinging double doors, passing a nurse exiting the emergency area. "Where is he? Where did they take him?" she wailed.

The nurse grabbed her arm. "You can't go in there. You'll have to wait out here."

"I must see Phil," Rachel insisted.

"Are you family?" the nurse asked.

"Yes," she fibbed.

"The doctor will speak with you when he can," the sympathetic nurse assured her. "Can you give me any information on the patient? Name? Address? Age?" Rachel answered as many questions as she was able.

Rachel recalled the day she paced within the hospital walls in Oregon City worrying about Gerald. He had not survived. She plopped into a chair and intertwined her hands, praying for a different outcome for Phil. She located a telephone and called her mother. When Kathryn answered, Rachel told her she didn't yet know anything about Phil's condition. "What if . . .?"

She dismissed the thought. "I'm staying here all night if need be." Rachel could hear the anxious kids shouting.

Rachel experienced pure torture waiting for information. She alternately paced and sat, inhaling deep breaths. She laced her fingers together, looking upward. "Please spare Phil."

As the wall clock approached eleven, Rachel rested on the firm cushions of a two-seat chair. She leaned her head against the wall and closed her eyes. Exhausted from worry and the tiresome day at the clinic, she laid her head on the armrest. Before long, rhythmic breathing hummed from her slumbering body.

Hours later, as daylight peeked through the windows, a nurse gently shook Rachel. She opened her eyes and stretched. Confused, she scanned the room. She jumped up when she realized she'd fallen asleep. She glanced at the wall clock. Five fifteen! She was glad the hospital staff hadn't kicked her out. "How is he? Phil DeLuca." She held on to the woman's arm. "Where is he?"

"He's stable and in room 115, but it's not visiting hours. You'll have to wait." The nurse disappeared through the double doors.

Rachel walked down the hall into the restroom. She did her business and then splashed water on her face. After emerging, she scanned the hallway, then crept around the corner to 115.

Rachel's fingers covered her gaping mouth, and her eyes opened wider. Phil's left arm was hooked to an IV drip. Stitches appeared on his right temple and the right eye was swollen shut. Black and blue bruises coated both arms. Rachel had an overwhelming desire to wrap the sleeping man in her embrace. She approached the bed and touched his chest, then put her hand on his right leg. Instead of feeling soft flesh, Rachel's fingers felt something hard. She held up the sheet and peeked underneath. A cast!

Rachel bent close to Phil. "It's Rachel. I'm here." She pulled a chair next to the bed and held his hand. She remained in this position for almost an hour until she heard a weak groan.

Phil opened his left eye. Seeing Rachel, he squeezed her hand and tried to lift his head. He murmured in a soft voice, "I will love you forever and a day."

Rachel whispered into his ear. "What did you say?"

"I will love you forever and a day."

Rachel's pulse quickened. She turned and gazed out the window at the sunrise. *I will love you forever and a day* . . . the words her husband spoke to her a bazillion times! Phil voicing that exact sentiment. This was the thumbs-up from Lee!

Rachel couldn't suppress her honest emotions. "All this time, I struggled with guilt until you made me face it. I'm finally accepting I'm not at fault for Lee's death, and I'm free to allow another man into my life. I can't deny I've fallen for you, especially after I had a bit of jealousy."

"Jealousy?"

"We can talk about it later."

He gave her a weak smile. "No, now."

Rachel sighed. "I saw you hugging an attractive woman when I came out of Meing's the day before the barbecue. And she kissed you on the forehead."

Phil grimaced as he tried to quell a chuckle. "That explains your mood change when you left the store. I'm flattered you were jealous. That woman is the daughter of my next-door neighbors. I've known her since she was in first grade. She told me she and her hubby are expecting. The news thrilled me."

"Oh."

"Now, what were you saying about allowing a man into your life?"

"I convinced myself I didn't deserve another man's love after what I did to Lee. Until we talked."

"And now?"

"I'm ready."

"For what?"

"A new beginning. You." Rachel planted a fervent kiss on his lips as a surprised nurse entered.

Chapter 35

After a few days of constant begging, Rachel brought the eager children to visit Phil. Unbeknownst to the hospital staff, Gina snuck Leo into the room. The cat snuggled against Phil's chest as though he was apologizing for causing the accident.

"You're not mad at him, are you?" Gina asked.

Phil rubbed his hand through the cat's orange and white fur. "Of course not."

Gina breathed a sigh of relief.

Barry touched the stitches on Phil's temple. "Hey, you might have a scar like me!"

"I hope not, but like you, I won't let it bother me."

Phil objected, but the doctor kept him "prisoner" in the hospital for a few more days. He planned to remove the stitches a week after discharge.

Rachel told Phil to plan on recuperating at Aunt Regina's house. "She won't take no for an answer."

For the next seven days, the constant attention of the entire family overwhelmed Phil. "I appreciate your efforts, everyone, but it's time for me to go home." Cliff volunteered to drive Phil to his house.

"No need, Cliff. Rachel will do the honors." Kathryn tossed a packed overnight bag into the back seat. Winking, she told Rachel she'd stay with the kids.

The pair exited the car and reached the stairs. Phil stopped to admire the sunset. "Beautiful, like you." He positioned himself and the crutches to climb up the four steps. His strength was returning, his swollen eye almost normal, and the bruises fading. The only prominent remaining sign of his injuries was the thigh-high cast.

Once inside, Phil stared at his mother's portrait. "I'm so glad to be back in one piece," he remarked. Rachel opened a couple of windows to freshen the stuffy air. "Hope I'm recovered by basketball season. I hate not being available to coach Little League."

"It's almost July. You've got almost five months. You'll be fine by then, thank God. Now, do you want anything? How 'bout a bowl of soup?"

"I'm not hungry, but a glass of wine or a beer sounds inviting. I'm a little tired. Going to lie down in my bedroom."

"The doctor recommended no alcohol due to your medications."

"One glass won't hurt."

Rachel took two glasses from the cupboard and filled them with cold water and ice cubes. As she headed out of the kitchen, she spotted an unopened bottle of Chardonnay. What harm would a few sips of wine cause? *None.* She dumped the water and rummaged through several drawers for a corkscrew. She uncorked the bottle and poured a few ounces into the glasses.

When she entered the bedroom, Phil was sprawled on the bed, eyes closed.

Rachel set the glasses on the bed stand and leaned to kiss his forehead. As she turned to let him sleep, Phil gripped her hand. "Where's the liquid refreshment?"

Rachel pointed to the glasses as she sat on the edge of the mattress. "I thought you were asleep." She smiled at the rudimentary drawings the kids had sketched on his cast. "Gina did a decent job drawing Leo. I'm sure you'd rather see no reminders of him."

"On the contrary. I love that cat!" He rubbed his fingers over Gina's drawing. "Because of him I fell, which resulted in you allowing me into your heart. Enduring the pain was worth it."

"Leo is also responsible for the car accident," Rachel said. "Our first meeting. An accidental one. Literally."

Phil pulled Rachel close to him and held her tight. Intoxicated by the sweet fragrance of her gardenia-scented perfume, he whispered into her ear. "Stay." He tossed his shirt on the floor, then smothered Rachel with kisses. She brushed her hands along his bare back, but when Phil began unfastening her blouse, she slid away from him. "Call me old-fashioned, and believe me, I'm aching for you, but I need to be married before I make love."

Phil pointed to a stick figure Barry had drawn on his cast with the word "Dad" scribbled above it. "The kids told me they want me to be their dad. The feeling is mutual. That can happen if you're my wife."

"Are you proposing?"

Phil gestured to the top drawer of his dresser. "There's a ring box inside. Please bring it to me." He removed an antique emerald and diamond ring from the case and slipped it onto Rachel's finger. "The ring belonged to my mother. She told me–no, ordered me–to give it as a gift from her to the lucky woman who captured my heart. I wish Mom was alive. She would love you as much as I do." He wrapped his hands around hers. "What are the odds an accidental encounter between strangers would lead to love and, I hope, marriage?"

"Zilch."

He ran his fingers through her hair. "I've got a confession. You hooked me from the night I recognized you after the basketball game. I initially became involved with the kiddos as an excuse to see you. But I grew to love them as though they are my own children. I want to adopt them if you'll agree."

"I remember the night at *Dea's* when you asked me my name. That's when the barrier I erected around my heart began to crumble, but I resisted. I've been a fool and I regret it took me so long to admit I needed a man in my life to fill the emptiness." She had a second chance at love. Phil was the right man for her and the children. She reached for the wine and offered a toast. "To the future father of my children." They clinked the glasses together. After a few sips, he set the glasses down. Rachel welcomed his gentle pecks up her left arm. He smelled clean, like soap. His kisses continued to her lips, intensifying. A powerful current of arousal gripped Rachel.

"Cast or not, a cold shower may be necessary. We'd better tie the knot ASAP. I don't want to wait," Phil said, planting yet another impassioned kiss on Rachel's lips.

In silence, Rachel turned off the lamp and disrobed. She was ready to give herself to the man she at long last allowed into her heart.

Maneuvering with the heavy cast proved awkward, but their bodies melded together. With their lovemaking, all traces of Rachel's guilt vanished. Their love was pure, unselfish, and undemanding. An eternity later, they lay facing one another, their hearts pounding and bodies moist. "Is this a dream, or am I lying here with you?" Phil asked.

Rachel pinched him. "I'm here in the flesh and *I* will love *you* forever and a day." She rested her head on his chest, intending to spend the night.

Word of Rachel's upcoming nuptials spread like wildfire throughout Alder Creek. Everyone in this close-knit community planned to attend the wedding. So much for a small, intimate ceremony.

"Mom!" yelled Barry. "A guy named Howie is on the phone!"

Howie? She hadn't heard from him since leaving Philadelphia. "How are you?" Rachel asked.

"All right," Howie answered. "I should have kept in touch. Vince told me you're getting married in a couple of weeks. He gave me your phone number. I'm inviting myself if you don't mind. It's about time I visited my best friend's widow and his kids. I'll bet they've grown like weeds."

"You'll be shocked at how tall Eddie and Barry are. Gina is quite mature for her age. Of course, I'm biased."

"We'll reminisce and catch up on everything. Give me your address and the date and time of the wedding."

"Are you bringing your wife and children?"

"No." He paused. "Shirley moved out with the kids. We're divorced. Tina and Paul took it hard." He offered no details.

The news surprised Rachel. They seemed the perfect couple.

"So sorry." Then, "Howie, did Lee enjoy playing cards with you and the guys all those Friday nights?"

"Of course. Why do you ask?"

"Ah . . . never mind."

"Looking forward to seeing you. And Rachel, I found a ring you may recognize."

Chapter 36

———◆———

"Rachel!" Howie said as he approached her inside the airport terminal. He gave her a tight bear hug. "You're as lovely as I remember." Turning to the man standing beside Rachel, he said, "You must be Phil." He shook his hand. "How'd you break your leg?"

"I fell off a ladder while trimming the ivy bear."

"Say what?"

"I'll explain later when we arrive at Rachel's."

"You're a lucky man. Rachel insisted she'd never marry again. How'd you persuade her?"

Phil wrapped his arm around Rachel's shoulders, kissing her head. "It wasn't easy to crack through her barrier. Combining my charm and prodding from her three kiddos, mother, and Aunt Regina, we outnumbered her. She had no choice."

"True," Rachel admitted. She bent her head upward to meet Howie's eyes. "Got any luggage?"

"Only a carry-on. I'm booked on an early morning flight Sunday morning."

"We'll be on our honeymoon. Cliff or Mom can take you to the airport," Rachel said. She drove the Frazer toward Alder Creek. Phil sat in the rear, positioning his broken leg the length of the seat. He grinned as he listened to the pair reminiscing about the exploits of Howie, Lee, and their naval buddies. "Lee and I were as close as any two friends. Lee's death shocked me. I thought he was a healthy dude." Patting Rachel's shoulder, Howie said, "I'm sorry I didn't spend more time with you after his passing."

"Don't be. Lee's wonderful family was there for me and the children. They pleaded with me to move to Vineland, or at least stay in Philly." Minutes later, Rachel turned into the driveway.

"Whoa! What an enormous bear," Howie said. "How spectacular. Is this the ivy bear you referred to when you said you fell?"

"Yep," Phil answered.

"Who created it? And why all those chairs in front of it?"

Rachel and Phil smiled at each other. "Our wedding will take place there tomorrow. Gerald, a cherished family friend who died last year, built it. Aunt Regina insisted Mom rename the café *The Ivy Bear* in honor of Gerald's creation." She pointed to the huge hand-painted sign atop the roof. "He was the children's surrogate grandfather. Phil and I wouldn't think of any other place to exchange our marriage vows."

"Is everything ready for the ceremony?"

"Yes. My mother, Aunt Regina, and Betty Ann, the kids' babysitter, took care of everything with input from me. You'll meet them later. Right now, let's get you settled. Take your pick. Sleep in Gina's room, on the couch, or at Aunt Regina's."

"The couch." Howie set down his carry-on. "I want to take a closer peek at this unique structure." He advanced toward the bear. Phil and Rachel exchanged questioning glances.

Howie knelt, lifting a layer of the lush ivy. He leaned closer to examine underneath the leaves.

"What are you looking for?" Phil asked.

"Curious if all this ivy stems from one primary source and what material he used for the inside skeleton if you will. Sturdy wood like Douglas fir I'll bet. Quite impressive." He tried to stifle a sneeze as he reached into his pants pocket. "Allergies." He withdrew a cloth handkerchief. As he did, a tiny plastic bag fell out, landing on the ground. Howie picked it up and handed the bag to Rachel.

"What's this?" Rachel asked.

"A ring. I suspect it's Lee's."

Rachel removed the jewel and stared at it. She recognized at once the gold ring with the small diamond.

Phil saw the pain in her eyes. "What's wrong?"

Rachel rubbed the ring, ignoring both men. She held it up. "Howie, where did you find this?"

"A few months ago, I cleaned the garage. I pulled the workbench away from the wall and when I swept, I noticed a shiny object among the dirt and dust. A ring. I didn't know whom it belonged to or how it got there. Then I remembered Lee had been over the night before he died to replace my car brakes. I figure he took the ring off and put it on the windowsill and forgot to take it when he left in a hurry. We," he hesitated, exhaling a deep breath, "had a heated discussion. I'll never know how or when it landed on the floor behind the workbench. All this time, it's been in my garage."

Rachel recalled the guys decided not to play cards that Friday because it was Easter weekend. "I remember Lee said he was going to your place to replace your brakes." *Or to spend time with his lover.* Could Howie's explanation be true? Lee *never* removed his ring except to work on vehicles. She leaned against the chair back, sighing.

"This explains why the ring wasn't among his personal effects. With the trauma of his sudden death, I didn't realize it was missing until weeks later." Rachel paused. "Did Lee ever complain about my stance on his beer drinking?"

"He mentioned once or twice that you had an unreasonable hatred for beer," Howie answered. "He talked so much about you and the kids, he bored us. The guys all had no doubt you and the kids were his whole life."

Rachel still believed her attitude about drinking drove Lee to stray. Could she ever come to terms with his painful betrayal? She stood and stuffed the ring inside the bag, then hurled it toward the ivy bear. It disappeared among the abundant ivy leaves.

Howie's mouth fell open. "Why did you toss the ring? Aren't you pleased you got it back?"

"Lee betrayed me. The ring has lost its significance. I'm still dealing with . . ." She hesitated, then confronted Howie.

"You were his best friend. He didn't go to your house every Friday to play cards, did he? Admit he was unfaithful to me."

"What gives you such a ridiculous idea? You're kidding, right?"

"No. I wouldn't joke about something that has haunted me for three years. I found a note in his wallet from a DK."

"Oh, shit!" Howie cried out. He bowed his head and walked to the last row of chairs. He sat, burying his face in his hands, turning his head back and forth.

Phil approached him. Before Phil had a chance to utter a word, Howie rose and rushed to Rachel. He placed his palms firmly on Rachel's shoulders. "Lee loved you from the depths of his soul. There was no way he would be unfaithful. It was . . ."

Rachel stepped away from his hold.

Howie stared at Phil, now standing beside Rachel. He stepped a couple of feet back and pivoted, facing away from Rachel. He ran his fingers through his thick, graying hair and then turned to stare at Phil.

"Phil knows about the affair. I keep no secrets from him."

Howie thumped his thumb into his chest. "*I* had the affair."

"You?"

"Yes."

Rachel pounded Howie's chest with every ounce of strength she could muster. "Do you comprehend what I've gone through believing Lee betrayed me? You son-of-a-bitch!" She slapped his cheek.

Phil stepped forward and pulled Rachel away from Howie. Rachel leaned against his chest, the tears flowing like Niagara Falls. Phil guided her to a chair and tried soothing her.

"Lee was aware of my, ah, transgression," Howie said. "When he came over to replace my brakes, I showed him the note. I told him I was going to break it off. He went ballistic, saying if the woman was pregnant, I couldn't dump her and I'd be responsible for the child. We argued. He grabbed the note so Shirley wouldn't see it, then stomped out the garage door. Unfortunately, he didn't destroy it before he died the next day." He stood inches from Rachel, wrapping his hands around hers. "Who would fathom you'd see the note and assume the worst about Lee? If I'd known, I would have explained everything. I regret the mental anguish you endured. Forgive me?"

Forgive. That word again. Rachel darted away from the men. Howie ran after her.

"Let her be alone for a few minutes," Phil said.

Rachel settled herself on one of Gerald's carved benches behind the café. She placed her intertwined hands onto her head, rocking back and forth. She scolded herself for believing even for a second that her beloved Lee committed adultery. Her eyes focused on the bright blue sky. "Lee, you proved your love for me every single day. Please forgive me for assuming the worst." She tilted her head back, closed her eyes, and inhaled deep, relaxing breaths. Serenity enveloped her as she sensed Lee's forgiveness. And she couldn't remain angry with Howie. He had no knowledge she had read the note and mistakenly believed Lee's infidelity. She headed back to Howie and Phil.

Rachel stared deep into Howie's eyes. "Not aware I found the note, there'd be no reason for you to mention anything to me. I'm ashamed I believed Lee committed adultery."

"I'm sorry my actions caused you distress."

"Let's put this behind us. But I'm wondering. The affair. Is that why you're divorced?"

"Yea. I confessed to Shirley, but she said she couldn't trust me." Howie rubbed his neck. "Biggest mistake of my life. I'm hoping one day she'll trust me again. I want her back."

"Who is DK and was she pregnant?"

"No one you knew. When she told me she concocted her possible pregnancy hoping I'd divorce Shirley, I wasted no time cutting ties with her."

A breeze wafted through the air, providing slight relief from the late afternoon's increasing temperature. Phil stood by, overlooking the annoying itching inside his walking cast.

"How'd you pull off meeting DK on Fridays?" asked Rachel.

"Wayne would park his car a block away and walk to my house. We told Shirley his wife dropped him off. When we disbanded for the night, I pretended to drive Wayne home. I'd drop him off at his car and head to DK's apartment. Shirley knew it was about an hour and a half roundtrip to and from Wayne's, so I had plenty of time to, ahem, visit DK."

"So, all the guys knew about your affair? Including Lee?" Rachel shook her head and stroked her throat.

Howie's shoulders slumped and he bowed his head. "Rachel, I'm not proud of what I did. I'm mortified you thought Lee was unfaithful and how it affected you." He exhaled a heavy breath. "Besides losing Shirley, Lee died before we patched up things between us. My angry words are the last ones I spoke to him. It's a load I've carried all this time."

"I'm positive you and Lee would have reconciled."

Smiling, Howie said, "I'm going to believe you're right." He peered at the ivy bear. "Do you want me to search for Lee's ring?"

"No." *I'll decide one of these days what to do about the ring.*

Relief swathed Rachel. She hadn't disclosed the heart-wrenching misinterpretation to anyone besides Phil. Lee's stellar reputation remained intact. He was her first love and the father of her precious children. She would close the chapters of her life with her dear Lee and leave them on the shelf of her memory. She sensed Lee's blessing on the future chapters with Phil.

Gina handed her mother a bouquet of pink roses and baby's breath. She strolled ahead of her mother, tossing rose petals. Barry, carrying Leo, and Eddie escorted their mother to the base of the ivy bear for the early evening nuptials. Rachel wore a modest knee-length white dress with pink roses stitched across the bodice. Phil, wearing a pair of fancy shorts that complemented his decorated cast, stood next to Cliff, his best man.

Rachel's co-workers, the entire Alder Creek community and Phil's colleagues witnessed the exchange of vows. Jo and her parents, much to Cliff's delight, flew out to represent the Favretto clan. "Gives me a chance to check out where my daughter is threatening to move," commented Jo's father. Vince and Maggie surprised Rachel. "There's no way I would miss your wedding," Vince said. "The wish I made when I tossed the three coins into the Trevi fountain on my honeymoon came true. Phil is a blessed guy. God's blessings on you, my dear sister-in-law."

Rachel's eyes fixated on Phil's glowing face as they held hands. She expressed words from the depths of her soul. "I remember when you rescued my family after our car accident. You were so caring. You convinced Barry he was brave." Phil winked at Barry. "I never expected you'd reappear in my life. Thanks to Eddie's basketball obsession, you did." Eddie pumped his fist into the air. "You came at the right time. I needed someone like you. You brought sunshine back into my life and helped me free myself from guilt and learn to forgive. Lord knows I didn't make it easy for you to destroy the barrier around my heart. I didn't think I could be happy again, but I am. Words can't express how much I love you."

"Me, too!" Gina jumped up and wrapped her arms around Rachel and Phil. Phil motioned for the boys to join them. "Be careful not to squish Leo," Barry said.

When Father Juliano pronounced the couple husband and wife, Eddie proclaimed, "That's our new dad!" Spontaneous clapping and cheering rocked the serene Alder Creek hamlet. Ming and Chang wagged their tails and barked approval. Howie was the first person to offer his sincerest congratulations. "Much happiness. You deserve it."

Dr. Abbott's wife, Eleanor, snapped a series of formal pictures in front of the ivy bear. The guests gathered inside the café's party room. Kathryn had prepared a variety of salads and cold cuts. Eleanor roamed throughout the room, taking informal snapshots. The camera caught Barry sampling the frosting with his finger as the bride and groom stood poised to cut the three-tiered chocolate cake.

Afterward, Rachel sat near Aunt Regina. "Thank you for being my maid of honor. And your words of wisdom. How can I ever repay you?"

"Your happiness is all I need." She shooed Rachel back to her guests and stepped outside. She ambled toward the ivy bear and sat on Gerald's carved bench creation. Removing her silk scarf and gazing upward at the twilight sky, she addressed Lee out loud. "Your family is in excellent hands. Phil loves Rachel and the children with every breath of his being. They'll always be his priority, believe me. And I've provided for them in my will, Kathryn and Cliff, too." She leaned back, closing her eyes, a vision of Gerald entering her mind. "My beloved, what a tribute to you Rachel and Phil married in the shadow of your ivy bear." Aunt Regina took her cane and walked to the bear. Rubbing her frail hands along the plentiful ivy leaves, she felt Gerald's presence. "I still miss you as much as ever. Now that Rachel's life is secure, I'm ready to join you whenever God calls me."

Inside, Rachel hugged her children before departing for a brief honeymoon in Seaside.

Pointing to her brothers, Gina said, "We're wondering if you're gonna–"

". . . have a baby!" Eddie belted out.

Rachel and Phil exchanged tender glances. "Kiddos, I assure you we're planning on it," their new father beamed.

"I hope it's a boy!" Barry declared.